Jacob & Esau's War

Paulette Chartrand

Razzberry Press
Plainfield, IN

Jacob & Esau's War

Razzberry Press Edition
Perfect Bound Edition
© Tamuz 5771 (July 2011) by Paulette Chartrand

Razzberry Press
P.O. Box 231
Plainfield, IN 46168

Visit our website at www.razzberrypress.com

Cover Design by Paulette Chartrand

Images courtesy of dreamstime.com:
Cover images:
Jewish Scroll image by Howard Sandler
Qur'an w/prayer beads image by Paul Cowan
Judaism & Islam symbols image by Roman Smitko
Interior images:
Bismillah in Farsi by Wan Ashhar Marsuki Wan Mustaffa
Islam symbol image by Roman Smitko

Printed in the United States of America
2011 First Edition

ISBN 978 - 0 - 9824591 - 2 - 6

Dedicated...

To my Jewish brothers and sisters.
May your eyes be opened to find
the love and Salvation in
Yeshua HaMashiach!

To my brothers and sisters in Messiah (Christ),
which includes my Amish brothers and sisters.
May He open your eyes to see everything
that our Jewish God, Jesus, has for you!

To my Catholic friends and family.
May your eyes be opened to the Truth
and you find true Salvation in the One
who loves you - Yeshua - Jesus -
the Only mediator!

To my family and friends who are Mormon,
Muslim, New Age, Atheist or any other religion.
May your eyes be opened to the Truth
and you find Salvation in the One
who loves you - Yeshua - Jesus -
the One and Only!

And last, but definitely not least,
this work of fiction is thankfully dedicated
to the LORD Jesus,
Yeshua the Jewish Messiah and King.
May His great Name
be exalted forever and ever!

List of Characters

The Good Guys
God
Jesus
Holy Spirit
Adam
Eve
Abram / Abraham
Isaac
Jacob / Judah Jacob / Israel Jacob / Jew Jacob / Children of
    Jacob - Jewish people
Messianics / Messianic Jacob - Jewish people who believe in
    their Messiah Jesus
Gentile Messianic Jacob - Gentiles who believe in Messiah
    Jesus (at end of book both Jew & Gentile are called
    Messianics)

Not-so-Good Guys
Gentile Catholic - Gentiles separated from Messianics,
    formed own church
Protestant Jacob - Gentiles separated from Gentile
    Catholics - beginning to discover Truth
Crusaders - Secular soldiers promised salvation for
    fighting for the Gentile Catholics
Knights Templar - A group of secular crusader soldiers
    who devoted themselves completely to protect the
    Gentile Catholic pilgrims going to Jerusalem

The Bad Guys
Esau - Jacob's brother; spirit of Satan - antichrist spirit
Edomites - descendants of Esau
Ishmael - Esau's cousin; spirit of Satan - antichrist spirit
Amalekites - descendants of Ishmael
Idumeans - proselytes & Esau's cousins
Zealot Jacobs - those Jews who actively tried to force the
    Messiah to come forth (Judas Iscariot was a Zealot)
Abdul Odnan - Esau's puppet - the antichrist / al-Mahdi

The False Trinity
Isa - Arabic name for Islam's Jesus (not real Jesus)
al-Mahdi - Islam's savior - the Antichrist
Satan - Evil itself

Jacob & Esau's War

Part I

The first two thousand years

*A*ll that is about to happen from this point on is by *divine design*. Everything that will happen in the next six thousand years or so, has a purpose. God is not a God of disorder and chaos - everything He does is for a *divine* reason.

Using His divine language, the alphabet that existed before the creation of the world, God began to create the earth using the raw materials of the twenty-two characters of Hebrew. He began to create all that is on the earth, but He had a *small* interruption - Lucifer.

Lucifer was a foolish angel. He was the highest ranking of all the angels, and he was the brightest, most beautiful angel. But when Lucifer thought God wasn't looking, he tried to take over His kingdom, daring to think he had the right to take God's throne. But God was mightier and much wiser than Lucifer, who was a creation of His. But also being all knowing, God knew what Lucifer was planning all along.

So Lucifer, and a third of the angels who became his followers, were thrown out of the kingdom for their disobedience. They were no longer angels - they were fallen angels, or demons of darkness. Since he wanted a kingdom to rule, God sent Lucifer to a far off land and made him ruler over this land, called earth - for the next six thousand years of earth's existence. Lucifer would not only be ruler of this land, he would be ruler over the air around it. He was in essence *the prince of the power of the air, the spirit who now works in the sons of disobedience.* God then changed Lucifer's name to *Satan.*

God then continued with His plans. Known only to God and His angels, His spiritual language was an eternal language, and it was what He used when He spoke things into being. Since sending Satan to earth had caused the earth to become dark, God gave the earth a couple of lights in the sky for night and day, giving it a not-so-bright light that caused the rest of the sky to become darkness for the night, and the brightest light ever for the light of the day. He created grass, trees, bushes and all that is green, and that grows on the earth. He also created animals, birds and creeping things.

Then God created His best creation ever, one who would be in His own image - a man-person. God planted a garden in the East, a place He called Eden, and He put the man-person in it. God told the man-person that he wasn't to eat of the tree in the middle of the garden, or he would die. It was the tree of the knowledge of good and evil.

God didn't want man to be alone, so He gave Him a helper, a counterpart. He put the man into a deep sleep and took a rib from him, and from that rib God created another person in His own image - a woman-person to be the man-person's companion. The man-person called her Woman because she came from Man. They would complement each other, she would be strong where the man-person was weak, and he would be strong where the woman-person was weak.

God clothed Man and Woman with His glory. They did not know they were naked because of God's glory that surrounded them night and day.

These two people knew nothing of evil, for even though Satan had been sent to this same land, long ago, he had not yet deceived them. Satan had taken the form of a snake, and he slithered onto a branch of a tree that was nearby where Woman was standing. He deceived Woman, causing her to eat of the tree of the knowledge of good and evil. Although Man had told Woman about not eating from the tree of the knowledge of good and evil, she had not heard God say this herself. So when Satan suggested that perhaps Woman didn't hear Man correctly, she began to second guess herself. She reasoned she would be wiser, like God, if she ate from this tree. So Woman took the fruit from this tree in the middle of the garden, and took a bite. And then she gave the fruit to Man, who was standing there with her. Man was not deceived, for he knew exactly what he was doing. He knew about the tree in the middle of the garden, but then he ate of the tree of the knowledge of good and evil anyway, for he wanted to please Woman.

Man and Woman were in trouble now! God's glory disappeared the moment they took a bite of the fruit of the tree of the knowledge of good and evil. Now they were both naked and they both knew it, and they began to have horrible feelings, like shame, embarrassment, guilt and fear! They had never felt these feelings before. When God came in the evening to walk in the garden with them, He knew what they had done and where they were, but since they were hiding He asked Man and Woman, *"Where are you?"*

Man answered God, "I heard your voice in the garden, and I was afraid, because I was naked, so I hid myself."

God then said, *"Who told you that you were naked? Have you eaten from the tree from which I ordered you not to eat?!"*

God continued to question them, and Man and Woman finally admitted to what really happened. God was grieved in His heart. Satan had deceived God's creation, and now sin had entered into His new created world. And so, God went ahead with His plans, for He had already known what would happen.

God pronounced sentence over Man and Woman. To Woman He said, *"I will greatly increase your pain in childbirth. You will bring forth children in pain. Your desire will be toward your husband, but he will rule over you."*

To Man God said, *"Because you listened to what your wife said and ate from the tree about which I gave you the order not to eat from it, the ground is cursed on your account; you will work hard to eat from it as long as you live. It will produce thorns and thistles for you, and you will eat field plants. You will eat bread by the sweat of your forehead till you return to the ground."*

⊱⊰

Man, who was now called Adam, named his wife Eve, which meant *life*, for she was the mother of all living. God made garments of skin for Adam and his wife to clothe them, since they no longer had His glory to clothe them. Then God banished them from the garden, and put angels in place to guard the garden so Adam and Eve could not enter it again.

God would eventually send His Son to this land in order to destroy Satan. But the *Plan* for His Son to come to this land wouldn't happen for another four thousand years. So until the time was right for His Son to come and give people the power to rule over him, Satan would rule the air over this land. Satan knew God had prophesied the coming of His Son from an early time in his rule, saying to him, *"Because you have done this, you are cursed more than all livestock and wild animals. You will crawl on your belly and eat dust as long as you live. I will put animosity between you and Woman, between your descendant and her descendant. He will bruise your head, and you will bruise His heel."* Even though God had just stated Satan's destiny, he didn't really believe it would happen. He planned to rule this land forever.

⊱⊰

Satan was evil, and he was a spirit. In fact, he was evil itself. He was restrained though and could not truly control the first two humans God made. Until now. Satan had managed to trick these two humans and they more or less gave him the key to his *chains*. He had been on the earth for a long time, but had no one to deceive. Now he had been released to do as he pleased - for the most part.

Satan exercised his newfound freedom, sending his demons all over the land to wreak havoc. But Satan himself was now their leader and could control his demons whenever he wanted. His first order of rule would be to possess the first son of Adam, causing him to commit the first murder of the land. Satan caused this man to kill his own brother. Cain killed Abel, his younger brother, because of jealousy.

Thinking he was truly in control of this land, Satan and his demons spent the next two thousand years doing as he pleased. He spread his depravity in many cities, but somehow God would come along behind him and destroy those cities. Although Satan was the ruler over this land, God had made this land and was ultimately still in control. God had simply given Satan the rule over those who *let* him take control over their lives, limiting Satan to some extent. Satan worked overtime in heaven, accusing God's people of this and that transgression - asking for God's permission to touch them and their lives because of these transgressions. God had to uphold His own Law, and granted Satan permission to do these things - sometimes with restrictions though.

><><

God continued watching his creation for a *day*, which was a thousand years for Adam and Eve, and their family. Adam lived almost the whole one thousand years. He didn't die until he was nine hundred and thirty years old. So Adam was still alive when Enoch was born. Even though Adam had sinned, he repented and still followed God, for he had known Him personally. Although most people did not follow Adam's example of following God, Enoch did. Enoch was born about the year six hundred twenty-two, or when Adam was six hundred twenty-two years old.

And so, Enoch was different. He didn't follow after all the strange gods that everyone else did. He worshiped God because he could hear Him speak to him. People laughed at Enoch, but somehow he knew he was on to something very holy. So Enoch listened to God, talked with Him and walked with Him. And because he walked with God, Enoch did not die like the rest of mankind, for God took him to heaven alive. This would be mankind's *pattern* for what was to come at the end of the earth's age.

God knew that mankind, being made of flesh and having free will, wouldn't work out very well. So God shortened mankind's days so he wouldn't live so long. God said, *"My Spirit shall not strive with man forever, for he is indeed flesh; yet his days shall be one hundred and twenty years."*

God saw that the wickedness of mankind was great in the earth, and that every intent of the thoughts of mankind's heart was only evil continually. So God had a heavy heart and grieved over what He had to do - sorrowful that He had made man on the earth. His creation had broken His heart. There were so many people now on the earth, but in only one thousand years, only a *day* to God, only two people had truly heard Him and worshiped Him, and walked with Him. So God said, *"I will destroy mankind whom I have created from the face of this earth, both mankind and beast, creeping thing and birds of the air, for I am heartbroken and sorrowful that I have made them."*

Another four hundred years had gone by and Noah was born. Noah was Enoch's great, great grandson. And Noah was different too. Noah was like his great, great grandfather, and so he walked with God, too. He worshiped God, and talked with Him and walked with Him on this earth. Satan could not find anything wrong with this man, so he could not possess him. But Satan would continue trying to trip Noah up, using those people around him.

The earth was corrupt before God, and the earth was filled with violence. All flesh had corrupted their way on the earth. But Noah had found grace in the eyes of God. Noah knew what God was planning to do to the earth because He had talked with Noah. So God said to Noah, *"The end of all flesh has come before Me, for the earth is filled with violence through them; and behold, I will destroy them with the earth. Make yourself an ark of gopher wood; make rooms in the ark, and cover it inside and outside with pitch."*

God continued on, telling Noah the exact measurements and instructions on how to make this ark, and then He concluded with how He would destroy mankind, *"I Myself am bringing a flood of waters on the earth, to destroy from under heaven all flesh in which is the breath of life; and everything that is on the earth shall die. But I will establish My covenant with you; and you shall go into the ark - you and your sons, your wife, and your sons' wives with you.*

And of every living thing of all flesh you shall bring seven of every sort into the ark, to keep them alive with you; they shall be male and female. Of the birds after their kind, of animals after their kind, and of every creeping thing of the earth after its kind, seven of every kind will come to you by twos, to keep them alive. And you shall take for yourself of all food that is eaten, and you shall gather it to yourself; and it shall be food for you and for them."

And Noah did all that God commanded him. Noah was five hundred years old at the time he and his three sons, Shem, Japheth and Ham, began building the ark. All the people harassed Noah while he and his sons built the ark, for they thought he was crazy - especially when the ark took one hundred years to build!

Noah and his sons endured this harassment all that time. There were times when Noah's sons doubted why they were building the ark because they had not heard God themselves. But Noah reassured them that God was indeed going to destroy the earth. Noah just told his sons to ignore the people who were harassing them. God would deal with them.

When the time came, and the ark was finished, God commanded Noah and his family to enter the ark. The animals came to the ark by themselves, so Noah and his family guided them to their places within the ark. One week before it started to rain, *God closed the door of the ark* so no one else could get in. Noah and his family then sat and waited. But they didn't have to wait long, for after seven days it did indeed begin to rain, and soon the waters of the flood had come upon the earth.

It rained forty days and forty nights, and water gushed up from the bottom of the oceans. Now the earth was completely covered with water. The water even covered all the high hills and mountains that were on the earth.

All flesh that had been left on the earth had died. God had destroyed all living things which were on the face of the ground of the earth, just like He said He would do. Only Noah and those who were with him in the ark remained alive.

After it stopped raining, and the bottom of the ocean was sealed up where the water was gushing up, the waters stayed on the earth for one hundred and fifty days. Then God made a wind to pass over the earth, and the waters receded. After the waters had receded for about three months, the ark came to rest on the mountains of Ararat.

For another four months Noah waited to be sure the land was dry again. Then God spoke to Noah and said, "*Go out of the ark, you and your wife, and your sons and your sons' wives with you.*" He also told them to free the animals, birds and creeping things from the ark, so Noah did so.

Noah then built an altar to God and offered Him burnt offerings on the altar. God smelled a soothing aroma, and said, "*I will never again curse the ground for man's sake, although the intent of man's heart is evil from his youth. Nor will I again destroy every living thing as I have done.*"

And so it came to be that Noah and his family would be like Adam, and God had established His covenant with Noah. "*Thus I establish My covenant with you; never again shall all flesh be cut off by the waters of the flood; never again shall there be a flood to destroy the earth,*" said God to Noah.

Then He told Noah the sign of the covenant, "*This is the sign of the covenant which I will make between Me and you, and every living creature that is with you, for all your generations: I set My rainbow in the cloud, and it shall be for the sign of the covenant between Me and the earth. It shall be, when I bring a cloud over the earth, that the rainbow shall be seen in the cloud; and I will remember My covenant which is between Me and you and every living creature of all flesh; the waters shall never again become a flood to destroy all flesh.*" But keeping it to Himself, God had reserved the earth for fire - the next time.

God also said, "*While the earth remains, seedtime and harvest, cold and heat, winter and summer, and day and night shall not cease.*" And so God told Noah and his sons to multiply and fill the earth.

Noah's sons did indeed multiply and filled the earth. Noah lived another three hundred fifty years after the flood. And his sons and descendants lived long lives for another four generations, in order to multiply the earth. But then mankind's lives were shortened, as God had promised. Eventually man did not live more than one hundred twenty years. And at the end of the age, only seventy or eighty years did man have life on this earth.

It came to pass that Noah's youngest son, Ham, who was the father of Canaan, did not respect his father. So Noah cursed Canaan, Ham's son. Noah then said, "May God enlarge Japheth; he will live in the tents of Shem, but Canaan will be their servant." God honored Noah's words, and gave Canaan's land to Shem's ancestors.

*G*od knew mankind would become evil again, so He finalized His plans for the earth, for He had already prophesied what would happen and He needed to make sure that mankind knew of His plans for the future. God would give mankind His plan in His Tabernacle, His Feasts and in His written Word - none of which would come for another thousand years. And He would use everything that happens on the earth as a *pattern* for the things to come. God knew He would always find at least one man on earth who would listen to Him, so He had no doubt His plans would succeed.

><del></del><

The whole earth had one language after the ark landed, and Noah and his family multiplied and filled the earth. It came to pass that all the people journeyed from the east and came to a land called Shinar, and they dwelt there.

They were of one mind, and made bricks and mortar to build with. And they said, "Come, let us build ourselves a city, and a tower whose top reaches into the heavens, making a name for ourselves.

But the Lord came down to see the city and the tower which they had built. And the Lord said, "Indeed the people are one and they all have one language, and this is what they begin to do?! Now nothing that they propose to do can be withheld from them. Come, let Us go down and confuse their language, that they may not understand one another."

So God scattered them abroad from there over the face of all the earth, and they ceased building the city. Therefore, the name of that city is *Babel*, which means *confusion*, because God confused the language of all the earth, and scattered the people.

He did this because it was not time yet that they should come together as one. There would be an appointed time in the future when all mankind will be able to understand each other again. And then nothing they do can be withheld from them.

><

God needed someone whose seed His Son would come through to be born in this land. But He needed someone who had a heart for Him. And so, after another *day* (almost another thousand years to those on the earth), along came Abram. Abram was very careful not to let Satan into his life, and God noticed this. God had made His covenant with Noah, but it wasn't the final covenant. There would be one more covenant before the last. God's last covenant would be through His own Son.

Each covenant would carry over, but each new covenant

would include those things to be carried over, leaving out those no longer needed. So God chose Abram to make His second covenant with. God called this covenant an *everlasting covenant*, which it would be - until His Son would bring the *final* covenant to the earth. Abram would become the father of many nations. God told Abram that he would have a son and His Promise would be through this son.

Now Abram was quite old and so was his wife Sarai. Abram believed God would fulfill His promise, but when it didn't happen for many years he thought that maybe he should help it along. Sarai agreed and gave her maidservant to Abram, and she conceived a son by Abram. God was not happy. This son was not the son of the promise. This son was Ishmael, and he was Hagar's son, not Sarai's.

So God reminded Abram, "*I am Almighty God. Walk in My presence and be pure hearted. I will make my covenant between me and you, and I will increase your numbers greatly.*" Abram fell on his face, and God went on, "*As for me, this is my covenant with you: you will be the father of many nations. Your name will no longer be Abram, but your name will be Abraham, because I have made you the father of many nations. I will cause you to be very fruitful. I will make nations of you, and kings will descend from you.*

I am establishing my covenant between Me and you, along with your descendants after you, generation after generation, as an everlasting covenant. I will be God for you and for your descendants after you. I will give you and your descendants after you the land in which you are now foreigners, all the land of Canaan, as a permanent possession; and I will be their God."

Then God gave Abraham instructions, *"As for you, you are to keep my covenant, and the sign of this covenant will be circumcision. Generation after generation, every male among you who is eight days old is to be circumcised. This is the sign of the covenant, and anyone who will not be circumcised will be cut off from his people."*

Then God spoke to Abraham about his wife, *"As for Sarai your wife, you are not to call her Sarai; her name is to be Sarah. I will bless her; moreover, I will give you a son by her. Truly I will bless her: she will be a mother of nations; kings of peoples will come from her."*

Abraham laughed and thought it impossible since Sarah was ninety years old, and he one hundred. Abraham said to God, "If only Ishmael could live in Your presence!"

But God answered, *"No, but Sarah your wife will bear you a son, and you are to call him Isaac. I will establish my covenant with him as an everlasting covenant for his descendants after him.*

But as for Ishmael, I have heard you. I have blessed him. I will make him fruitful and give him many descendants. He will father twelve princes, and I will make him a great nation. But I will establish my covenant with Isaac."

One year later, Sarah conceived and brought forth Isaac. Isaac was the true *son of the Promise.* After Isaac was weaned, Sarah saw Ishmael making fun of Isaac, so Sarah had Abraham send Hagar and her son, Ishmael away.

God was with Ishmael and blessed him. Ishmael grew into

a strong young man. He lived in the desert and became an archer. He lived in the Paran Desert, and his mother chose a wife for him from the land of Egypt.

After about thirty years, God tested Abraham. He said to Abraham, "*Please take your son, your only son Isaac, whom you love, and go to the land of Moriah, and offer him there as a burnt offering on one of the mountains of which I shall tell you.*" God was about to set the stage for another *pattern*, for He was not asking of Abraham anything that He wouldn't do also to *His* Son. God would one day offer His own Son for a sacrifice, too.

God had set up *patterns* or *rehearsals*, for the future. These *patterns* would be signs of His salvation, neatly woven within the lives of mankind. And He had every one of these *patterns* written down, so they would be passed down from generation to generation, and also so that mankind of the future would find them in His written Word.

Abraham rose early in the morning and saddled his donkey, and took two of his young men with him, and Isaac, his son. He took wood for the burnt offering, and went to the place which God had told him.

Abraham told the two men to stay at the bottom of the hill, and he took Isaac with him. The two of them went up, and as they were walking, Isaac asked about the lamb that they did not have with them for the offering. Abraham assured Isaac that God would provide the lamb for the burnt offering. But Isaac knew what God had asked of Abraham, and still went willingly for he trusted God would indeed provide a lamb.

When they arrived at the top of the mountain, Abraham bound Isaac and laid him on the altar, upon the wood. With tears rolling down his face, Abraham stretched out his hand and took the knife, and he was ready to slay his son. But an angel of the Lord called to him before he could slay Isaac, and stopped him. And then Abraham saw the ram stuck in a thicket by its horns. Abraham quickly unbound Isaac, and took the ram and offered it up to God as a burnt offering - instead of his son. God now knew that He could trust Abraham - a man after His own heart.

⌒⌒

Isaac was now ready for a wife, so as was the Jewish custom, Abraham, his father, sent his oldest servant to find a wife for Isaac. But he was not to take a wife for Isaac from the Canaanites, for Abraham had dwelt in the land of Canaan, and knew of God's plans for this land and its people.

The servant found Rebecca from among Abraham's own people of Mesopotamia, in Nahor. Isaac was forty years old when he took Rebecca as his wife. But Rebecca was barren and could not give Isaac any children. So Isaac pleaded with God, and He granted Isaac's plea, and Rebecca conceived after twenty years.

Isaac was sixty years old when his sons were born. There were two sons born, twins. Jacob and Esau were at war with each other even in Rebecca's womb. And when they were born, the first came out red and hairy, which was Esau. Then the second followed and grabbed onto the heal of the first one, which was Jacob.

So the two boys grew. Esau was a skillful hunter, a man of the field; but Jacob was a mild man, who did not hunt. And as parents should never do, Isaac and Rebecca had their favorites. Isaac loved Esau, and Rebecca loved Jacob.

One day Jacob, who had become clever and cunning, tricked his brother Esau. He knew Esau would give anything for a bite to eat of the stew he had just cooked, since he was so tired and thought he was about to die after having been out hunting for several days. But as clever and cunning as Jacob was, Esau didn't have much interest in his birthright, for he did not believe the promises of God. Esau despised his birthright.

And Esau said to Jacob, "Please feed me with that same red stew, for I am weary."

But Jacob said, "Sell me your birthright as of this day."

And Esau answered Jacob, "Look, I am about to die; so what is this birthright to me?"

Jacob still needed confirmation, so he said to Esau, "Swear to me as of this day." So Esau swore to him, and sold his birthright to Jacob. Jacob then gave Esau bread and the stew of lentils. Esau ate and drank, arose, and went his way.

Their mother, Rebecca, was in on this birthright *conspiracy*, and helped Jacob disguise himself as Esau in order to be blessed by his father, Isaac. Rebecca helped Jacob make himself appear and feel hairy like Esau, so Isaac would mistake him for Esau, for Isaac was quite old by this time, and his sight was failing him. Isaac's blessing would pass on the *Covenant of Promise* to his *firstborn* son.

Esau later accused Jacob of stealing his birthright and his blessing, but it was too late. Isaac had just blessed Jacob, thinking he was Esau. Esau begged his father for another blessing, and Isaac did have another blessing, but it wasn't the blessing of the covenant God had given to him. That was given to Jacob.

So Esau hated Jacob because of the blessing with which his father gave him, and Esau said in his heart, *"The days of mourning for my father are at hand; but then I will kill my brother Jacob."* Esau had just opened the door for Satan to possess his life, for hate opens that door every time.

Jacob and Esau were now at war - for the next four thousand years.

Part II

The third & fourth

thousand years

$\mathcal{J}$acob and Esau were twins. So in reality they were born on the same day, making them both eligible for their father's blessing. A few minutes didn't make much difference in God's eyes, but the Hebrews tended to take the things of God to the extreme sometimes. And Isaac was one of those Hebrews, for he considered Esau to be his firstborn and he loved him more than Jacob.

But Jacob had tricked his father Isaac into blessing him instead of Esau, and Isaac gave him this blessing, the same blessing God gave Abraham, "Surely, the smell of my son is like the smell of a field which the Lord has blessed. Therefore may God give you of the dew of heaven, of the fatness of the earth, and plenty of grain and wine. Let peoples serve you, and nations bow down to you. Be master over your brethren, and let your mother's sons bow down to you. Cursed be everyone who curses you, and blessed be those who bless you!"

But once he discovered that he had blessed Jacob, and not Esau, Isaac knew the blessing had gone to his rightful heir.

Jacob would be the one to carry the *Promise* of God to future generations. And many nations would discover that this blessing from God was profound and true, for the last line in the blessing came to be true over and over again, throughout history, that *"Cursed be everyone who curses you, and blessed be those who bless you."* Those nations who cursed *Jacob* would be cursed, and those who blessed him would be blessed.

⤞⤝

"Esau wouldn't really kill me, would he?" Jacob thought. But that's exactly what his mother had told him she overheard Esau say. And Jacob trusted his mother. So far she had proven she would do anything for him to be heir of the *Promise.* So he would go. She had told him to go hide out at her brother's place, so to Laban's he went.

Jacob wondered if his father loved him. After all, his mother did conspire to have him blessed instead of Esau. His mother had told him that he and Esau had struggled even within her womb, so she knew they would struggle in life too. She also told Jacob what God had said to her shortly before he and Esau were born, *"Two nations are in your womb, two peoples shall be separated from your body; one people shall be stronger than the other, and the older shall serve the younger."*

So Jacob knew his mother loved him, because she knew of the future God had foretold for him. But he knew that his father favored Esau because he was a hunting man, while Jacob was more of a farmer. *"I wonder why mother never told father what God told her?"* he wondered. *"Maybe then he would not hate me so."*

Isaac finally understood that Jacob was his rightful heir, for Esau had foolishly given up his birthright - and the blessing of the *Promise*. But his boys were now at war with each other, so Rebecca was right in sending Jacob away.

Rebecca had said to Jacob, "Now therefore, my son, obey my voice: arise, flee to my brother Laban in Haran. And stay with him a few days, until your brother's anger turns away from you, and he forgets what you have done to him; then I will send and bring you from there. Why should I be bereaved also of you both in one day?"

Then Isaac, Jacob's father, said to him, "You shall not take a wife from the daughters of Canaan. Arise, go to Padan Aram, to the house of Bethuel your mother's father; and take yourself a wife from there of the daughters of Laban your mother's brother." Then Isaac blessed Jacob and sent him away to Padan Aram.

But then Jacob's father *did* give him another blessing as he was leaving home, "May God bless you, and make you fruitful and multiply you, that you may be an assembly of peoples; and give you the blessing of Abraham, to you and your descendants with you, that you may inherit the land in which you are a stranger, which God gave to Abraham."

⤛⤜

On his journey to Padan Aram, Jacob thought about all that had happened to him in the last few days. He did trick his brother into selling his birthright to him, but it wasn't really a trick for he knew Esau didn't care much for the fact that he was born a few minutes earlier than Jacob. Esau thought his birthright was all a big joke. But Jacob took it seriously, for it was from God. And he wanted his father's blessing of the *Promise*. And so, Jacob justified in his mind what he had done to his brother.

Jacob soon came upon a well in a field, and there were flocks of sheep lying by it. There were also men with them, seeming to be waiting for something. As he came upon them, Jacob said to them, "My brethren, where are you from?"

And they said, "We are from Haran."

Since Jacob was on his way to Haran to his uncle's land, he then asked the men, "Do you know Laban the son of Nahor?" And they told him that they did indeed know Laban.

"And look, his daughter Rachel is coming with the sheep," the men added, as they pointed in the direction of a woman with many more flocks of sheep, coming in their direction. Jacob looked to see Rachel, and for him, it was love at first sight!

Jacob told Rachel that he was her father's relative and that he was Rebecca's son. So she ran and told her father. Laban came and embraced Jacob as soon as he heard his sister's son had come.

Jacob loved Rachel, so after he had been there for a month, he said to Laban, "I will serve you seven years for Rachel, your younger daughter."

To which Laban replied, "It is better that I give her to you than that I should give her to another. Stay with me."

And so Jacob stayed with Laban for seven years, serving him for Rachel. When the seven years were up Jacob said to Laban, "Please give me my wife, for my days are fulfilled."

It was the custom to throw a big party for the bride and the groom, so Laban gathered together all the men of the place and made a wedding feast. In the evening, when it came time for Jacob to consummate the marriage, Laban sent his veiled daughter Leah, his oldest, to Jacob, and he went in to her. But in the morning, Jacob discovered that it was Leah he had married, and not Rachel.

So he said to Laban, "What is this you have done to me?! Was it not for Rachel that I served you? Why then have you deceived me?!"

And Laban replied to him, "It must not be done so in our country, to give the younger daughter before the firstborn."

So then Laban suggested that Jacob serve another seven years, and then he would give Rachel to him also. So Jacob reluctantly agreed, and served Laban another seven years. Laban did not trick Jacob this time, and gave his daughter Rachel to him. And of course, Jacob loved Rachel more than Leah.

Jacob eventually made plans to leave Laban's land, and he had made an agreement with Laban to take only the streaked, speckled, and spotted flocks of Laban's flocks. Laban had been greatly blessed since Jacob had come to live with him, so he was more than happy to give some of his flocks to Jacob - those that he thought were blemished, of course.

But God prospered Jacob's flocks, and every single lamb

born from that day forward was streaked, speckled, and spotted, and eventually Jacob possessed most of Laban's flocks. Jacob now possessed large flocks, female and male servants, and camels and donkeys. So when he left Laban, he was quite prosperous.

When Laban heard that Jacob now possessed most of his flocks, he became angry. Jacob had lost favor in his sight, so he conspired to leave without telling Laban, taking his wives, his children and all he owned with him. Jacob set off to go back to the land of Canaan.

But Jacob didn't know that Rachel had taken the family idols of her father with them, for her father was Syrian and did not know the God of Abraham, Isaac and Jacob. So after about three days, Laban went after Jacob, thinking it was he who had taken the idols.

When Laban had caught up to Jacob, he confronted him and said, "What have you done, that you have stolen away unknown to me, and carried away my daughters like captives taken with the sword? Why did you flee away secretly, and steal away from me, and not tell me; for I might have sent you away with joy and songs, with timbrel and harp? And you do not allow me to kiss my daughters. Now you have done foolishly in doing this. It is in my power to do you harm, but the God of your father spoke to me last night, saying, '*Be careful that you speak to Jacob neither good nor bad.*' And now you have surely gone because you greatly long for your father's house, but why did you steal my gods?"

Jacob responded and told Laban that he was afraid he

would have been angry that he had taken his daughters away from him. He also told him he knew nothing of Laban's gods, and suggested Laban search everyone and the person who was hiding the idols should be put to death, for he didn't know that Rachel had taken them.

But Laban did not find the idols Rachel had taken, and so, after much discussion with Jacob, Laban reluctantly agreed to let Jacob take his daughters and all that he once possessed with him. They made a covenant and placed a barrier on the land, which neither one would pass to get to the other. This they both promised by an oath and a covenant.

Jacob and his family were now well on their way to Canaan, but had to pass through the land of Seir, the country of Edom. Edom belonged to his brother Esau, and Jacob was afraid he would run into him. It had been twenty years since he last saw Esau, but he wanted to be sure there were no hard feelings between him and his brother. He had no idea if Esau still hated him.

Jacob sent messengers to Esau, and they came back with this report, "We went to your brother Esau, and he also is coming to meet you, and four hundred men are with him."

So Jacob was afraid and distressed by this news. So he divided his people, flocks and herds into two groups, and sent them in different directions. And he said to them, "If Esau comes to the one group and attacks it, then the other group which is left will escape."

Jacob then prayed, "O Lord, God of my father Abraham and of my father Isaac, the One who said to me, '*Return to your country and to your kindred, and I will deal well with you.*' I am not worthy of the least of all the mercies and of all the truth which You have shown Your servant; for I crossed over this Jordan with my staff, and now I have become two groups. Deliver me, I pray, from the hand of my brother, from the hand of Esau; for I fear him, lest he come and attack me and the mothers with my children. For You said, '*I will surely treat you well, and make your descendants as the sand of the sea, which cannot be numbered for multitude.*"

So Jacob stayed there that night, awaiting his fate. He prepared a gift for Esau, two hundred female goats and twenty male goats, two hundred ewes and twenty rams, thirty milk camels with their colts, forty cows and ten bulls, twenty female donkeys and ten foals. Jacob then delivered them to his servants and gave them instructions to go before him, to present his gift to Esau.

That night, Jacob took his two wives, his two maidservants, and his sons, and crossed over the ford of Jabbok. He sent them ahead of him over the brook, and he was then left alone. While he was alone, Jacob met an angel of the Lord, whom he wrestled with for a blessing. But the angel of the Lord would not bless him, so Jacob wouldn't let the angel go. But finally the angel of the Lord blessed him, saying, "*Your name shall no longer be called Jacob, but Israel; for you have struggled with God and with men, and have prevailed.*"

Jacob understood that he had just seen the *face* of God, and lived. But he did not go unscathed, for the angel of the Lord touched his hip, which gave Jacob pain in his hip. From that day forward, Jacob had a limp, but it didn't matter much to him, for he, a sinful man, had survived in the presence of God.

><del>~~</del><

The next morning Jacob saw Esau coming toward him, with his four hundred men. Jacob feared for his and his family's lives, so Jacob divided his children among Leah, Rachel and the two maidservants. He put the maidservants and their children in front, Leah and her children behind them, and then Rachel and Joseph last. He then went before them all and bowed himself to the ground seven times, until he came near to his brother.

But Esau ran to meet him, and embraced him, and fell on his neck and kissed him, and they wept, for Esau had forgotten that he hated his brother Jacob.

><del>~~</del><

The angel of the Lord said to Hagar, "*I will multiply your descendants exceedingly, so that they shall not be counted for multitude. Behold, you are with child, and you shall bear a son. You shall call his name Ishmael, because the Lord has heard your affliction. He shall be a wild man; his hand shall be against every man, and every man's hand against him. And he shall dwell in the presence of all his brethren.*"

These were the words God said to the mother of Esau's

cousin, Ishmael. Esau understood that they were words for him as well, but he also remembered his own blessing, "*Behold, your dwelling shall be of the fatness of the earth, and of the dew of heaven from above. By your sword you shall live, and you shall serve your brother; and it shall come to pass, when you become restless, that you shall break his yoke from your neck.*" But Esau didn't think this was a blessing at all, and still had too much hatred for his brother buried deep within his heart.

*A*t first, Esau's hatred for Jacob was so great, at times the thought of what Jacob had *done to* him was overwhelmingly suffocating. But as time went by, and his focus began to turn toward his family and providing for them, Esau came to almost forget about Jacob - and what he had done. His hatred wasn't quite as consuming any longer.

Esau, who was now called Edom, had taken wives from the daughters of Canaan. There was Adah, Aholibamah, and Basemath, his cousin Ishmael's daughter. Both Esau and his cousin Ishmael did not worship the God of their fathers, but the gods of the Canaanites were their gods. And so, even though Esau's hatred had moved to the back of his mind, the spirit within him was quite different than the spirit of Jacob.

Esau was blessed with five sons and Eliphaz was Esau's firstborn son, born of Adah. And his second son was Reuel, born of Basemath. Aholibamah bore Esau three sons, Jeush, Jaalam, and Korah. But it was his first two sons who carried on Satan's spirit because they went on to become the Edomites. But there was one of Eliphaz's sons, Amalek who would become even more evil than the Edomites, if that was possible. Esau's son Eliphaz had six sons, and Reuel, Esau's second son, had four sons. Eight of those sons became the Edomites.

Esau's hatred for Jacob may have dissipated, but that evil spirit had found other vessels, his sons and grandsons. Amalek, who was the son of Timna, who was the concubine of Eliphaz, was one of those evil vessels. It was Amalek who eventually became the people called the Amalekites. The Amalekites considered themselves enemies of Jacob.

Now when Eliphaz, Amalek and Reuel were young, they would hear their grandfather, and father respectively, speak of Esau's hatred of his brother Jacob. So they clung to this hatred and made it their own, and passed it on down to their sons, grandsons and all their descendants.

By the time Esau and Jacob had met and mended their relationship, Esau's sons were on their own and did not agree with Esau's reconciliation. Eliphaz, Amalek and Reuel had decided that they would keep Esau's hatred alive, even if their fathers wouldn't.

>~~~<

But turning back to Jacob and Esau's meeting, twenty years had gone by, and as it turned out, Esau greeted Jacob with an embrace. There didn't seem to be any hard feelings between them any longer. Esau even refused Jacob's gift at first, but then eventually took it when Jacob insisted. And so the brothers decided to dwell in the same land, on the outskirts of Canaan. But it soon became apparent that the size of each of their livestocks became so large that the land could not contain both of them. So Esau went back to his own land, Edom, in the mountains of Seir. God blessed Edom for this reconciliation, and Edom eventually became "Greater Edom" which stretched southward to Teman, on the West coast of Arabia.

><><

God appeared to Jacob again, and blessed him. And He said to him, *"Your name is Jacob; your name shall not be called Jacob anymore, but Israel shall be your name."* And so from then on, God called Jacob's name *Israel*. Then God said to *Israel*, *"I am God Almighty. Be fruitful and multiply; a nation and a company of nations shall proceed from you, and kings shall come from your body. The land which I gave Abraham and Isaac I give to you; and to your descendants after you I give this land."*

Jacob did indeed multiply, for he now had twelve sons, with the very youngest being Benjamin, who was Rachel's youngest. Ten of Jacob's sons, by Leah, were full of jealousy and hatred for their younger brother Joseph. Joseph was Jacob's favorite, for he was Rachel's oldest son, and so Jacob had given him a special coat. Joseph, being young and naive, enjoyed pointing out to his brothers how much his father favored him. Joseph's brothers were down with the flocks in the valley, but Joseph was excited and wanted to show them his new coat. It was apparently many colors and Joseph's brothers could see him coming from afar off - because of the many colors of his coat. So he headed out to the valley to join his brothers. Joseph had no idea how his brothers felt about him.

Because Joseph's brothers were very jealous of him, and although they conspired to do so, they couldn't kill him. So they got rid of him another way, and they convinced their father that Joseph was killed by a wild animal.

Joseph's brothers then sold him to the Ishmaelites, Esau's cousins. And then *they* sold Joseph to the Egyptians as a slave. Eventually, Jacob and the rest of his sons would also end up in Egypt and then they would also become slaves in Egypt. They multiplied greatly, but also remained in Egypt as slaves.

After four hundred thirty years in captivity, God raised up Moses to deliver His people from slavery. First God delivered nine plagues onto the Egyptians: waters turning to blood, frogs, lice, flies, diseased livestock, boils, hail, locusts and darkness. The tenth plague was to be the death of the firstborns in all Egypt.

God then told Moses how the children of Jacob would be able to save their households from this next plague. They were to choose a lamb on the tenth of this month, Nisan. The lamb was to be unblemished, and male, and they were to keep it until the fourteenth of the month to make sure is was indeed unblemished. At sundown they were to kill the lamb.

They were then to take the blood of this lamb and put it on the two doorposts and the lintel of the door of their households. They were also to eat the lamb in their homes, and were supposed to be ready to leave, having everything ready to go at a moment's notice. They were not supposed to allow time for their bread dough to rise - they were supposed take it with them and eat it unleavened. God was going to have the Egyptians release them.

God said, *"For I will pass through the land of Egypt on that night, and will strike all the firstborn in the land of Egypt, both man and beast; and against all the gods of Egypt I will execute judgment: I am the Lord. Now the blood shall be a sign for you on the houses where you are. And when I see the blood, I will pass over you; and the plague shall not be on you to destroy you when I strike the land of Egypt."*

So it came to pass at midnight that the Lord indeed did pass over Egypt and strike all the firstborn of Egypt - including the Pharaoh's firstborn son. This *Passover* was a *pattern* for when the true Savior would come.

Pharaoh was so distraught that he let the children of Jacob go. The Egyptians sent with them their flocks and their herds, and gave them articles of silver, gold and clothing, insisting that they leave now in case all Egypt would die. And so, Moses led the children of Jacob out of Egypt.

When Pharaoh had finally let the people go, God did not lead them by way of the land of the Philistines, although it was the closest way to go. God said, *"Lest perhaps the people change their minds when they see war, and return to Egypt,"* for He knew their hearts.

So God led the people around the Philistines' land and they went by way of the desert of the Red Sea. So they went on their way, and the Lord led them by going before them by day in a pillar of cloud, and by night in a pillar of fire to give them light, as they traveled in the night. This the Lord did while the children of Jacob were in the desert.

While the children of Jacob were traveling, Pharaoh had changed his mind, and sent his armies after them. So the Egyptians pursued the children of Jacob and caught up to them just before they reached the Red Sea. When the children of Jacob saw the Egyptians not too far off, they were very afraid, and the children of Jacob cried out to the Lord.

And then the children of Jacob grumbled to Moses, saying, "Because there were no graves in Egypt, have you taken us away to die in the desert? Why have you so dealt with us, to bring us up out of Egypt?"

They continued complaining, stating that they had said these very words to Moses when they were still in Egypt. At that time, they thought it would have been better for them to serve the Egyptians than that they should die in the desert.

But Moses ignored their grumblings and said, "Do not be afraid. Stand still and see the salvation of the Lord, which He will accomplish for you today. For the Egyptians whom you see coming after you today, you shall see again no more forever. The Lord will fight for you, and you shall hold your peace."

Then God said to Moses, *"Why do you cry out to Me? Tell the children of Jacob to go forward. But lift up your rod, and stretch out your hand over the sea and divide it. And they shall go on dry land through the midst of the sea.*

I will harden the hearts of the Egyptians, so that they will follow them. So I, the children of Jacobs' Lord, will gain honor over Pharaoh and over all his army, his chariots and his horsemen. Then the Egyptians shall know that I am the Lord." Then the Angel of God moved and went behind the children of Jacob, causing the pillar of cloud to be behind them, instead of before them. It was a cloud of darkness to the Egyptians, but it was a light to the children of Jacob at night. The Egyptians did not come near the children of Jacob all night.

The next morning Moses stretched out his hand over the sea, and the Lord caused the sea to go back by a strong east wind all the night before, and now the sea was made dry land before the children of Jacob. So they went into the midst of the sea on the dry land, and the waters were a wall to them on either side of them.

After the children of Jacob had crossed the Red Sea, the Egyptians then tried to cross it too. While they were in the midst of the Sea, the Lord caused the army of the Egyptians to be troubled, and the wheels of their chariots fell off. The Egyptians knew then that the Lord fights for the children of Jacob and they became afraid. They attempted to turn around and flee back the way they came, but then the Lord said to Moses, "*Stretch out your hand over the sea, that the waters may come back upon the Egyptians.*" So Moses did so.

The waters returned and covered the chariots, the horsemen and all the army of Pharaoh. Not one of them remained. So the Lord saved the children of Jacob that day, delivering them out of the hand of the Egyptians. This was the Lord's revenge for four hundred thirty years of enslaving His people.

The children of Jacob were now in the desert of Shur. All that they had were the clothes on their backs, so there was no water nor was there food to eat. They also had all their flocks and herds, and all the articles of silver, gold and clothing that the Egyptians had given them before they left Egypt.

After they had traveled for three days in the desert, the only water they had come upon was bitter so they could not drink it. The children of Jacob murmured against Moses, so when he cried out to the Lord for them, the Lord showed him a tree and he cast the tree into the waters and they were made sweet.

For the rest of their journey, the Lord made sure the children of Jacob had water to drink. When they had traveled to the Desert of Sin, which was between Elim and Sinai, they murmured against Moses again, saying, "Oh, that we had died by the hand of the Lord in the land of Egypt, when we sat by the pots of meat and when we ate bread to the full! For you have brought us out into this desert to kill this whole assembly with hunger."

Then the Lord said to Moses, *"Behold, I will rain bread from the heavens for you. And the people shall go out and gather each day only enough for the day, that I may test them, whether they will walk in My law or not. And on the sixth day they shall gather twice as much as they gather daily.*"

This God did because the children of Jacob had murmured against Him, and He was not only testing them, He was also giving them a day of rest. But they did not understand this. And each time the children of Jacob murmured against the Lord, He gave them what they wanted.

All the while they were in this desert, God made sure their clothing and their sandals did not wear out. And He made sure they always had water to drink, and food to eat. He was teaching them to completely rely on Him for their provision.

⤸⤷

When Jacob's people came out of Egypt, they were tired and weary, so the Amalekites attacked their rear ranks. Because the Amalekites did not fear God, they killed all the stragglers at their rear.

When Moses was telling the children of Jacob of the Law, he told them that God said, *"Remember what Amalek did to you on the way as you were coming out of Egypt,...Therefore it shall be, when the Lord your God has given you rest from your enemies all around, in the land which the Lord your God is giving you to possess as an inheritance, that you will blot out the remembrance of Amalek from under heaven. You shall not forget."*

But the Amalekites did not know of this prophecy and probably wouldn't have believed it anyway, so the spirit of Esau continued with his attacks on Jacob, the *children of Israel.* Moses commanded Joshua to go fight the Amalekites because of what they had done, and Joshua defeated the

Amalekites in the battle at Rephidim. Unfortunately, it wasn't quite the end of the Amalekites.

But God had sworn that He would have war with Amalek from generation to generation, and would eventually *utterly blot out the remembrance of Amalek from under heaven.* But this *final* war was for an appointed time in the future.

✂︎～✂︎

In the third month after the children of Jacob had come out of the land of Egypt, they came to the Desert of Sinai. So they camped at the bottom of the mountain of Sinai, and Moses went up to the top of the mountain to speak to God.

God said to Moses while he was up on the top of the mountain, *"If you will obey My voice and keep My covenant, then you shall be a special treasure to Me above all people; for all the earth is Mine. You shall be to Me a kingdom of priests and a holy nation. These are the words you shall speak to the children of Jacob."*

So Moses went back down the mountain and called for the elders of the people, and told them all these words which the Lord commanded him. Then all the people answered together and said, "All that the Lord has spoken we will do!" So Moses brought back the words of the people to the Lord.

God then told Moses He would come upon the mountain of Sinai, but the people should not touch the mountain while He was there or they would surely be put to death. God gave Moses instructions for the children of Jacob so they would be able to stand before Him, for He would come upon the mountain to be near His people.

God's presence caused the mountain to quake, and there was smoke over the whole mountain because the Lord descended upon it in fire. God called Moses and Aaron, his brother, to the top of the mountain, for they were the only two God would allow into His presence. When the Lord spoke to them, there were thunderings, lightnings, the sound of a shofar, and the mountain was smoking - which the people all witnessed and they trembled and were afraid. They were afraid for God to speak to them, and told Moses he could speak with God, and then they would listen to Moses.

So Moses went up on the mountain alone and was only gone for forty days. God gave Moses His words of the Ten Commandments, which He wrote on two tablets of stone. He also told Moses all the laws they were to follow, and He gave him the plans to build a tabernacle. For God wanted to dwell with His people, and He would dwell in the tabernacle. This tabernacle would be the *pattern* for the salvation of the children of Jacob, which would be fulfilled in another thousand years.

But when Moses came down he discovered that his brother Aaron had made a golden calf for the people to worship! Because of this great sin, the Lord said, "*To your descendants I will give the land that I swore to Abraham, Isaac and Jacob.*" So this generation would not set foot in the land that God promised to them and He caused them to wander in circles in the Desert of Sinai for forty years. This generation would die before the children of Jacob went into the land the Lord had promised to them.

Near the end of the forty years of wandering in the desert, Moses called all the people together and said to them, "The Lord will establish you as a holy people to Himself, just as He has sworn to you, if you keep His commandments and walk in His ways. He chose you out of all the peoples of the earth, and through you all the peoples of the earth will be blessed.

All the peoples of the earth will see that you are called by God, and that you alone has He chosen to reveal Himself."

And so, it was established that the children of Jacob had been chosen by God to represent Him on the earth. He gave them His Laws and commandments. Eventually, all mankind would be given the choice to be blessed through God's chosen people - to share in all His promises to them.

So Moses wrote the Law and delivered it to the priests, and commanded them, "At the end of every seven years, at the appointed time, in the year of the Jubilee, at the *Feast of Tabernacles*, you shall read this Law before all Israel, the children of Jacob.

You will gather them together, men, women and little ones, and the stranger within your gates, that they may learn to fear the Lord your God and carefully observe all the words of this Law, as long as you live in the land which you cross the Jordan to possess."

The Amalekites left Jacob alone for awhile, but now Jacob's people wanted a king to rule over them, and most importantly, to protect them against all their enemies. Before there were kings, there were judges over the children of Jacob. Samuel, the High Priest and previous judge, had two sons whom he placed as judges over Jacob's people, but these two sons were evil and corrupt. Esau hadn't left at all. He just found himself a couple other subjects through which he could harass Jacob's people.

So the children of Jacob did not want Samuel's sons to rule over them. Samuel went to God, even though it displeased him that the people had asked for a king, for Samuel thought they had rejected *him*. But God told Samuel to heed the voice of the people, for it was God that the children of Jacob were rejecting, for up to this point God had been their King. So the Lord told Samuel to forewarn the children of Jacob about the king that will be appointed over them, for their king will be handpicked by God.

The children of Jacob had been disobedient to the Lord ever since He had brought them up out of Egypt, so the king God would choose for them was not exactly their *ideal* person. Samuel told the children of Jacob all that their king would do to them, but they insisted, "No, but we will have a king over us, that we also may be like all the nations, and that our king may judge us and go out before us and fight our battles!"

And so a king was chosen from the sons of Kish, from the tribe of Benjamin. Saul was chosen by God to be king over the children of Jacob, but because he was chosen from the smallest tribe, they had objections. But Saul also didn't want to be king at first, so on the day he was to be chosen, he hid. But eventually he conceded and did prove himself to the people and they crowned him king over them.

Samuel gave the children of Jacob one more warning from God, after he had put before them a witness that he himself had not done the people wrong. "If you fear God and serve Him and obey His voice, and do not rebel against the commandment of the Lord, then both you and the king who reigns over you will continue following God. However, if you do not obey the voice of God, but rebel against the commandment of the Lord, then the hand of the Lord will be against you, as it was against your fathers.

Now therefore, stand and see this great thing which God will do before your eyes. Is today not the wheat harvest? I will call to God, and He will send thunder and rain, that you may perceive and see that your wickedness is great, which you

have done in the sight of God, in asking a king for
yourselves."

Then Samuel called to God and He sent thunder and rain
that day, and all the children of Jacob feared God and Samuel.
The people said to Samuel, "Pray for your servants to God,
that we may not die; for we have added to all our sins the evil
of asking a king for ourselves."

Samuel promised to pray for them, but also comforted
them that God would not turn away from them, even
though their wickedness was great. But he warned them, "Fear
only God, and serve Him in truth with all your heart; for
consider what great things He has done for you. But if you
still do wickedly, you shall be swept away, both you and your
king."

><del></del>><

Saul had been king for about a year, and had proven
himself to be a bad king. Saul was scared, for the Philistines
had come to the edge of town after being attacked by his son
Jonathan. They, and all the children of Jacob, thought Saul
had attacked the Philistines, but he had not and now he didn't
know what to do. He waited for Samuel, for he was the priest
and he would sacrifice before God for Saul. But Samuel had
not come yet so Saul could not wait any longer for him, and
sinned before God, for he himself went before God sacrificing.

Samuel finally did come and saw what Saul had done. He
said to Saul, "You have done foolishly. You have not kept
the commandment of God, which He commanded you. For
now the Lord would have established your kingdom over the

children of Jacob forever. But now your kingdom shall not continue. God will replace you with a man who is after His own heart." Then Samuel left.

><><

Meanwhile the Philistines were still camped in Michmash, and they didn't want the children of Jacob to make swords or spears. The children of Jacob went to the only blacksmith around to have their weapons sharpened, in the town of the Philistines, and the prices were high. So on the day of the battle, no spear or sword was found among the children of Jacob's people.

So Jonathan and his armorbearer went to the Philistines, and they killed about twenty men, and retrieved all the children of Jacob's weapons. The rest of the Philistines were then driven back from Michmash to Aijalon by Jacob's people. For the time being, they were no longer in danger from the Philistines.

But Saul continued to pursue the Philistines, and finally established his sovereignty over the children of Jacob. He fought against all his enemies on every side, against Moab, against the people of Ammon, against Edom, against the kings of Zobah, and against the Philistines. Wherever he turned, Saul harassed his enemies.

Saul was in perpetual war with the Philistines. And whenever he saw any strong man or any valiant man of the Philistines, he took him for himself - to be in his own army. Saul had become fierce and won many battles against his enemies. But he had also established himself as a cruel king.

>ᴙ~ᴙ

Samuel had another thing to say to Saul before his reign was over, "Thus says God: '*I will punish what Amalek did to the children of Jacob, how he laid in wait for them on the way when he came up from Egypt. Now go and attack Amalek, and utterly destroy all that they have, and do not spare them. But kill both man and woman, infant and nursing child, ox and sheep, camel and donkey.*'"

So Saul gathered his army to attack the Amalekites. And Saul came to the city of Amalek, and lay in wait in a valley. He even warned anyone who was not an Amalekite to leave the city so that they would not be destroyed also. Then Saul attacked the Amalekites, and he took Agag their king alive, but he utterly destroyed all the rest of the Amalekites. Saul not only spared Agag, all his best sheep, oxen and lambs were spared also. Everything else he utterly destroyed.

Then the word of God came to Samuel, "*I greatly regret that I have set up Saul as king, for he has turned his back from following Me, and has not performed My commandments.*"

Samuel was grieved and prayed to God all night in hopes that He might be lenient with Saul. The next morning Samuel went looking for Saul and found him in Gilgal. When Samuel arrived Saul yelled out, "Blessed are you of God! I have performed the commandment of God."

But Samuel heard the sheep and the oxen and knew that Saul had *not* performed the commandment of God. Saul tried to explain that they were spared to sacrifice to God. But Samuel just hung his head in shame for Saul, and told him that he had indeed not done the commandment of God. "God sent you on a mission, and said, '*Go, and utterly destroy the sinners, the Amalekites, and fight against them until they are exterminated.*'" Samuel then asked Saul why he didn't obey God. He accused Saul of doing evil in the sight of God.

Saul insisted he had done what God commanded of him, even stating that he had brought back King Agag with him, but that he had destroyed the rest of the Amalekites. But Samuel told Saul that he had sinned, and now his kingdom would for sure be taken away from him. What Saul did not realize is that if Agag was spared, it might be possible that not all the Amalekites were destroyed. There the possibility that some of Agag's children had been spared also. Saul had not trusted the Words of God - instead he trusted in his own power. He had fallen for the age-old deceit of the lies of Esau - "God didn't really say....did He?"

The Amalekites would live on - Esau would raise up a new enemy of the children of Jacob. Five hundred years later the Amalekites would become the Agagites - and they would still want to destroy Jacob's people.

><><

Samuel had no choice now. He had to do as God had told him, but it greatly saddened him. Samuel mourned for Saul, and God Himself was sorrowful that Saul had not worked out as king.

God said to Samuel, "*How long will you mourn for Saul, seeing I have rejected him from reigning over Israel? Fill your horn with oil, and go; I am sending you to Jesse the*

Bethlehemite. For I have chosen a king among his sons."

Samuel was afraid to go because he thought Saul would kill him if he found out. But God told Samuel to take a heifer with him to sacrifice, so that when he was questioned he would tell whoever questioned him that he had come to sacrifice.

Jesse had eight sons, and had brought his seven oldest before Samuel. Samuel thought sure God's anointed one would be the oldest or the tallest. But God told Samuel that none of the seven were the one God had chosen, and He said to Samuel, "*Do not look at his appearance or at his physical stature. For the Lord does not see as man sees; for man looks at the outward appearance, but the Lord looks at the heart.*"

Then Samuel asked if there was another son, and Jesse said he had one more son, his youngest who was out in the field with the sheep. Jesse sent someone to bring in his youngest son David, for Samuel said he would not sit down to eat until he saw David.

David had ruddy cheeks, red hair and bright eyes, and he was a good looking fellow. Just then God said to Samuel, "*Stand up and anoint him, for he is the one.*" Samuel took the horn of oil and anointed David, pouring the oil on his head right there in front of his brothers. From that day on, the Spirit of God would fall upon David with power.

Now David did not become king right away, for Saul was still king. But God took His Spirit away from Saul and put an evil spirit on him. Someone suggested that Saul have someone who played the harp to come play for him, so he would be comforted, for the evil spirit harassed him night and day. So David was brought to Saul because he was the best harp player around.

So David came to Saul and Saul loved him, and made David his armorbearer. And David would play his harp whenever Saul felt distressed by the evil spirit. As David would play his harp the evil spirit would leave Saul, and he would be comforted and refreshed.

One day when Saul and all of the children of Jacob were out in the Valley of Elah, they prepared to battle the Philistines. The Philistines sent out their champion and his name was Goliath. Goliath was a giant of a man, about nine feet plus a few inches tall! He was a bit scary looking, to say the least. Goliath yelled to the children of Jacob and challenged them to send out just one man to battle with him only. When Saul and the children of Jacob heard this, they were dismayed and greatly afraid.

The three oldest sons of Jesse had followed Saul to the battle. David would occasionally leave Saul's house to go feed his father's sheep at Bethlehem. So he came home this day and Jesse sent David to his brothers to bring them food at the camp where Saul was.

When David arrived he ran to his brothers, and it was about this time that Goliath had challenged them - and David heard the words of the big man. David then persuaded Saul's men to let him go out to meet with Goliath. Then David took his staff in his hand, and chose five smooth stones from the nearby brook. He put the stones in his shepherd's bag, and his sling was in his other hand. David was quite a marksman with his sling, which he told Saul's men when he was persuading them to let him go.

So the Philistine began drawing near to David on the field. When Goliath saw David, he belittled him because he was just a youth, and not very strong-looking. Goliath said to David, "Am I a dog, that you come to me with sticks?"

So David responded, "You come to me with a sword, with a spear, and with a javelin. But I come to you in the name of the Lord of hosts, the God of the armies of Israel, whom you have defied. This day the Lord will deliver you into my hand, and I will strike you and take your head from you. And this day I will give the carcasses of the camp of the Philistines to the birds of the air and the wild beasts of the earth, that all the earth may know that there is a God in Israel. Then all this assembly shall know that the Lord does not save with sword and spear; for the battle is the Lord's, and He will give you into our hands."

With that David chose one of the stones from his bag, put it in his sling and slung it around his head and then released it - it struck Goliath in the forehead. Goliath blacked out and fell down. David then ran and stood over the Philistine, took Goliath's sword and killed him with it, and then cut off his head. When the Philistines saw that their champion was dead, they turned and fled from the valley.

>──<

After his success with Goliath, Jonathan, Saul's son became David's friend. David soon married Saul's daughter, Michal, and he made a name for himself whenever he would go with Saul's men to battle the Philistines. David behaved more wisely than all the servants of Saul, so that his name became highly esteemed.

Then Saul's distressing spirit came over him and he sought to kill David. So Jonathan warned David, and went to his father on David's behalf and convinced him not to kill David. David went with Saul's men several more times to battle the Philistines, and each time he struck them down, and they fled.

Saul then sought to kill David again, this time while David was playing his harp for him. From then on Saul sought to kill David. David hid in Michal's room, and she helped him escape from her father.

Jonathan was very loyal to David and helped him often. David soon found himself on the run, and came to a place called Nob. David went to the priest and asked him for some bread for himself and for his men that were now traveling with him, because they were hungry.

The priest was reluctant, but gave David five loaves of the showbread from the Tabernacle, for that was all the town had to offer. Goliath's sword was also there, and the priest gave David the sword. Saul eventually came to this same priest, and killed all the priests there because of David.

David was on the run from Saul for many years after this. He even came upon Saul in battle and spared his life. But still Saul sought David's life.

During this time Samuel died, as he was an old man. David was there for the burial, and he and all the children of Jacob lamented for Samuel. They mourned him, and then David went down to the desert of Paran.

David has several more escapades in his travels, and even ends up sparing Saul's life again. He battles the Amalekites, and when they were delivered into his hand, he then went to Ziklag. He sent some of the spoil to the elders of Judah, and to his friends. He also sent some to all the places he and his men were accustomed to rove.

Meanwhile, the Philistines battled with Israel again, and they followed hard after Saul and his sons. The Philistines killed Jonathan, Saul and two of his other sons. David mourned their deaths greatly.

Then David was anointed king by the people of Judah, after the death of Saul and Jonathan. The people of Israel were still loyal to Saul, so they made Ishbosheth their king, over Israel. So the children of Jacob became two kingdoms.

After about seven and a half years, Ishbosheth died and David became king over both Judah and Israel. He remained king for forty years. He brought the Ark back to Jerusalem and God made a covenant with David to build a house for the Lord.

David's reign is full of color and life: he commits adultery with Bathsheba, has her husband killed, has a son with Bathsheba, and then his son dies - the consequence of his sin.

David was then told by God that he could not build the house of the Lord because he had shed blood in battle. But his son Solomon, who would be king after David, would build the house of the Lord. And David's sons after this did not exactly do right in the sight of the Lord.

In the four hundred and eightieth year after the children of Jacob had come out of the land of Egypt, in the fourth year of Solomon's reign over all of Israel, he began to build the house of the Lord. Eleven years later it was finished, and it was the grandest of buildings ever built. The splendor of the temple in Jerusalem was beyond anything the children of Jacob had ever seen.

Solomon walked in the ways of the Lord for most of his life, becoming wise beyond his years because of the wisdom of the Lord. But near the end of his life, his many wives had turned his heart from his God, and toward their gods. Solomon's heart was not loyal to the Lord his God, as was the heart of his father David.

Solomon worshiped at the high places of Chemosh and Molech, the abominations of Moab and Ammon. God became angry with Solomon, because his heart had turned from the Lord God of Israel, the land of the children of Jacob. God had appeared to Solomon twice, and had commanded him concerning this very thing, that he should not go after other gods. But he did not keep the commandment of the Lord.

So God said to Solomon, *"Because you have done this, and have not kept My covenant and My statutes, which I have commanded you, I will surely tear the kingdom away from you and give it to your servant. Nevertheless, I will not do it in your days, for the sake of your father David; I will tear it out of the hand of your son. But I will not tear away the whole kingdom. I will give one tribe to your son, for the sake of David and Jerusalem.*"

And so, like his divided heart, Solomon's kingdom became divided also. After Solomon died, his son Rehoboam reigned in his place. But Israel and Judah became separated, because Israel rebelled against the house of David. The only ones who remained loyal to the house of David, was the tribe of Judah. Later, the tribe of Benjamin joined them. Jeroboam, a servant of Solomon from the tribe of Ephraim, was made king over the other ten tribes of Israel.

The prophet Ahijah came to Jeroboam and told him what God said to Solomon, "*....But I will take the kingdom out of his son's hand and give it to you - ten tribes. And to his son I will give one tribe...*" God goes on to tell Jeroboam the same things as He told Solomon about walking in His ways, and keeping His commandments. Jeroboam reigned in the northern part of Israel, while Rehoboam ruled Judah in the southern part of Israel.

Jeroboam rebelled against Solomon and then God, and did evil in the sight of the Lord, causing Israel to sin. Because of this God struck Israel, and He uprooted them from their land, and scattered them beyond the Euphrates. But the Lord will reunite them with the children of Judah in the future, according to the prophets of God.

><

After Solomon, there were twenty more kings of Judah during the next five hundred years. Some were good, in that they followed the commandments of God. But most did evil in the sight of the Lord.

During the reign of kings Uzziah, Jotham, Ahaz and Hezekiah, there were no less than four prophets that God sent to warn the children of Judah Jacob's people. But they did not heed the warnings. So God then sent three more prophets during the reigns of kings Josiah, Jehoahaz, Jehoiakim, Jehoiachin and Zedekiah. Zephaniah warned the people during the reign of Josiah only, but Jeremiah prophesied during the whole time of those last five kings. But still the children of Jacob did not heed the warnings of God's prophets. So God delivered Judah Jacob's people into the hands of the Babylonians.

Seventy years Judah Jacob's people were in captivity under the Babylonians. During their captivity, both Daniel and Ezekiel prophesied to Judah Jacob's people. They told them of future events, some that will come to pass soon, and were also patterns for those things that were to come to pass at the end of the age. Although Judah Jacob's people were still a rebellious people, at the end of their captivity, Persia had conquered much of the Babylonian lands, and was now the new empire. Cyrus, the king of Persia released the Judah Jacobs and allowed them to return to Jerusalem to rebuild their temple and city.

There were actually three groups of people that returned to Jerusalem from their captivity in Babylon. The first group was led by Zerubbabel, who planned to rebuild the temple. Zechariah, a prophet during the reign of King Darius, encouraged Judah Jacob's people as they built the second temple in Jerusalem. The hope Zechariah gave the people of

Judah was the hope of the coming Messiah. Though still to come in another twenty-five hundred years, it was still enough to motivate the rebuilding of the temple, which suffered several setbacks, but was finally finished after sixty years - from the first year of King Cyrus to the sixth year of the reign of King Darius.

The second group was led by Ezra, who arrived shortly after the temple was finished. He came to rebuild the spiritual condition of the Judah Jacobs. Ezra was a priest and a skilled scribe. He was an expert in the Law of Moses, and taught the statutes and ordinances of the Law to those now in Jerusalem.

Now that the temple was finally completed, it was rededicated, and then the children of Judah Jacob celebrated the *Passover* for the first time, since before their captivity.

King Artaxerxes had given Ezra silver and gold, and a freewill offering for the temple. He also offered to the people wheat, wine, oil, salt and anything else the people of Jerusalem might need.

Ezra soon discovered that the Judah Jacobs who already returned to Jerusalem had not separated themselves from the peoples of the lands. They had intermingled with the Canaanites, the Hittites, the Perizites, the Jebusites, the Ammonites, the Moabites, the Egyptians and the Amorites. They had taken some of their daughters as wives for themselves and their sons, so that the holy seed was mixed with the people of those lands.

When Ezra heard these things being told to him, he tore his garment and his robe, and plucked out some of the hair of his head and beard, and sat down in mourning. He eventually sacrificed to the God of the Judah Jacobs, because of the transgression of those who had done this thing.

Then Ezra arose, and made the leaders of the priests, the Levites, and all Judah Jacobs swear an oath that they would do according to the word of the Lord, that Ezra would bring to them after three days time.

Then three days later, Ezra stood up and said to the people of Jerusalem, "You have transgressed and taken pagan wives, adding to the guilt of Judah Jacob's people. Now therefore, make confession to the Lord God of your fathers, and do His will: separate yourselves from the peoples of the land, and from the pagan wives."

And so they gave their promise that they would put away their wives; and being guilty, they presented a ram of the flock as their sin offering.

It was heartbreaking to separate from their families, but they must obey the Lord God. For only an obedient people will escape sin and calamity. They came so close to another captivity.

><><

The third, and final group to return to Jerusalem was led by Nehemiah, who challenges his countrymen to arise and rebuild the shattered wall of Jerusalem. This took place during the twentieth year of King Artaxerxes. Although there were also setbacks during the rebuilding of the wall, it took only fifty-two days to complete.

Ezra was asked to bring the Book of the Law of Moses,

and he read from it before the men and women and those who could understand; and the ears of all the people were attentive to the Book of the Law.

All the people wept when they heard the words of the Law, for they had never heard these words before. They bowed their heads and worshiped the Lord with their faces to the ground.

They found in the Book of the Law of Moses that they were to live in temporary shelters during the feast of the seventh month. Since it was now the seventh month, they did as was commanded them in the Book of the Law. And they lived in these temporary shelters, and celebrated the *Feast of Tabernacles*.

It was a bittersweet experience, because although there was joy, they were also sad since they had missed out on this wonderful feast since the days of Joshua.

Ezra continued to read from the Book of the Law of God, during this seven day feast, and on the eighth day there was a sacred assembly. And they celebrated this feast each year, for many more years.

*T*he spirit of Esau would never give up. And now he had a new subject to do his bidding, Haman the Agagite. Haman would probably not have been around if it were not for the disobedience of King Saul, over five hundred years earlier. King Saul was supposed to destroy every one of the Amalekites, but he spared King Agag, and apparently some of his children had escaped.

Five hundred years after this Amalekites incident, Haman the Agagite emerged and had a place in the Persian King Ahasuerus's court. King Ahasuerus, son of Artaxerxes, ruled over one hundred twenty-seven provinces, from India to Cush.

One day, while he sat on his royal throne which was in the Shushan capital, he decided to give a banquet for all his officials. The armies of Persia and Media, for this was the Persian-Media Empire, and all the officials of the provinces and the nobles were in attendance. King Ahasuerus continued to display all the dazzling wealth of his kingdom, and the splendor of the banquet for one hundred eighty days. Then he gave another banquet in the courtyard of the royal palace garden for seven days, for all the people in the Shushan capital.

Queen Vashti gave her own banquet for the women in the royal house. On the seventh day of the King's banquet, the King ordered seven officers that were at the banquet, to bring Queen Vashti to come before him, in order to show the people her beauty. But Queen Vashti refused to come, and King Ahasuerus was furious.

King Ahasuerus asked his seven princes from Persia and Media what he should do to Queen Vashti according to the law. Queen Vashti did not obey the command of the King, and so she must be punished. The seven princes told the King their fears that because of Queen Vashti's behavior, all the ladies of Persia and Media will hear of it and there will be excessive contempt and wrath toward their own husbands.

The seven princes suggested, "If it pleases the king, let a royal decree go out from him, and let it be recorded in the laws of the Persians and the Medes, so that it will not be altered, that Vashti shall come no more before King Ahasuerus. Let the King give her royal position to another who is better than she." It was thought that if this was done then all wives would honor their husbands knowing what would become of them if they did not obey their husbands. The King did according to the word of his princes.

King Ahasuerus had beautiful virgins sought for him from all the provinces of his kingdom. These women were gathered and brought to the women's quarters of Shushan. They were put under the custody of Hegai, the King's eunuch. He gave them beauty preparations for twelve months. Six months they were given *oil of myrrh*, and another six months they were given perfumes and preparations for beautifying women.

There was a young woman whose name was Hadassah, who was brought up by her cousin, Mordecai. Hadassah's father was Mordecai's uncle, and when her parents died, Mordecai took her in and cared for her as his own daughter.

Hadassah was just the right age to wed, so she was taken when the other virgins were taken to King Ahasuerus's palace. Hadassah called herself Esther, a more Persian name, so her people would not be revealed to those in the palace, because Mordecai had warned her not to reveal who they were.

Each of the women would be given a turn to go in to King Ahasuerus after she completed the twelve months of *beauty preparation*. Each young woman was also given the opportunity to take whatever she wanted from the women's quarters to the King's palace. Esther had used her year of preparation wisely, in holiness and prayer to her God, so when Esther's turn came to see the King, the wisdom of God came to her and she requested nothing but what Hegai advised. Because of God's wisdom and her unselfishness, Esther obtained favor in the sight of all who saw her. Esther found grace and favor in the King's sight especially, much more than all the other women. Esther was taken to King Ahasuerus, into his royal palace, and it was love at first sight for him. He loved her more than all the other women, so King Ahasuerus asked her to marry him, and of course Esther accepted, for she too had fallen in love with the King at first sight!

At their marriage, King Ahasuerus placed the royal crown upon Esther's head, making her Queen of Persia and Media. There was a great feast for all the King's officials and servants and this day, which the King called the *Feast of Esther*, was proclaimed a holiday in the provinces. And the King gave gifts to all who attended this feast.

Not long after the marriage of King Ahasuerus and Esther, two of the King's eunuchs became furious and they plotted to lay hands on the King. Mordecai had made it his custom to sit within the King's gate so he could be close to Esther, and he overheard the two eunuchs plotting. He told Queen Esther about the plot to kill the King, and she informed the King in Mordecai's name. When an inquiry was made into the accusations, it was confirmed, and both the eunuchs were hanged. This account was written in the book of the chronicles in the presence of the King, giving Mordecai credit for exposing the plot against the King.

><><

Haman, the Agagite, was promoted by King Ahasuerus, and he was advanced above all the King's princes. All the King's servants bowed and paid homage to Haman, for the King had commanded this. But Mordecai would not bow or pay homage to Haman, knowing that he was an Agagite - an enemy of the Judah Jacobs.

Haman was filled with wrath when he was told that Mordecai would not bow to *him*. Haman rationalized that all the Judah Jacobs in town would not bow to the King, since they would not bow to him, so he began a plan to stir up the King's pride. He wanted King Ahasuerus to know that the Judah Jacobs did not follow the King's laws, and therefore would not bow to the King. Mordecai had told Haman that he was a Judah Jacob, so Haman sought to destroy all the Judah Jacobs who were in the King's kingdom.

Haman went to King Ahasuerus and said, "There is a certain people scattered and dispersed among the people in all the provinces of your kingdom. Their laws are different from all other people's and they do not keep the King's laws. Therefore it is not fitting for the King to let them remain alive." Haman then suggested that the King write a decree to destroy all these people in his kingdom.

And so, not knowing that Haman was speaking of Esther's people, King Ahasuerus took his signet ring from his hand and gave it to Haman. The King then said, "The money and the people are given to you, to do with them as seems good to you." The King's scribes were then called to write a decree according to all that Haman commanded. In the name of King Ahasuerus it was written, and sealed with the King's signet ring. A copy of the document was issued as law in every province. It was published for all people, that they would be ready for the day mentioned in the decree.

Mordecai went into mourning when he heard the news of the new law against his people. He cried out with a loud and bitter cry to God. There was also great mourning among the Judah Jacobs. They fasted before God, with weeping and wailing. Mordecai knew something must be done to help the Judah Jacobs.

Esther went to talk to Mordecai at the King's gate, but he could not come in because he was in sackcloth. So Esther had one of the King's eunuchs go out to him to find out what the matter was. Mordecai told the eunuch that he must command Esther to go in to the King to make supplication to him and plead before him for her people. When the eunuch did this, Esther told him that everyone knows that any man or woman who goes into the inner court to the King unsummoned, will be put to death, except that one to whom he holds out the scepter. And it had been a month since Esther herself had been called to see the King.

These words were then told to Mordecai and he responded to Esther with these words, "Do not think in your heart that you will escape in the King's palace any more than all the other Judah Jacobs. For if you remain completely silent at this time, relief and deliverance will arise for the Judah Jacobs from another place, but you and your father's house will perish. Yet who knows whether you have come to the kingdom *for such a time as this?*"

The Judah Jacobs were Esther's people too, but she had not yet told the King. But before she went to see the King unsummoned, she asked Mordecai to gather all the Judah Jacobs together for a fast, and to pray.

Mordecai did all that Esther commanded him. After three days of fasting and prayer, Esther put on her royal robes and stood in the inner court of the King's palace, across from and facing the entrance of the King's house, knowing that the King was inside sitting on his throne.

The King saw Queen Esther standing in the court, and she found favor in his sight immediately. King Ahasuerus held out the golden scepter to Esther, and she came into the royal house and touched the top of the scepter. The King then said to her, "What do you wish, Queen Esther? What is your request? It shall be given to you - up to half my kingdom!"

Then Esther answered him, "My petition and request is this: if I have found favor in the sight of the King, and if it pleases the King to grant my petition and fulfill my request, then let the King and Haman come to the banquet which I will prepare for them, and tomorrow I will do as the King has said."

Haman had seen Mordecai on his way home, and when Mordecai did not bow or tremble before him, Haman was filled with indignation. But he did nothing, because he was so glad about the Queen's banquet, thinking he was about to be promoted again. Haman was joyful with a glad heart, and when he arrived home, he told his wife that Queen Esther had invited him to attend a banquet tomorrow, along with the King.

Then Haman told his friends to build a gallows so he could hang Mordecai first, then go onto the banquet with the King and Queen. So his friends built the gallows. The next morning Haman checked to see the progress of his friends, and was glad to find that the gallows was finished.

King Ahasuerus could not sleep the night before the

banquet, so he went to do what he always did when he could not sleep. He commanded the book of the records of the chronicles be brought to him, and they were read to him. The record of Mordecai telling of the plot to kill the king was written there, and the King asked, "What honor has been bestowed on Mordecai for this?" The King's servants, who were reading to him, said, "Nothing has been done for him."

It was morning by this time, and the King asked who was in the court. It just so happened that Haman had just entered the outer court of the King's palace to suggest that the King hang Mordecai on the gallows that he had prepared for him. The King's servants told him that Haman was standing in the court, so the King summoned him to come in.

So King Ahasuerus asked Haman, "What shall be done for the man whom the King delights to honor?"

Haman naturally thought it was himself that the King wanted to honor, so he answered the King, "For the man whom the King delights to honor, let a royal robe be brought which the King has worn, and a horse on which the King has ridden, which has a royal crest placed on its head. Then let this robe and horse be delivered to the hand of one of the King's most noble princes, that he may array the man whom the King delights to honor. Then parade him on horseback through the city square, and proclaim before him: 'Thus shall it be done to the man whom the King delights to honor!'"

King Ahasuerus was delighted with this suggestion and said to Haman, "Hasten, take the robe and the horse, as you have suggested, and do so for Mordecai the Judah Jacob who sits

within the King's gate. Leave nothing undone of all that you
have spoken." For the King did not know it was the Judah
Jacobs that Haman sought to destroy.

So Haman did all that, and when it was over he quickly
went to his house to mourn. But shortly after, the King's
eunuchs came to bring Haman to the banquet which Queen
Esther had prepared. Reluctantly, Haman went with them.
Although he was overjoyed with being chosen to attend the
banquet with the King and Queen, he was overwhelmed
with contempt for Mordecai the Judah Jacob, and having had
to parade him around such as he did.

Haman sat there at the table observing the King and
Queen, when the King asked Esther once again, "What is your
petition, Queen Esther? It shall be granted you. And what is
your request, up to half my kingdom? It shall be done!"

Then Esther, after hesitating a moment, answered the
King, "If I have found favor in your sight, O King, and if it
pleases the King, let my life be given me at my petition, and
my people at my request. For we have been sold, my people
and I, to be destroyed, to be killed and to be annihilated. Had
we been sold as slaves, I would have held my tongue."

King Ahasuerus was confused and bewildered with this
request, for he did not know that Esther and her people were
Judah Jacobs. Neither did he know the identity of the people
Haman sought to destroy. So he asked Esther, "Who is he,
and where is he, who would dare presume in his heart to do
such a thing?"

Esther slowly stood up, and then dramatically answered

the King, "The adversary and enemy is this wicked Haman!" Esther was now pointing in Haman's direction, to add more emphasis to her statement, and the gravity of what Haman had done. She then humbly sat back down.

Haman was terrified now. He could not understand why the Queen would accuse him of such a thing. The King was angry and stood, then left the banquet, going into the palace garden to think about what he had just heard. Haman stood and went before the Queen, pleading for his life for he could tell that the King's wrath was for him, and the King was determined against him.

Haman fell across the couch where Esther was sitting, and when the King came back in, he was astounded at Haman's actions. He said to Haman, "Will you also assault the Queen while I am in the house?"

One of the King's eunuchs then noticed the gallows that Haman had built for Mordecai and said to the King, "Look! The gallows which Haman has made for Mordecai, who spoke good on the King's behalf, is standing at the house of Haman."

Then the King said, "Hang him on it!" The King quickly went to Esther and put his arms around her to comfort her. Later, King Ahasuerus gave Queen Esther the house of Haman. Mordecai came before the King, for Esther had told the King that he was related to her. So the King gave his signet ring to Mordecai, and Queen Esther appointed him over the house of Haman.

But there was still the matter of the law which was to be

carried out on the thirteenth of Adar. The decree could not be reversed, so Esther once again went before the King to plead for her people's lives. Then King Ahasuerus said to Queen Esther and Mordecai, "You yourselves write a decree for the Judah Jacobs, as you please, in the King's name, and seal it with the King's signet ring; for a letter which is written in the King's name and sealed with the King's signet ring no one can revoke."

These new letters stated that the Judah Jacobs had the right to gather together and protect their lives. They had the right to destroy all the forces of any people or province that would assault them, and to plunder their possessions on the one day that had been previously decreed to do just that to the Judah Jacobs.

But these letters were more than just letters, for the God of Judah Jacob would give His people the power to protect themselves on that day. And that they did, throughout all the provinces of King Ahasuerus's kingdom. Haman's ten sons were also hanged, at Esther's request. Many enemies of the Judah Jacobs were killed because they dared to go up against the God of the Judah Jacobs.

Afterwards, the Judah Jacobs rested on the fifteenth day, and made it a day of feasting and gladness. From then on the Judah Jacobs celebrated each year on the fourteenth and fifteenth days of Adar, as days of gladness and feasting, and as a holiday where everyone would send gifts to one another. Mordecai wrote all these things down, and made it a decree for all of the Judah Jacobs. And so these two days became days of remembrance and celebration. This holiday was named *Purim*, and it was established in the writings of the chronicles of the Law of God.

Mordecai also wrote all these words in letters, and sent them to all one hundred and twenty-seven provinces of the kingdom of Ahasuerus, along with words of peace and truth. Queen Esther then made sure that Mordecai was honored properly. Mordecai was promoted for his greatness, and made second only to King Ahasuerus, and was great among the Judah Jacobs and well received by his people and all those in King Ahasuerus's kingdom.

Esau was very disappointed, for he had thought this plan to annihilate the Judah Jacobs would work this time. After all, why were Haman's people spared, if not to carry out the destruction of the Judah Jacobs? But, Haman and all ten of his sons were gone now, so there were no more of the Agagites to rile up against the Judah Jacobs. Esau would find someone else to possess - he always did.

Part III

The fifth thousand years

$\mathcal{J}$udah Jacob knew the story well. It had been passed down from generation to generation, for two thousand years: the world is to exist six thousand years. Tradition held that from Adam until Abraham, almost two thousand years had elapsed. The next two thousand years the Torah flourished; and the last two thousand years is to be the Messianic era, for their Messiah would come and rule during this time.

Judah Jacob had been born one hundred sixty years after Abraham was born, so he knew the Torah, plus he grew up knowing the God of Abraham and Isaac, for these family stories and traditions were passed down to each generation. Since it had now been four thousand years, Judah Jacob was watching every single day for his Messiah.

In the 49th year of a Jubilee, with the following year being the actual forty-second Jubilee year since Abraham, something amazing happened. It was the month of Tevet, when the angel Gabriel came to visit Mary. She was betrothed to Joseph, of the house of David, and when she first saw the bright light she thought maybe it was Joseph coming to visit her. But the light was much too bright to be from a candle or a torch, so Mary was a little frightened now that she determined it couldn't possibly be Joseph. And then she saw him - in the midst of the bright light - an angel! He spoke to her, "Shalom, favored lady! God is with you!"

Mary wasn't quite sure what to make of this visit. *"Why is an angel speaking to me? And what kind of a greeting is this?"* she wondered to herself. She was definitely frightened now. She had always been as good a Judah Jacob as she knew how, following all of God's commandments, but here was this angel of God - coming to *her*!

Then the angel spoke again, *"Don't be afraid, Mary, for you have found favor with God. Look! You will become with child, you will give birth to a Son, and you are to name Him Jesus. He will be great, He will be called the Son of the Highest. God will give Him the throne of His forefather David; and He will rule the House of Jacob forever - there will be no end to His kingdom."*

"How can this be," asked Mary of the angel, "since I am a virgin?"

The angel answered her, *"The Holy Spirit will come over you, and the power of God will cover you. Therefore the holy Child born to you will be called the Son of God."*

The angel also told Mary that her cousin Elizabeth had also conceived a son in her old age, and she was now in her sixth month. This was wondrous news, for Elizabeth had been barren all these years. Mary was overjoyed at this news. Mary spoke to the angel, "I am the servant of God. May it happen to me as you have said." Then the angel Gabriel left her.

Mary was excited, but she also wanted to see if it was true about Elizabeth. And if it was true about her cousin, then it must be true for her, too! She also had not seen her cousin in quite awhile, so she immediately set off to visit her cousin Elizabeth. It was the rainy season in Nazareth and a bit colder, but after telling Joseph, Mary bundled up and headed to the town in the hill country of Judah, where Zacharias lived. When she saw her cousin, Mary ran to her and greeted Elizabeth with a hug and a joyful greeting. Elizabeth jumped back, for when she hugged her and heard Mary's greeting, the baby in her womb leaped, and instantly Elizabeth was filled with the Holy Spirit.

Elizabeth then said to Mary, "How blessed are you among women! And how blessed is the child in your womb! But who am I, that the mother of my Lord should come to me? For as soon as the sound of your greeting reached my ears, the baby in my womb leaped for joy! Indeed you are blessed, because you have trusted that the promise God has made to you will be fulfilled."

"*Then it is all true!*" Mary thought. And she then went on to sing a song of joy, and danced around the room with Elizabeth. Over the next three months, the two of them danced around and sang every time they looked at each other, they were so happy and excited. But Mary finally announced she needed to return home to Joseph, and of course, for the Passover season. Elizabeth gave birth to a son shortly after Mary left, and he was called John. Her neighbors and other relatives heard how good God had been to her, and they rejoiced with her.

Mary had to tell Joseph, and she wasn't sure how to do it, for she feared he would not believe her. She was now three months along but did not show yet. When she arrived home, Mary told Joseph about the angel who had come to her, and about her visit to her cousin Elizabeth and what she had said. Joseph had this strange look on his face, and just turned and walked out of her house.

Joseph was a just man, and he did not want to make Mary a public example, so he made plans to break his engagement with her quietly. While he thought about these things, he dozed off and an angel of God appeared to him in a dream, saying, "*Joseph, son of David, do not be afraid to take Mary home with you as your wife; for what has been conceived in her is from the Holy Spirit. She will give birth to a Son, and you are to name him Jesus, (Yeshua, which means 'God saves,') because He will save his people from their sins.*"

Joseph was told that this was to happen in fulfillment of Isaiah's prophecy, "*Behold, a virgin shall be with child, and bear a Son, and they shall call His name Immanuel, which is translated, 'God is with us.'*" So Joseph awoke and did what the angel had told him to do - he took Mary home to be his wife. But he promised to not have intimate relations with her until after she had given birth to her Child.

><><

"This donkey is so uncomfortable, Joseph," said Mary quietly. She did not want to complain, but the ride was becoming unbearable now that she was so close to delivering her Child. It was the first day of the month of Tishrei, and they were traveling to Bethlehem for the census that had been decreed by Caesar Augustus. It had been said that all the world should be registered, and it was the first of this kind so all were expected.

Quirinius, the governor of Syria made it very clear that everyone should register in his own city. So Joseph and Mary went up from Galilee, out of the city of Nazareth, into Judea, to the city of David, because Joseph was of the house and lineage of David. Mary, who was Joseph's wife by this time, and was also with child, would also have to be registered in Bethlehem.

Joseph said to her, "It won't be long now. I think I see the outskirts of the city." Joseph lead the donkey slowly, for he knew that Mary was almost due and he didn't want to make it any more uncomfortable for her than was necessary.

When they arrived in town, Joseph tried to find a room at an Inn, but they were all full because of the census. Finally, Joseph found a man who would rent out space in his barn, which was a barn that housed the unblemished animals of sacrifice. So Joseph took Mary into the barn. He gently helped her down from the donkey, and made sure she was comfortable. It wasn't long before she gave birth to her Son.

Mary had come prepared, and wrapped her Son in swaddling cloths, as was the Jewish custom. But she did not have a bed to lay Him in, so Joseph made a bed out of one of the animal troughs. Mary laid her Son in the trough.

Shortly afterward, several shepherds came to see the Child, for after an angel had come to them telling them of the Messiah being born, they said to each other, "Let us now go to Bethlehem and see this thing that has come to pass, which God has made known to us."

The shepherds found Mary and Joseph, and the Child exactly as described by the angel. So they quickly spread the news of what the angel had told them about the Child. And all those who heard it marveled at those things which were told them by the shepherds. But Mary treasured those things the shepherds said, and pondered them in her heart, for she wasn't sure what they meant.

Mary and Joseph knew they had missed the *Feast of Shofars* because Jesus was born that day, and they had stayed in Bethlehem another day. Fortunately, it wasn't one of the feasts where Joseph was required to attend temple. Joseph and Mary then took the Child up to Jerusalem to present him to God - as it is written in the Torah of God, *"Every firstborn male is to be consecrated to God."*

So on the eighth day, when it was time for his circumcision, the Child was given the name Jesus, which is what the angel had called him before his conception. They were to offer a sacrifice of a pair of doves or two young pigeons, as required by the Torah of God. Joseph and Mary had chosen to sacrifice two doves for Jesus, and the lamb of a goat for their sin sacrifice, and did so on the *Day of Atonement,* just two days later.

While they were in Jerusalem, there was a man whose name was Simeon, and this man was just and devout, and waited eagerly for God to comfort Israel, and then the Holy Spirit came upon him. It had been revealed to him that he would not see death before he had seen God's Messiah.

So he had come to the temple, and when Joseph and Mary brought Jesus into the temple, Simeon took Him up into his arms and blessed God and said, "Lord, now You are letting Your servant depart in peace, according to Your word. For my eyes have seen your Salvation which You have prepared before the face of all peoples, a Light to bring revelation to the Gentiles, and the glory of Your people Israel!"

Joseph and Mary marveled at the things this man Simeon had spoken of their Son. Simeon then blessed Joseph and Mary and said to Mary, "Behold, this Child is destined for the fall and rising of many in Israel, and for a sign which will be spoken against. Yes, a sword will pierce through your own soul also, that the thoughts of many hearts may be revealed."

Then there was a woman who was about eighty-four years old, and was a widow, and her name was Anna. She did not depart from the temple, but served God with fastings and prayers night and day. When she saw Jesus with His parents, she bore witness that He was the One whom the Scriptures spoke of, and she told everyone to look for redemption in Jerusalem, for He had come!

Mary and Joseph stayed in Jerusalem awhile longer, because the *Feast of Tabernacles* was to begin in less than a week, and Joseph was required to attend temple for this feast. They stayed for the full seven days of the festival, performing all the things that were required according to the Law, and then Joseph and Mary returned to their home in Nazareth.

But they pondered all the things that had been said of their Son by the shepherds, the old man and the old woman at the temple. Occasionally these things would come to mind, but for the most part they tucked these things in the back of their minds, for they had a Son to raise, and didn't completely comprehend who their Son really was.

><

When Jesus was about twelve years old, his parents took Him up to Jerusalem in the Spring, as they always did this time of year according to the custom, for the festival of Pesach, which is the Passover. After the full eight days of Pesach, Unleavened Bread and Firstfruits, Joseph and Mary headed home in the caravan they had come in. They had traveled a day before they realized that Jesus was not with any friends or relatives in the caravan, so they went back to Jerusalem to find Him.

On the third day Joseph and Mary found Jesus - he was sitting in the temple court among the rabbis, not only listening to them, but asking questions, too. Everyone who heard him was astonished at His insight and His responses, even His parents. As soon as they could interrupt, Joseph and Mary were shocked and said to Him, "Jesus, why have you done this to us? Your father and I have been terribly worried looking for you!"

But Jesus gave them a confused look and then said, "Why did you have to look for me? Didn't you know that I had to be concerning Myself with my Father's affairs?" But Joseph and Mary did not understand what he meant. So Jesus went back to Nazareth with His parents, and was obedient to them. He had not realized that He had worried them so much. But Mary stored all these things in her heart, for she wondered what Jesus had meant by saying he had to be *"concerned with his Father's affairs."* It had been twelve years, and Mary still did not realize who her Son really was.

Jesus grew both in wisdom and in stature, and continued learning the Torah, and the whole Tanakh. He gained favor with the other people, and with God. Then, when He was about thirty years old, Jesus knew it was time. So he set out to find his cousin, John. As was the custom of the Judah Jacobs to be immersed completely in water for spiritual cleansing and consecration, Jesus sought to be cleansed for righteousness. Jesus knew His cousin was known as an Immerser, and was preaching, "Turn from your sins to God, for the kingdom of heaven is near!"

When John saw Jesus walking into the water and coming toward him to be immersed, he yelled out to the crowd of people standing on the banks of the river, "Behold! The Lamb of God!" And then said to Him, "But My Lord, You are coming to me? You should be the One to immerse *me!*" But Jesus explained, "Let it be this way now, because we should do everything righteousness requires." And so, John immersed Jesus in the water. As soon as Jesus had been immersed, as He came up out of the water, heaven was opened up. Jesus then saw the Holy Spirit coming down upon Him like a dove, and a Voice from heaven said, *"This is my Son, whom I love. I am well pleased with Him."*

><~><

After He was immersed by John, Jesus gained many followers, but most didn't truly believe in Him as the Messiah. Still, Jesus did only those things His Father told Him to do.

Jesus was then led by the Spirit into the desert, in order that He may be tempted by the devil. Jesus fasted forty nights and forty days, and then He became hungry. And it was at this time the devil thought He was weak, and came to tempt Him.

The devil said to Jesus, "If You are the Son of God, command that these stones become bread."

But, being the Son of God, Jesus knew what the devil was up to, so He said to him, *"It is written, 'Man shall not live by bread alone but by every word that proceeds from the mouth of God."*

The devil tried several other ways to tempt Jesus, but failed every time. And now Jesus was led by the Spirit out of the desert into Galilee, fulfilling the prophecy that there would be light come to Capernaum. Jesus was that light. And He proceeded to spread the message of the good news that the Messiah had come, and that the kingdom of heaven had come to their city - a message straight out of the Tanakh. He began by saying, "*Repent, for the kingdom of heaven is at hand.*"

Jesus preached wherever He went, and He healed the sick, in some cases raised the dead. He told them they were breaking commandments even in their thoughts, and proclaimed to all that He had come to fulfill the Law, and all the Scriptures speaking of the Messiah.

He taught many things about living a holy life, how to pray to the Father, and reminded them to seek first the kingdom of God, and their lives would be blessed for it. He also warned them of the things that would happen at the end of the age, using the Jewish wedding ceremony as an analogy many times. He wanted to be sure they and all in the future, would know these things so they could be ready. The Rabbis questioned Him about many of the things He was teaching, and most of them did not like Him, because He said He was the Son of God. Because they had taught many traditions of men, and Jesus was contradicting these things, they did not like Him. They continually accused Him of blasphemy.

And after three and a half years Jesus had done what the Father sent Him to do, and went into Jerusalem to celebrate the Passover with His apostles. He told His apostles that He would be delivered up to the Rabbis to be killed, but they did not understand what He meant. Jesus and His apostles had the *Passover* meal early that day, shortly after sundown. As they sat around the table, after they had finished eating, Jesus took the unleavened bread, blessed it and broke it, and gave a piece to each of the men there at the table.

Then He said, "*Take this bread, eat it, for this is My body which is broken for you. Do this in remembrance of Me, whenever you come together for this Passover celebration.*"

Then He took the *Third Cup*, the *Cup of Redemption*, and His disciples watched in wonder as He did this, for no one ever touched *that* Cup. Jesus then gave thanks to the Father, took a drink from the *Cup of Redemption* and then passed it around the table for the others to also take a drink. After they had done this, He said, "*This is My blood of the new covenant, which is shed for many for the remission of sins. Do this also whenever you come together for this Passover celebration, in remembrance of Me.*"

His apostles knew He was referring to when Moses sprinkled the blood that was sprinkled on the children of Israel, meaning Jesus was speaking of sealing a covenant with blood - that His own blood would be poured out for the covenant of God. The apostles also understood Jesus was telling them to add the breaking of the unleavened bread and the drinking of the *Cup of Redemption* in remembrance of Him, to their Passover celebration each year from this point on.

Although the *Cup of Redemption* wasn't in the Torah, the blood covenant was, and this *Third Cup* had become a part of their Passover season. The breaking of the unleavened bread and the drinking of the wine had always been a part of the Passover meal, as far as they could remember. They had always thought the cup of wine was symbolic of the first Passover blood covenant, and also the sealing of the covenant

God made with Abraham. But they didn't truly understand what the *drinking* of the *Cup of Redemption* meant *now* - they thought that when Jesus spoke of His death, it too was symbolic.

After Jesus's death and resurrection, His disciples would add the tradition of the *afikomen* ceremony with the bread, to their Passover meal celebration. The *afikomen* ceremony symbolized the death, burial and resurrection of Jesus.

They were also about to discover that the Spring *Feasts of God* would have much more meaning after Jesus fulfilled them - which He was about to do. Then they all sang a hymn, and then went outside to the garden of Olivet to pray.

After He had prayed several times for He knew what was about to happen, Jesus was betrayed by one of the men who were closest to Him, and He was handed over to the mob who had come to take Him to Caiaphas the High Priest. Although it was the priests of the Judah Jacobs who accused Him so He would be arrested, Jesus was not killed by the Romans or the Judah Jacobs. Of course, Esau made it to appear that way, but in fact Jesus willingly *gave* His life, as was His Father's plan from the beginning of mankind. Jesus was *born to die* as the *Passover Lamb*, for the sins of mankind - He was to fulfill the sacrificial system of the Tabernacle.

So when the soldiers led Him up to Golgotha to be crucified, and even though they thought they knew what He was doing when He picked up the *Cup of Redemption*, His apostles had thought it was all symbolism, including His death that He had spoken of. But no one truly understood, not even Jesus's followers. He tried to tell them what would happen, but still they did not understand for they thought Jesus had come to rescue them from the Romans. They didn't understand that God Himself would come to earth, to make a way for the Judah Jacobs' *eternal* salvation. But some would understand and believe, in time.

And so it happened exactly as God had planned - His sacrifice was His only Son. And just as everything in the Torah and Prophets foretold of past events, they also foretold of future events, in that they were *patterns of the things to come.* Just as God tested Abraham in that He asked him to sacrifice *his* only son, and Abraham was obedient because he knew that God would raise his son from the dead, for he was the son of the *Promise* - God Himself had sacrificed *His* only Son - and then raised Him from the dead.

The second Jesus died, war broke out in heaven, between the archangel Michael and his angels, and Satan and *his* demon-angels. Satan's side lost, and they were cast out of heaven for good - no longer able to accuse God's people.

Before Jesus died, Satan had access to heaven and it was his daily practice to accuse God's people before Him, all day long. Satan also had access to earth's people - he could do to them whatever he wanted, but he needed God's permission to touch God's people. All that changed when Jesus died on the cross, taking all sin with Him. Satan could no longer accuse God's people before Him in heaven, and he could not kill His people either, for death was defied with Jesus's resurrection.

But he was so angry at being locked out of heaven,

chained-up so to speak, he became more deceptive than ever. He and his demon-angels worked overtime, whispering lies in the ears of God's people constantly, causing them to believe they were sick, and causing many to kill themselves, or want to kill others. Plus he is always there to remind those who have been forgiven, of all their past sins. He couldn't wait to be released from his chains, so he could do even greater damage to God's people again. He was angry and knew he didn't have much time left.

><<

Jesus died on Passover, was buried on the first day of Unleavened Bread, and on the third day, which was the day of Firstfruits, God raised Him from the dead. Jesus became the *Firstfruits from the dead.* Not only did Jesus take all mankind's sins onto Himself, removing them forever, death had also been defeated when He was raised from the dead.

Esau's plan to kill Jesus had backfired on him. He had not known of God's plan - that it was His plan for Jesus to die, for blood had to be shed for the remission of the people's sins - pure blood, as according to the *pattern* of the Tabernacle. And the only pure blood was God's blood. Jesus was truly the Hope of *all* of Jacob's people. And He would soon also be the Hope of the Gentiles, too.

No one truly understood the love of God - only those who finally understood what Jesus had done. When Adam brought sin into this world, God was separated from His own creation. He loved Adam, and it broke His heart that He could no longer have Adam and Eve in His presence. He had to fix the mess they had gotten themselves and mankind into.

So God came to earth as a Man - a Man who would sacrifice His own pure blood for the sins of His people. Jesus was that Man. It was now all a matter of the true Word of the Tanakh, the good news of Messiah come to earth, being spread so that the whole world would know what God had done for them.

～～

Judah Jacob pondered recent events. There was this Jesus who claimed to be the Messiah. But He was crucified and died. There were those who claimed he rose from the dead, but the Rabbis said his followers stole his body so they could claim he was alive. *"Why would his followers do that?"* Judah Jacob wondered. *"But weren't his followers Judah Jacobs too?"* It was all very confusing, *"But the Rabbis would know, wouldn't they?"* he asked himself.

Judah Jacob didn't believe these followers of Jesus. They had no proof, no signs to show him. There were thousands who had seen this Man after He was supposedly risen from the dead, but still Judah Jacob did not believe.

Still, there was the expectation that the Jewish Messiah would come after four thousand years of time. The Rabbis said Messiah would come no later than eighty-five Jubilees, and Jesus was born at the beginning of the eighty-second Jubilee. Judah Jacob continued to wonder and question.

There is so much tension among the Judah Jacobs right now. Rome had sent cruel rulers and lawmakers to rule over Judea. This yoke was most oppressive and the Judah

Jacobs thought sure a leader, their Messiah, would be sent by God to free them from this Roman tyranny. And so they waited.

Many of the Messianics, as the followers of Jesus were now calling themselves, because they knew the Messianic age had just been ushered in, were going from town to town telling Judah Jacobs of what God had done, sending His Son to earth to be their Messiah. Even though these followers of Jesus showed the Judah Jacobs everything written about Him, many of the Judah Jacobs ignored all the Scriptures pointing to Jesus, arguing that they weren't speaking of Him at all. But Judah Jacob wondered about those scriptures in Isaiah:

"For unto us a Child is born, unto to us a Son is given; and the government will be upon His shoulder. And His name will be called Wonder of a Counselor, Mighty God, Father of Eternity, Prince of Peace. Of the increase of His government and peace there will be no end, upon the throne of David and over His kingdom, to order it and establish it with judgment and justice from that time forward, even forever. The zeal of the Lord of Hosts will perform this."

"Didn't all Jewish women desire to be chosen to bear this Child?" Judah Jacob asked himself. He had memorized many Scriptures as a boy, and he knew there were other Scriptures that spoke of the Messiah, but at the moment he couldn't think of any others. He tried to remember those Scriptures he had memorized as a boy, and then he remembered a Scripture in Zechariah that he thought spoke of the Messiah.

"*For dogs have surrounded Me; the assembly of the wicked has enclosed Me. They pierced My hands and My feet; I can count all My bones. They look and stare at Me. They divide My garments among them, and for My clothing they cast lots.*"

"*And I will pour on the house of David and on the inhabitants of Jerusalem the Spirit of grace and supplication; then they will look on Me whom they have pierced; they will mourn for Him as one mourns for his only son, and grieve for Him as one grieves for a firstborn.*"

But then Judah Jacob remembered that the Rabbis had said that these Scriptures were not speaking of their Messiah. "*Then who were they speaking of?*" Judah Jacob asked himself. Part of him wanted to believe, but another part of him did not. He reasoned that this Man Jesus could not have been the Messiah.

The Messiah is to come and rule and bring peace with him, according to the Rabbis. Jesus didn't bring peace to his people and Jerusalem. He brought division, for Judah Jacob's people were now divided - those that believed in this Jesus as the Messiah, and those that did not. Judah Jacob was very confused.

Judah Jacob's real confusion was because Jesus was not the only one in this day that declared he was the Messiah. For there were a great many who claimed to be Israel's deliverer. And that number grew after the death and resurrection of Jesus.

Many Judah Jacobs did not believe that the Messiah would

be divine. They believed their savior would be like the deliverers of old. It was thought that the true Messiah would do at least three things: He would build the true temple of God, He would deal with the *Gentile problem*, and he would establish the kingdom of God. However, most Judah Jacobs understood these things from an Abrahamic covenant perspective.

They fully expected their savior and king to build a temple made of stone. And then He would bring a violent end to the Gentiles, sinners occupying the promised land, and he would establish a revitalized Abrahamic covenant Israel. They had conveniently forgotten one of the many prophecies about the Gentiles in Isaiah, "*I, the Lord, have called You in righteousness, and will hold Your hand; I will keep You and give You as a covenant to the people, as a light to the Gentiles.*"

⋙⌒⋘

But Jesus *did* come as the Messiah, and Messianic Jacob believed. Because Jesus gave His Spirit to His believers on the day of the *Feast of Shavu'ot*, they now had Him on earth to help whenever they needed Him. It was a fitting gift on the day the Torah was given - the Word Himself came to dwell inside each believer! His Spirit now lived within each believer, which made each believer a part of the *temple of God*. Not until many years later, would it be proved that when one becomes a true follower of Jesus, it is a scientific reality - not just a chosen belief system. In believing, their dead spirits, separated from God, had been brought back to life so they could go boldly before the throne of God with Jesus as their only mediator.

What Judah Jacob did not understand is that God would do a *spiritual* thing, in that Jesus brought a New Covenant to the Judah Jacobs. Even though the Scriptures spoke of a new covenant, not all of the Judah Jacobs truly believed Jesus was the Messiah, that the New Covenant was *in Him*.

And so Jesus's followers were instructed to turn to the Gentiles. They were to do this in order to make the Judah Jacobs jealous. When the Judah Jacobs saw that the Messianics were still following the Tanakh and worshiping Messiah, they would return to God - but apparently, not right away.

So the Messianics took their message to the Gentiles. Jesus's believers were now a mixture of Judah Jacobs and Gentiles, but they all called themselves *Messianics* because they were followers of the Messiah. They continued to spread the word about the Messiah, creating new synagogues all over Asia Minor, Greece and other nearby countries. *The Way*, as the followers of Jesus called it, was growing faster than the persecutors could keep up with.

God then chose some of the Messianics to reveal Himself, so others may know who He is. Jesus commissioned all His followers to tell others of Himself fulfilling the sacrificial system of the Tabernacle, prophecy and His Father's Feasts. They were to go to the synagogues first, so the Judah Jacobs could hear the good news first. But then they were also to go to every nation, so all the Gentiles would hear the good news, too. And so, every town they came upon, they first went to the synagogues to tell the Judah Jacobs first, and then they went out to those Gentiles who wanted to know Him. According to prophecy, even the Gentiles would be blessed and saved, through the Judah Jacobs.

Matthew, Mark, Luke, John, Paul, James, Peter, and Jude were inspired by God to not only write to the leaders of the congregations, but to reveal God within their words - so that their words would complete the Tanakh. They did as they were inspired, and their own written pages were put with those of the Tanakh, copies hidden for safekeeping in large storage urns - to be found many, many years later.

*I*t grieved God's heart to watch His people sin - again - and He could only hold back His judgment from them for forty years. Judah Jacob's people had been given forty years to accept God's Messiah, but they didn't. Forty years, as so often it is in God's Word, is symbolic of chastisement and probation. Their disobedience to God is what brought this terrible tragedy upon them.

God allowed their temple and their city to be destroyed, and He scattered the Sanhedrin. Had they accepted His Messiah, His Son Jesus, they would not need the temple any longer anyway. But Judah Jacob's people did not know what to do. They could no longer do their sacrifices with no Sanhedrin and no temple.

Some describe what happened to Herod's Temple as simply *destroyed*. But it was much more sorrowful than a mere word. Titus surrounded the city during the Passover Feast, so the number of people in the city was double the normal number. It was one of the most horrific sieges in history.

And then God put blinders on those Judah Jacobs who did

not accept His Son. They would stay blinded until an appointed time in the future - in about two thousand years.

>~>~<

Shortly before the destruction of the temple, Paul had spent a couple years in Rome in a rented house, where he had preached the gospel to those who would meet with him. Linus had come to Rome to be with Paul in his last days, and just before he was executed, Paul passed the "baton" to him. Paul intended Linus to lead the meetings when the believers in Rome came together.

But once Paul had passed on to be with the Lord in heaven, Linus was not the best leader for he quickly fell into teaching false doctrines. But it wasn't easy being a Gentile Messianic Jacob in Rome, surrounded by all the Greek philosophical teachings, and the pagan festivals and such, that were constantly trying to infiltrate all that he knew. And Linus did in fact fall prey to the Spring festival of the Roman god Eastre, and began to have his congregation celebrate Jesus's resurrection on the Sunday *following* the Passover, rather than *during* the Passover season with the Judah Jacobs. He wanted this celebration to coincide with the Roman holiday. Clement joined Linus there in Rome, and he also agreed that to keep peace with the Romans, that they should celebrate Jesus's resurrection in this manner. But although they in Rome were celebrating the Roman's Eastre day with the Romans, hoping to convert the Romans, the Gentile Messianic Jacobs in the east still celebrated the Jewish Passover season with the Judah Jacobs, as they were the festivals when Jesus died and was resurrected. They still celebrated the resurrection of Jesus on the day of Firstfruits.

>✦✦✦<

Twenty years after the Messiah had come and ascended to heaven, Roman general Pompey and his army came to Jerusalem. Roman occupation of the Holy City had truly begun. They were pagans occupying the *Promised Land*. They brought with them strange gods and strange ways of thinking and living. Roman generals *did* allow Judah Jacob's people to practice their religion, but Roman paganism and Caesar worship were constantly threatening to intermingle with Jewish and Messianic beliefs.

The Jewish priests performed a daily sacrifice for Caesar's health and for the symbol of Rome, Caesar's golden eagle that Herod had placed on top of the great gate to the Temple. This abomination to God, the unbearable tax burden upon the Judah Jacobs, combined with the constant persecution of Judah Jacobs, believers and unbelievers of Jesus alike, made Jewish rebellion inevitable.

During the second half of the first century, Judah Jacob, Messianic Jacob and Gentile Messianic Jacob coexisted in Jerusalem - barely. There was much unrest in the city, because of the Roman occupation. Even before the *big rebellion*, little *wars* broke out against the Romans, but eventually the Judah Jacobs and Messianic Jacobs, and Gentile Messianic Jacobs turned against each other and they had a civil war on their hands.

Before 70 AD, the Messianic Jacobs were still considered a

sect of Judaism. But the real problems began to develop somewhere around 66 AD, with the Jewish revolt against Rome. At this time the Gentile Messianic Jacobs and the Messianic Jacobs in Jerusalem fled to Pella in Perea, which was about sixty miles northeast of Jerusalem. Although some from Jerusalem returned after the war, Messianics from this point on were regarded as traitors to the *Jewish Cause*.

⥲

The rebellion covered more than ten years, and in the process Judah Jacob's people were suffering from Roman cruelty, famine and heartache. But it wasn't only the Romans. Judah Jacob was at odds with his own people and priesthood. Such petty arguments arose over the most silly of things, and then turned out memorably tragic. Many Judah Jacobs were slaughtered - by each other. By all appearances, God had *forsaken* His own people - because they had rejected His Son. To God it was only *two days*, but to Judah Jacob it was the longest two thousand year captivity ever!

Not only was there a change in the Messianic situation, there was also now a drastic change in the Judah Jacob situation. The Jewish temple, the sacrificial system, and numerous customs and practices of Judaism were about to come to an abrupt end.

There were pockets of armed resistance against Rome, and skirmishes between the Romans and Judah Jacobs, but it really wasn't the Romans who caused the most devastation. The Idumeans, who were distant relatives of the Judah Jacobs, and cousins of Esau, had been recruited by the Zealot Jacobs. So once again, Esau was showing his ugly face.

Judah Jacob's people were still restless and fed up with the brutality of the Romans. This tyranny simply cannot go on - at least that's what the Zealot Jacobs were saying.

At the beginning of the revolt, Herod Agrippa II, an Idumean by blood, gained control of the Upper City, while the High Priest Eleaser took over the Lower City - and a civil war broke out. Agrippa made a futile effort to restore peace, by gathering the people in the Chamber of Hewn Stone, but the Zealot Jacobs and Idumeans set fire to the palaces of Agrippa and his sister, Bernice. They also set fire to the house of the High Priest. Eventually Agrippa fled from Jerusalem, which enabled the Zealot Jacobs to capture the Fortress Antonia and Herod's palace.

To add insult to injury during these civil wars, in one skirmish someone accidentally set fire to the city's grain reserves. Jerusalem normally had enough in reserve to endure a long siege, and a Sabbath year. However, the loss of these reserves led to a devastating famine in the land. Bands of cutthroats roamed the streets murdering entire families just for a morsel of food.

Also during these battles, there were many of Judah Jacob's people who tried to leave the city, to escape being caught in the middle of this pointless rebellion - away from the Zealot Jacobs. But their flight was proved difficult, since the Zealot Jacobs guarded every passage out of the city. Those that were caught trying to leave, were slain because they were thought to be deserting over to the Romans.

But the Zealot Jacobs were easily swayed by those who had money to give - those that could afford to bribe the Zealot Jacobs were allowed to leave - leaving the poor, who would not join the Zealot Jacobs in their cause, to be slain.

The Idumeans and Zealot Jacobs were more than barbaric, and seemed to kill just for the sake of killing. They wreaked their havoc in Jerusalem for several years and then, one day the Idumeans repented for what they had done, and just up and left out of guilt. But nothing had been solved. The Zealot Jacobs would not give up and they would not leave the city.

The Zealot Jacobs favored armed rebellion against Rome. They believed that God would deliver Israel with the sword. Their reasoning went back to the days of David - when there was a gentile problem, what did David do? He got out his sword and dealt with it, and God was on his side. The Zealot Jacobs were convinced God would raise up a new *Son of David* who would deliver them from the Romans. They were determined to force God's hand so the Messiah would come!

～～～

Titus, the son of Vespasian, began his final siege of Jerusalem. When the Romans came on the day of Passover, the city was divided among three warring factions - Esau had once again sent in his Idumeans and the Zealot Jacobs to go up against the Judah Jacobs. They were at each other's throats, literally. These groups were so self-involved with battling each other, that they paid no attention to the approach of the Romans. Titus surrounded Jerusalem while the Judah Jacobs were distracted by their own internal conflict and warfare. The Romans assaulted Jerusalem's walls, and gave the Judah Jacobs every opportunity to surrender and save their city from destruction.

In time, Titus breached Jerusalem's defenses and surrounded the temple. A battle broke out that could only be called ferocious, but Titus ordered his soldiers not to harm the temple itself. It was never clear who set fire to the temple structures. Some say it was overzealous Roman soldiers who were maddened by the resistance they encountered. But others say it was the Idumeans or the Zealot Jacobs in a final act of defiance.

There were great quantities of gold and silver in the temple, not only placed there for safekeeping, but there were also the temple elements. After the fire had run its course, the Romans tore the stone structures of the temple apart in order to recover the gold and silver. The gold and silver had melted and run down between the rocks and in the cracks of the stones, so the soldiers had to use long bars to pry the massive stones apart to get to it. So quite literally, not one stone was left on top of another, in their pursuit of these precious metals.

Judah Jacob, Messianic Jacob and Gentile Messianic Jacob, those that were left and had escaped to the outskirts of the city, watched the temple burning, frozen in place, unable to move. The Judah Jacobs showed no emotion at first, because they were in shock, but others who also watched were moved to tears. As they watched, the Judah Jacobs said to themselves, "Isn't this what that guy Jesus predicted about the temple?" The Judah Jacobs were confused and thought maybe that somehow, this Jesus had somehow stirred up His followers to make this happen.

But then the Judah Jacobs, as they watched flames shoot into the air, fell on their knees and sent up heartbreaking cries to God that matched the noise of the calamity. Then, just as suddenly, they were on their feet and dashed to the rescue, with no thought of saving their lives. Tired, hungry and bleeding, they ran to the temple. The reality had sunk in - that which they had guarded so devotedly was disappearing right before their eyes. But there was nothing they could do. Their temple and city were devastated - burning and in ruins.

><del>><

A new center of Judaism arose and continued by the Pharisees at a place called Yavneh, where the Sanhedrin provided for the spiritual needs of the Judah Jacobs. The Yavneh School accomplished many things. Considerable work was carried on toward establishing the official text of the Hebrew Tanakh. But they also established something else - the *Heretic Benediction* - which caused the division between Judah Jacob and Messianic Jacob and Gentile Messianic Jacob to become much deeper.

Around AD 90, the *Heretic Benediction* was adopted and came into regular use at synagogues. A condemnation of sects, the *Heretic Benediction* was not drafted specifically against the Messianics, but it did eventually include them. From this point on it would be exceedingly difficult for Messianic Jacobs and Gentile Messianic Jacobs to sit comfortably in the synagogues while their own Messiah was being cursed.

><<<

In the year 130, Emperor Hadrian visited the ruins of Jerusalem. He was sympathetic toward the Judah Jacobs at first, and promised to rebuild their city. But the Judah Jacobs felt betrayed when they discovered that Hadrian intended to rebuild the city, not as it was, but as a Roman metropolis. Hadrian planned to build a new temple on the ruins of the Judah Jacob's temple, and it was to be dedicated to Jupiter, a Roman god.

A Judah Jacob sage started a rumor that Simon Bar Kosiba could be the Judah Jacob's Messiah. He gave him a new name *Bar Kokhba* which means *"son of a star,"* based on the prophecy, *"There shall come a star out of Jacob."*

Messianic Jacob was still a minor sect of Judaism at the time, so most Judah Jacobs chose to believe in this Simon Bar Kokhba, who had a larger following. The belief of the Judah Jacobs that Bar Kokhba was the true *Messiah* sharply deepened the schism between them and the Messianic Jacobs, and the Messianic Jacobs could not be involved in what was to come next.

Judah Jacob leaders planned a second revolt so they could avoid the many mistakes during the first unplanned and spontaneous revolt, sixty years ago. In 132, Simon Bar Kokhba led the Judah Jacobs in this revolt, and they were somewhat successful, cutting off the Roman garrison in Jerusalem.

Although the Roman troops were many more than Titus had in the first revolt, the battle lasted for three years. But the revolt was brutally crushed in the end, Bar Kokhba and what was left of his army, withdrew to the fortress of Betar. But it also came under siege, and the Romans were triumphant. The Roman Emperor Hadrian defeated the Judah Jacobs in the Bar Kokhba Revolt.

His General plowed the Temple Mount with salt, to make it ready for rebuilding, and Jerusalem was renamed *Aelia Capitolina*. Hadrian also banned the Judah Jacobs from Jerusalem.

<hr />

Many of the Judah Jacobs in Judea and Samaria had either died in the Bar Kokhba Rebellion or had been carried off into slavery by the victorious Romans. There were Messianic Jacob synagogues throughout all Judea, Galilee and Samaria, but from the end of the Bar Kokhba rebellion on, all Judah Jacobs, and even Messianic Jacobs were forbidden to enter any part of Jerusalem.

Up until that time, the bishops of Jerusalem had all been Jewish. But Emperor Hadrian removed the Jewish bishops and replaced them with Gentile bishops. The Gentile bishops had already begun to think of themselves as having replaced the Judah Jacobs in God's eyes, and this change sealed it for them.

Hadrian attempted to wipe out Judaism, because he was convinced it was the cause of the continuous rebellions. He prohibited the Torah Law and the Hebrew calendar. In an attempt to erase any memory of Judea or Israel, Hadrian wiped the names off the map, made it one region and called it *Syria Palaestina.*

Being banned from Jerusalem, Judah Jacob's people were scattered to other lands. Many Roman leaders after this turned against Jesus's followers, and they were eventually executed by the Romans because they would not recant their beliefs. Yet the synagogues they started continued on, most of which were located in Asia Minor and Greece at this time.

><del></del><del></del>

Now that they were scattered to other countries, and because of the *Heretic Benediction*, Messianic Jacob no longer had a place in the synagogues. Most Messianic Jacobs were eventually chased out of the churches also, for teaching their Jewish ways, especially in Rome.

Most of the Gentile Messianic Jacob assemblies were no longer synagogues, and were all mostly Gentile Messianic Jacobs. But with the apostles being gone for over fifty years now, apostasy had already taken hold - and was spreading fast. Gentile Messianic Jacob drifted further and further away from his original Jewish ways. He soon had forgotten all the Jewish reasons behind the things of God.

*T*he Bible is a Jewish book, full of Jewish phrases and idioms. Without the knowledge of a Jewish heart and mind to guide them, the church was lost - left to their own Greek philosophies and intellectualism to help them understand Jewish writings. And this was impossible, for a Gentile mind has no understanding of a Jewish heart or a Jewish book. They were doomed to fail, and fail they did - straying far from the true doctrines and teachings of Jesus.

They were dead wrong to remove the Jewish element from their congregations, severing the *natural root* from the *wild branch*. But after the last apostle, John, died, this is exactly what they did. But God would choose a remnant out of this abominable lot, and bring them back to their Jewish heritage - to rejoin the *natural branch*. It may take two thousand years, but God would definitely bring them back to the Truth of His Word.

⤞⤝

Linus, Clement, Evaristus and Ignatius changed the course and direction of the first church dramatically. Although these men were later considered part of the *church fathers*, they did great damage and set things on a course for disaster for the church over the next fifteen hundred years.

Because of what they did, and their complete ignorance of the Word of God, it would be impossible for the church to get back on track without the Holy Spirit - who by this time, had chosen not to become involved, but watched from a distance. He grieved the loss of His church, but stuck around and watched so He would know when to intervene, according to God's plan.

Linus, Clement and Evaristus were bishops in Rome, and Ignatius was a bishop in Antioch, all about the same time. It has been said that these four men studied under the apostle John, but even though John was alive until about the year 100, their theology was so far off the mark there is no way they could have known him, or studied under him.

John, a devout Jew, with the true knowledge of the Jewish writings of the First Covenant, knew how Jesus fulfilled and fit in with the Scriptures of the very Jewish First Covenant, and would never have approved of their false theology, false teachings or their doctrines of devils.

The apostasies were a gradual thing, but these men brought them into the church, despite the fact they had copies of all the letters to the Messianic communities. The original apostles spent a lot of their time visiting and writing to the congregations of believers, mostly to straighten out their false teachings that they continually strayed into, and to get them back on track.

Once John went to be with his fathers, there was no one to keep these churches on the track of good doctrine. Just before the turn of the century Linus, Clement and Evaristus got together to discuss church doctrines concerning the day of the Sabbath, immersing in water and celebrating the Passover season, all of which included whether or not they should remove the Jewishness of the church. It seemed that these discussions were taking place a lot more frequently now that John was gone. And they even took their new ideas to Ignatius, who took them and ran with them in his own writings.

Ignatius was one of the first, if not *the* actual first, to claim the false doctrine of the *Lord's Supper*. Since he had separated his church from the Passover season, he now had to come up with an explanation for the unleavened bread and the wine. The more he read the gospel accounts of this event, the more Esau helped him get off track. He couldn't see that these things were connected to the whole Passover season. The original apostles had always taught that Jesus died on Passover, was buried on the first day of Unleavened Bread, was raised from the dead on the Day of Firstfruits, and gave His Spirit on the Day of Pentecost - completely fulfilling all of the Spring Feasts of God at His first coming.

And thus, Ignatius, and several of the others, determined this bread and wine thing must be a part of the New Covenant that Jesus brought. It was later determined to be the actual body and blood of Jesus coming back to life - once again blaspheming God's Word, "Now if we died with Messiah, we believe that we shall also live with Him, knowing that Messiah, having been raised from the dead, dies no more. Death no longer has dominion over Him. For the death that He died, He died to sin *once for all*: but the life that He lives, He lives to God.

For Messiah has not entered the holy places made with hands, which are copies of the true, but into heaven itself, now to appear in the presence of God for us; *not that He should offer Himself often*, as the high priest enters the Most Holy Place every year with blood of another - *He then would have had to suffer often* since the foundation of the world; but now, once at the end of the ages, He has appeared to put away sin by the sacrifice of Himself....so *Messiah was offered once* to bear the sins of many. To those who eagerly wait for Him He will appear a second time, apart from sin, for salvation."

To continually bring Jesus back to life in the way the *eucharist* suggests, would mean that He also has to continually die for our sins over and over again. But the bishops continued to stand by their decision in this. Ignatius once stated, "It is monstrous to talk of Jesus Christ and to practice Judaism," making it quite clear where he stood.

The original believers in Jesus had always celebrated the resurrection of Jesus during the Passover season with the Jews, both Jew and Gentile, but now it had been separated from the Passover celebration and moved to Sunday.

So the Passover season had split into two Roman traditions: Eastre, a Roman holiday that took the place of celebrating the resurrection day of the Lord; and the *Lord's*

Supper took the place of the rest of the Passover celebration, eventually evolving into the *eucharist* - which was actually a copy of a Roman Emperor ritual.

Immersing in water was always a Jewish custom of ritual cleansing for righteousness, but now it had become a *baptism* for salvation. Many other rituals arose around this *baptism*, and it soon became the norm to baptize an infant and then the child would be saved. But Salvation is through grace, given as a gift by God to those who *choose* to believe in Jesus.

These apostasies didn't happen all at the same time, but the bishops continually dissected and questioned past doctrines and teachings, and the Scriptures. They had copies of the letters to the churches, so there was really no excuse for these atrocities, except for the simple fact they did not understand the Scriptures. The changes these men made to the church were only a few of the things that they instituted into church doctrine, but the most damaging to be sure. Many of the writings of these four men superseded the writings of the original apostles, therefore changing the direction of the church indefinitely. Ignatius did the most damage, in that he wrote so many letters showing his own opinions, rather than sound doctrine.

Everything snowballed from there over the next several centuries, and every time one turned around a new doctrine was introduced as *Scriptural fact*. But the true fact was, none of these things were even in the Scriptures. With Esau's false teachings and Greek philosophies already well on their way to being deeply embedded in church doctrine, the second century had come upon the earth.

Without their Jewish roots, these Gentile *grafted-in branches* would not be *true branches* - branches of the *olive tree* that was Israel. Since they had absolutely no understanding of the Jewish Scriptures, the *church* turned from something holy, into something hideous.

><-

Clement was deeply firm in his belief of his position, being the head bishop in Rome, he was convinced he was also head of all churches. He started the ball rolling, and when Boniface III did in fact begin to call himself *pope*, in the seventh century, he had officially usurped the place of God - some *popes* even thought they were *Jesus on earth.*

From this point on, the person who stood in the pope's position, was thought of, for all intense purposes, as the only authority over God's Word - the pope's word became God's Word. And what the pope said, became what the church said, and therefore became doctrine.

Soon, the Greek word *"Cristos"* replaced the Hebrew word *Mashiach (Messiah),* so the derivative form *Christian* became more widely used now. Gentile Catholic Christians wanted nothing to do with the Jewish ways, nor their language, so they also began to call themselves *Gentile Catholics*, for they now felt their church was the only *universal* church.

><-

The bishops of the church in Rome were many in the second century. Evaristus, Alexander, Sixtus and Telesphorus were the bishops of the church in Rome, successively. They had each continued to try to persuade the churches in the east to celebrate *Eastre* with them on the same day, but were not successful in this. Although Hyginus, a bishop of Rome in the mid-second century, didn't have to contend with the rebellion of the Judah Jacobs that was going on in Jerusalem, he did have a few other problems of his own.

As always, Esau was playing both sides again, and he stirred up Valentinus, a Gnostic who was spreading heresies. Hyginus may not have been the first to excommunicate someone from the church, but his actions managed to make their way into the history books. Valentinus was excommunicated from the church for his false teachings - which just added to all the confusion in the congregations, which were already riddled with many heresies. Hyginus had gladly passed the leadership over to Pius, since he wasn't too keen on continuing the discussion of the never-ending *Eastre problem*, as well as deal with Valentinus.

Pius built the first actual physical church in Rome, and it was the residence of the reigning bishop until the early fourth century, when Constantine offered the *Lateran Palace* for the bishops to live.

Polycarp, a bishop of the church in Smyrna in the middle of the second century, visited Pius to discuss the differences that existed between the churches in Asia and Rome. These differences were centered on the timing of the Passover festivals, which the churches in Jerusalem and Asia Minor were still celebrating with the Messianic Jacobs. Polycarp was a disciple of the apostles directly after John, so he was still quite familiar with the Jewish ways that were supposed to be a part of the *Church*. Polycarp's church still celebrated all of the Messianic Jacobs' Passover festivals, as they were the true dates of the death and resurrection of Jesus. For some time now, the church in Rome had been celebrating *the resurrection* in combination with the Roman Eastre celebration.

Pius also considered himself the leader of all the churches, and felt he had the authority to decree that Passover should be kept on a Sunday, just as the Roman Eastre celebration. Upon Polycarp's departure, he and Pius agreed to celebrate the resurrection of Jesus as each pleased, but it was still a sore spot for Pius, and it was still not resolved.

In Rome, it was an entirely different story than in Smyrna. The Messianic Jacobs that were so much a part of the the synagogues in Jerusalem and Asia Minor, but in Rome were no longer a part of the *church*. In Rome, *Messianic Jacob* was now gone completely, so of course the church did not resemble the original Jewish synagogue of Messianic Jacob in any way, shape or form any longer.

The Gentile Catholics had created the new religion *Christianity* by this time, and the Gentile Catholic *church* officially replaced the synagogue. They still needed to get the churches in the east to see things their way, though.

Gentile Catholics eventually saw Messianic Jacob and Judah Jacob as enemies - the *'killers of our Lord.'* So, of course Gentile Catholic now saw himself as the replacement for Judah Jacob.

In the West, the *new religion* drew more direct inspiration from its Greek sources, and continued to be the religion of the intellectuals and administrators. This Greek philosophy had dug deep, and permanent roots for itself in ancient Greek philosophical culture - and *Christianity*. Sadly, by this time no one really knew what salvation was. No one truly knew if they were saved or not. They were never quite sure if they had done enough, or said enough prayers, or gave enough money - never really understanding that salvation cannot be bought with money or with works. Although the Gentile Catholic church would award salvation to many, in reality salvation could only be given by God.

><

In the third century, Origen was a pupil at the seminary in Alexandria, and was also considered to be another early *church father* of the Gentile Catholic church. But he was also considered to be a heretic, because of his crazy ideas and teachings - which were way off the map.

Many have thought there was no writer who did any more damage to the Hebrew roots of the Messianics than Origen, but he simply carried on where Linus, Clement, Evaristus and Ignatius left off. Origen's views of the implied differences between Judaism and *Christianity* were that Christians perceive the mysteries which are only hinted at in the Bible; but Judah Jacobs are only capable of a strictly literal understanding of the text. Origen didn't have a clue that God never intended there to be two religions, for Jesus never started *Christianity*, man did.

Origen was the father of the allegorical method of interpreting the Scriptures. Through his methodology, the biblical position of Israel and the Jewish people was allegorized and simply rendered irrelevant.

Origen was eventually excommunicated from the *Church* for other reasons, by the Council of Alexandria in 231. The council was attended by several bishops and priests, and was called by Bishop Demetrius for the purpose of declaring Origen unworthy of the office of teacher, and to have him excommunicated.

Although Origen was considered a heretic in his lifetime, his influence lived on and greatly increased. Most of the Greek fathers of the church in later centuries would remain under the influence of the spirit and works of Origen. It is Origen's system of interpretation of Scripture that deepened the *"anti-Judaic New Israel"* theology, where the Gentile Catholic Church replaces the Judah Jacobs in the plans and purposes of God.

By this time, a succession of bishops had confused Jesus with the Roman sun god, and they saw Jesus as the *"Sun of the Resurrection,"* and the *"Sun of Justice,"* confusing Him with the Roman god of the sun.

While the *church* in Rome was taking on a new identity, Pamphilus, obviously an instrument of Esau, and a Gentile Catholic, was establishing churches in Israel. He also established a theological school and library dedicated to teaching Origen's views as the true orthodoxy throughout the entire Church.

><del></del><

In the fourth century, Constantine became emperor over

the western part of the Roman Empire, and Maxentius was emperor of the east. They agreed to battle at the Milvian Bridge, and the winner would be the emperor over the whole empire. Winning the battle, which made him master of all the Western and Eastern Roman world, Constantine had hopes of uniting the eastern and western halves of the Roman Empire. So he professed his belief in the God of the *Christians* after he won that significant battle, but it was merely a means to unite a still divided world.

He believed Gentile Catholic's God had kept His promises (according to a dream where he too confused Jesus with his sun god Mithras), and in gratitude Constantine immediately rewarded the followers of this God. To Constantine, this God of the Gentile Catholics was just another god, in his polytheistic mind, but he issued the *"Edict of Milan,"* as it came to be called, which restored buildings and land that had been seized from the Gentile Catholics during past persecutions.

Constantine professed his belief in this now Gentile Catholic God, but his conversion was not as many have presented it. For though he professed himself a *"Christian,"* Constantine never did display any interest in Christian ethics, their way of life, their worship of their God, and never let anything of the Scriptures inflict their morals on himself.

Constantine was eager to consolidate his gains and was determined to quench the various divisions within *Christianity*. Two problems were particularly difficult, the *Arian Controversy*, which contested the divine nature of Christ, and the continuing divisions over the *proper* date and celebration of the Passover/Eastre.

To Constantine, the moral and theological squabbles that divided the new religion, were causing problems within his newly united empire, and he wanted these little battles to stop. What mattered to him was that the Gentile Catholic church should be one and closely identified with the state, and that the state should be its undisputed master. Constantine presided over the first council at Nicaea in an effort to do just that.

Constantine included this *"double Passover"* issue - which is how he referred to this age-old problem within the Gentile Catholic church of the two dates (Passover and Eastre) that they were still arguing over - at the *Council at Nicaea*. When the three hundred eighteen bishops had assembled, Constantine admonished them against disunity. He had united his empire, now he intended to deliver the Church from *"internal sedition"* as well. And so, Constantine ruled in favor of *his* Roman holiday, and *Eastre* on a Sunday had now *officially* replaced the true date of the resurrection of the Jewish Jesus, which used to be the Jewish eight-day Passover celebration, with the third day, Firstfruits, as the actual day of the resurrection of Jesus.

Although Constantine will be blamed in the future for changing the Church, he didn't really do all that much to change it. Many of the changes had already been introduced, as with the Eastre/Passover controversy, over two hundred years before Constantine's time. Constantine simply had a meeting to make a determination for one day to celebrate this holiday, and others. Since he was a Roman, of course he ruled that his Roman holiday, *Eastre*, is the holiday that represented the resurrection of the Gentile Catholic God, and it should be celebrated on a Sunday. And so, at the Council of Nicaea the *"Eastre"* problem was settled once and for all, and a more permanent separation was made from the Judah Jacobs and Messianic Jacobs, and *their* Passover.

At the insistence of the bishops during his time, Constantine eventually instigated the removal of all Jewish ways from the Gentile Catholic church, making it the law. It had now become official, and it was now illegal to celebrate Jewish festivals and to celebrate with any Messianic Jacobs - who still seemed to linger for another four hundred years after Constantine's time. Even though it was illegal in the Roman Empire, the two groups still managed to mingle somewhere on the earth.

✻✻✻

Religion and politics were virtually entwined, as was the Roman way. Constantine made himself head of the Gentile Catholic church, an empire like Rome itself, and like Rome, *eternal*. Constantine, who had become Esau's puppet, continued to change *his* new eternal religion so that it not only served him better, but so that it served his subjects better. He decreed a strict toleration of his old beliefs. Paganism remained a potent presence at the center of Roman life in his empire. Paganism gave the impression of dwindling, but in actuality, paganism simply melded in, changing the names of the gods to Christian names. But the Romans never really stopped worshiping these gods - and the rest of the Gentile Catholics embraced Constantine's gods with ease.

Constantine's militant interpretation of this *new religion* was founded on his Roman understanding of interactions between faith and power. A more accurate term is *religio*, which really cannot simply be translated as meaning '*religion.*' No, for the Romans, their religious life of the army as a whole was distinct from the soldiers' individual lives. As an army, they were people at war, and their faith was a link between them and the civilians. As a people, their rituals, which had the sanction of the state, were intended to build morale and ensure unity. And then there were their private rituals, where they recognized a multitude of gods, and many forms of worship.

These three separate beliefs and rituals were linked together to form the state *religio*. Performing the state rituals was essential as it ensured the public well-being, and Constantine believed it protected families and communities from harm. As Rome's powerful empire expanded, it absorbed the local rituals, too. They were not alternatives however, as much as they were supplemental to the Empire.

Constantine's cults continued to stand at the heart of the state's religious system for two centuries, and full participation of soldiers and civilians was essential. Divine support for the head of state was guaranteed only by correct and universal observance of ritual. So when Constantine embraced the Gentile Catholic God, this god was simply added to his already ingrained rituals and beliefs.

Prior to embracing the Gentile Catholic God, Constantine had changed his obsession with his gods of Mars, to the god of Claudius II Gothicus, Mithras, whom he claimed he and his father were descended from. Mithras later became known as the god who became one with the sun, and was now '*the Unconquered Sun god*' Mithras. Mithras was born on *December the twenty-fifth.* This day soon became a Gentile Catholic holiday, celebrating the birth of Jesus and Mithras, since Constantine thought they were *one and the same* god. Eventually the Gentile Catholics stopped including Mithras in this celebration, about the sixth century, and began calling it Christmas (Christ's Mass).

Constantine wrote a decree which was known as the "*Donation of Constantine,*" in which he transferred authority over Rome and the western part of the Roman Empire to the Bishop, upon his deathbed, about the year 337.

Although it was determined to be fraudulent in later years, this document was used by all bishops to confiscate large territories in Italy. Emperors have always held the title of "*Supreme Pontiff*," or "*Pontifex Maximus,*" a title Constantine had also assumed. Because of Constantine's *donation*, this title was used by the Gentile Catholic bishops as well, as a part of Constantine's gift of his authority - and was still used in later years, *after* the *donation* was determined fraudulent.

Constantine was baptized this same year, 337, by Julius, who had just become the bishop of Rome earlier in the year.

Constantine died shortly afterward, thinking he was saved and going to heaven. Esau went in search of his next puppet.

Constantine's power shift to the Holy Roman Gentile Catholic church after his death, may have appeared to be a great thing for the Gentile Catholic church, but it was the beginning of the end for the Holy Roman Empire itself.

><>

Although they thought they were the only *church*, the Gentile Catholic church was no longer *Godly*, and for the next seventeen hundred years or so, the Gentile Catholic church was very dark spiritually - for without the guidance of the Holy Spirit the *Church* was blind spiritually - and sadly, none of these people were really *saved*.

They tried to look pious, and commanded the respect of the peasants, but the Gentile Catholic bishops did not have the guidance of the Spirit of God anymore, and they didn't understand the Scriptures. The doctrines that the Gentile Catholic church clings to cannot be found in God's Word, and was never taught by any of the original apostles. What followed for the next seventeen hundred years was evidence enough of their brutality, and complete lack of Biblical knowledge.

><>

It was in the early fifth century that an argument arose between the bishops of the Gentile Catholic church about whether Mary was the *mother of Jesus*, or the *mother of God*. In the year 431, at the Third Ecumenical Council of Ephesus, with more than two hundred bishops attending, and was presided over by St. Cyril of Alexandria representing Bishop Celestine I, was when Mary was declared the *Mother of God* by the Gentile Catholic church.

This new *title* gave her similar qualities to God in their eyes. And it was determined that Mary was the mediator between mankind and Jesus. She was later given other godly qualities, and eventually became a person to be venerated, which blasphemed God and His First Commandment: *"I am the Lord your God, who brought you out of the land of Egypt, out of the house of bondage. You shall have no other gods before Me."* Mary was never supposed to be anyone but a very willing vessel of God.

And in the year 787, the Second Council of Nicaea convened. It was the Seventh Ecumenical Council, or Nicaea II, which was summoned by Emperor Constantine VI and his mother Irene, under Pope Adrian I, and was presided over by the legates of Pope Adrian. This council determined in favor of the *veneration of holy images*. Three hundred sixty-seven bishops were present. Again, breaking the Second commandment of God: *"You shall not make for yourself any carved image, or any likeness of anything that is in heaven above, or that is in the earth beneath, or that is in the water under the earth; you shall not bow down to them nor serve them."*

*A*lthough Esau had infiltrated the Gentile Catholic church, he began to fall for his own lies, and studied Gentile Catholic's ways, thinking they were God's true followers. He may have gotten the ball rolling, but mankind had changed God's Messianic community so much, that Esau felt he needed to know it better.

He decided to also attack it from the outside, too. His master plan was unveiling right before his eyes. He would not only attack Catholic Gentile, but he would also attack his ultimate enemy, Judah Jacob - using the Gentile Catholic church. Esau knew he would not fail now.

Although Esau planned to help the Gentile Catholic church to eventually destroy itself, he had even more evil plans. It was now three hundred or so years later, after Gentile Catholic's split from Messianic Jacob and Gentile Messianic Jacob, and now Esau's evil spirit was planning to take over another. Esau would have his new *puppet* pattern his *new* religion after Gentile Catholic's *Christianity*, including their version of eschatology, but with a touch of Judah Jacob's history, too. But it was to be a very twisted version, with just enough *truth* to sway people into believing.

><del>><del>

Esau possessed Muhammad in that sacred of all caves, in Mt. Hera. He caused Muhammad to have convulsions and seizures, and scared him half to death. But eventually Muhammad was convinced that whatever possessed him was *not* evil - it was who he thought was Allah, the head god over Muhammad's people's gods. But now Allah has become only *one* god. Although Esau would spread the lie that *Allah* means *God*, in reality it is the name of an already established Arab god - who was around long before Muhammad was even born.

Muhammad began his *career* as the world's worst enemy, but he began in the Arab world first. Muhammad first tried to convince his Arab neighbors of his revelation of this new religion which had only one god. Since they were polygiests, they of course thought him crazy.

He had a few followers, but eventually he was kicked out of Quraysh, his home town, and landed in Yathrib. Muhammad established his new religion by offering part of the booty of conquered lands, to those who would join him in his quest. With his new religion now established, he also renamed the city of Yathrib - it was now Medina.

After Muhammad's army of followers grew to over ten thousand, they made their way back to Quraysh and challenged the many there, to conquer it for Islam. From then on he forced his new religion, Islam, on all who crossed his path. In fact, all who were in the towns that he conquered and would conquer, would hear of his new religion - words directly from Allah. Those who followed Muhammad called themselves Muslims, meaning *"those who submit."*

><><

This Allah distorted the true Word of God, giving his own version of God's Word to Muhammad. This twisted version was recited to Muhammad, who passed it down verbally, until eventually it was passed to someone literate, who wrote it all down and these words became the Qur'an. Rather than being the *inspired word of God*, as is the Bible, the Qur'an claimed to be the *actual* words of Allah - whom Muhammad claimed to be the one and only *God*.

But it is an actual contradiction, or opposite of everything that God is. It is, in essence, the *ultimate false religion*. And Islam's Muslims will be at war with the people of the One True God for more than fourteen hundred years. Esau had finally found his ultimate weapon.

><><

Another part of Islam that existed long before Muhammad was born, is that Quraysh is a city of pilgrimage. In the center of the city stands a black shrine that houses an idol called *Hubal*. In the eastern corner of this shrine there is a black stone called the *al-hajar al-aswad*. This stone was built into a corner of the wall of the shrine and had become an object of veneration.

The rulers of Quraysh had made a great deal of money from the pilgrims who came there each year, and were afraid this new monotheistic religion of Muhammad's could possibly cut into their profits. Even though most of the people of Quraysh were polytheists, they eventually turned to Islam and this pilgrimage became a part of their Muslim belief system, as well as this strange shrine with the black stone.

The jealousy and resentment born from this new religion, Islam, created an unparalleled hate which ultimately set off wars and horrible cruelties for many years to come. The Bible is the *title deed* to the land of Israel, which God promised to Abraham, Isaac and Jacob's descendants, and it has always been the *source* of the friction between *Jacob* and *Esau*.

⤛⤜

The goal of Islam is to take over the world, not in the usual sense, but in that Muhammad and his Muslims truly believe that Islam is the true religion of the God of Abraham. They *know* that Allah wants all of mankind to be Muslims. And so, they set off to spread the word of their Qur'an. But their way of *spreading* this word, was by force, for this was the instruction of the Qur'an.

The original believers of Islam were Arabs, who descended from Joktan, the father of the Arabs, Peleg's brother. About five generations after Joktan, Abraham was born, the son of Terah and the father of the Hebrews, so the Arabs really have no claim to the *Promise of God*. But, the Arab people insist it was Ishmael not Isaac, whom Abraham was about to sacrifice on Mount Moriah when an angel stopped him. According to the Qur'an, the Abrahamic covenant, with its promises - including the *title deed* to the land of Israel - was passed down to Esau through his cousin Ishmael, rather than to the Judah Jacobs through Isaac.

Esau taught Muhammad that he was the rightful heir to Abraham's promise from God, so their eventual focus, and hatred, was on Judah Jacob. Esau caused the Muslims to believe that Judah Jacob changed and distorted the Bible in order to establish themselves as the heirs of Abraham's Covenant blessings.

So Islam began distorted, but things had become even more distorted after the Qur'an was passed down by only word of mouth for many years. While Ishmael is a direct descendant of Abraham, he was never an Arab, the people to whom Allah first gave the Qur'an. But that's only semantics, which are neither here nor there for the Muslims. This was a later claim anyway, and Esau was not concerned with those things. His new religion would spread to other nationalities anyway, so he was not concerned with foolish semantics. As far as the Muslims are concerned, the *Promise of God* belongs to them. And they will use any means possible to get people to believe in Allah.

In the year 638, Esau's Muslims conquered Jerusalem and claimed it as their third most holy site. About the year 688, they began to build a shrine on the temple mount. "Islam will have victory over the infidels!" yelled Esau's Muslims, as they stood atop the temple mount in Jerusalem, where the construction of the new shrine was getting under way.

Esau was now convinced he had triumphed over Judah

Jacob. Muhammad's followers had taken Jerusalem, and then they became much stronger after Muhammad died in 640. By this time, Islam had grown into a substantial entity. The fusion of religion and politics, which is the essence of Islam, and the idea that there cannot exist a law that is not the expression of Allah's will, gave the intensely unorganized Arabian tribes a unity they had never possessed before - they now had a single cultural identity. This false idea of unity though, would not last forever.

From the time Muhammad started the Islamic religion, the dimensions of the conflict between Judah Jacob and Esau began to enlarge even more than they were already. When Muhammad's followers laid claim to Jerusalem as their third holiest site, the die was cast for Jerusalem to become "*a burdensome stone for all the peoples.*"

>~~~~<

Muhammad had achieved exactly what the Emperor Constantine had hoped for, but ultimately failed to achieve at the Council of Nicaea. Constantine considered himself not only the Emperor, but also a divine entity. Romans worshiped their Emperors as deity. Unfortunately for Constantine, the Council of Nicaea didn't exactly obtain him this right.

But Muhammad had succeeded in achieving the complete identification of the secular realm with the sacred, and the corresponding elevation of the ruler to the position of being divinely chosen by Allah, and a divinely inspired being. Esau's Muhammad not only copied and reversed the religion of the

Gentile Catholics, he also copied and *surpassed*, Constantine.

There is only one law in Islam, and it is called the *Shari'a Law*, which is just another counterfeit - of the *Law of God*. In Islam, the *Shari'a* is the direct expression of the will of Allah, derived from the Qur'an and the Hadith. This Hadith was written by the community of scholars known as the Ulema. It relates to all of Allah's commands concerning the activities of man. And it is this *Shari'a Law* that will take over the world - making it a world under *One Law*.

The core of the Shi'a religious world view is the Hidden Imam, Muhammad al-Mahdi, "*The Guided One.*" While the stories of the first eleven Imams are historical, the history of the twelfth Imam seems more mystical and miraculous.

Shi'a doctrines revolve around this *Hidden Imam*, and are the doctrines called *Occultation and Return*. This *Doctrine of Occultation* is the belief that Allah hid Muhammad al-Mahdi away from the eyes of men in order to preserve his life. Abu'l-Kasim Muhammad (which is the name of the Prophet Muhammad himself) was born in 868. Hasan al-Askari, the Eleventh Imam, died in 874, and the seven year old Abu'l-Kasim Muhammad then declared himself to be the Twelfth Imam. Immediately after, he went into hiding in a cave, where Allah will sustain his life - so the story goes.

This cave is blocked by a gate which is called *Bab-al Ghayba*, or "*Gate of Occultation.*" The faithful gather here to pray for the return of the Twelfth Imam. The Shi'a believe Allah has miraculously kept Abu'l-Kasim alive since the day he was hidden in 874. Eventually Allah will reveal him as the *al-Mahdi* to the world.   The Sunni believe any Muslim could be al-Mahdi - and he will bring with him Isa, the false Jesus and false prophet.

><><><

Islam had transformed into a formidable conquering force. Before Islam,   the Greeks and their Roman heirs had been the only competing views of life, or competing faiths.   But now Islam had transformed the ancient struggle between Europe and Asia.   They battled and conquered their way into much of Europe and Asia by the end of the eighth century AD. Islam had definitely become a force to be reckoned with.

It was the invasion of Spain that caused Gentile Catholic to pay attention to this new enemy. By killing Rodrigo, the last king of the Visigoths, and absorbing their serfs and runaway slaves, Islam's Arab general Tariq ibn Ziyad was able to invade Spain, by way of the narrow strait that separates North Africa from Europe. This invasion by these *Moors*, as the Europeans called them, left the Gentile Catholics of the Mediterranean world completely surrounded by Muslim states. Soon after the Islam occupation of Spain, most of the Iberian Peninsula was under Muslim reign.

Spain had become a permanent battlefield, but it was also the *final* frontier, the place where Islam and Gentile Catholics met. In the centuries during which Spain was under Muslim rule, there were a very large number of conversions to Islam.

It was quite easy to convert a Gentile Catholic once they were surrounded by Moors.   It was inevitable that they would pick up the religious practices, the customs, the clothing and even the eating habits of these Moors, since they had no real foundation for their faith.

>∾∾∾∾∾<

Islam and Gentile Catholics continued to attack, and counter attack each other, each as barbaric as the other. And the Muslims continued to become more organized and strengthened. In a world of unceasing conquest and reconquest, of migration and deportation, ownership of a land was established not by who got there first, but by who could stay there the longest.

While the Gentile Catholics considered themselves *Christians* and the rightful heirs of God's kingdom, they were really just as much barbarians as those they battled. Those warriors of the First Covenant fought their battles against evil in the natural, once Jesus came this was not to be the case. The Gentile Catholics had abandoned Jesus for the most part, by this time. There was *an evil* entity guiding them now, but still using *"the name of Jesus."*

A strange myth, conjured up by the Gentile Catholics of Spain, had transformed James, one of the first followers of Jesus, into *Saint James the Iberian saint.* He became the symbol of the worldwide struggle against Islam. And so, the attack of the Moors on the city of Compostela, did not undermine the power of *"James the Moor Slayer."* In fact, the attack dramatically backfired. The *Moors* did not cause fear and disenchantment as had been intended, but had roused indignation and anger throughout the Gentile Catholic world.

Part IV

The sixth thousand years

*M*uch like the Muslims, the Gentile Catholics were one, concerning church and state. So it was with this mindset that they determined to get Jerusalem back. They must take back *their* land, for they still believed their people had replaced Judah Jacob as the true *Church*.

The Gentile Catholics felt the only way to win Jerusalem back was to create an army. They needed people who could be warriors and fight. They would shed blood just like David did, and still be true Gentile Catholics in God's eyes. And so, the *Crusader* army was created.

Secular soldiers were recruited, given a cloth cross and made to take vows. They were also promised salvation and penance for past sins, if they would fight for the Church. It was stressed that only those who were responsible for retaking Jerusalem would this be possible, causing an overwhelming popular support for the *first crusade*. Unfortunately, no one knew salvation wasn't theirs to give. But these secular soldiers were now '*Soldiers of the Church*.'

The Gentile Catholic Crusaders were determined to win back Jerusalem. They wreaked havoc in the name of *their* Jesus, but this was not what God had intended at all. The Crusaders were not acting according to the will of God, they were acting out of pure hatred, retaliation and greed. They aimed to take back Jerusalem for what they called the *Gentile Catholic Church for God*. They had suddenly been given a central place in the conception of the *just war* by the pope himself.

But most of these men, who were promised salvation, were not Gentile Catholics at all. They left their homes and families unprotected, to fight in this holy war, having no idea what they were getting into, nor who they were really fighting against. In most cases, the Gentile Catholic Church did not care about these men and their families, and confiscated their homes *legally*, assuming they were never coming back, and their families were turned out of their homes, or sent to convents. The Gentile Catholic church simply needed men to fight their so-called *just* battles, and it was only right the church *protect* the soldiers' property.

Since these crusaders, who called themselves *pilgrims of the cross*, or *soldiers of the Church*, truly did not know who their real enemy was, their first target was not the Muslims. It was the Judah Jacobs. The *Crusaders* had little, if any, understanding of theology or sacred history and none whatsoever of Scripture, and they were unable to distinguish clearly between the various *"enemies of Christ"* about whom they had heard so many tales from the equally ignorant priests. They considered Judah Jacobs, heretics and Muslims, all of whom they called *the enemies of God*, to be equally detestable. Much in the same fashion as Islam calls for, the Crusaders went to *"wipe out or to convert"* any non-Gentile Catholic they found in their path.

Many Judah Jacobs were annihilated by the *Crusaders*, in an effort to *clear the path* to Jerusalem. The rest of the Judah Jacobs went into hiding, but the *Crusaders* hunted them down, determined to rid Jerusalem of all of *God's enemies*. The *Crusaders* burned synagogues, destroyed Torah scrolls, and desecrated Jewish cemeteries wherever they went. The slaughtering continued for many years, and all this was done *in the name of Jesus*. It was truly the *"first holocaust."*

Having regrouped after having butchered the Judah Jacobs, the *Crusaders* moved into the Balkans, where the army, who were by this time completely out of control, first attacked the town of Zemun, and then they took Belgrade. Although many perished in the subsequent seizures of foreign lands and booty, certain groups of *Crusaders* made it as far as the now Seljuq city of Nicaea - where they were wiped out by the Turks.

In the following month, a more orderly group of men took up the cross of the *Crusaders*, and began the long and hazardous journey across eastern Europe toward Constantinople. From there the Crusaders headed to Nicaea, and then on to Antioch, and finally to Jerusalem. It took them over a year to arrive there, and by this time they were hungry, saddle-sore, weary and despondent. The *Franks*, as

Esau's Muslims called all Europeans, had at last penetrated the sacred soil of the *dar al-Islam*.

The Seljuq Turks, who ruled over the geographical area that was originally Judah Jacob's land, were now divided up into a number of semi-independent states. They were all under the rule of the caliph in Baghdad but they were all deeply suspicious of one another. In fact, they had been in a civil war for about thirty years at this point. The Fatimids, who controlled most of the Holy Land, had survived this struggle but were greatly weakened. For them, the disorderly and ill-equipped Franks seemed at first to be a far lesser threat than their own people.

The *Crusaders* moved swiftly and orderly, taking advantage of the Muslims' apparent failure to offer much effective resistance. Nicaea was surrendered without much of a fight. The *Crusaders*, now on the verge of starvation and marching in heavy armor under a burning sun, now set out for Antioch. Antioch was no longer the city it had been under Byzantine rule, but it controlled the route into Aram.

Miraculously, Gentile Catholic's *Crusaders* managed to defeat another of Esau's Muslim forces that had been sent in to stop them. They were on the march again. By nightfall, in June of the year 1099, Gentile Catholic's *Crusaders* had reached the walls of the holy city of Jerusalem - literally the center of the world.

Esau's Islam was thriving - and conquering. The Muslims ruled a vast region and had spread to the northern parts of Africa and as far east as Persia and Afghanistan. Things had been quiet for about four hundred years, but now they were preparing to battle those *Crusaders*. Esau could see them over the wall of Jerusalem, blazing their swords and riding directly toward the city gates. *"Silly infidels,"* he thought. *"They will never take Jerusalem. And besides, it never belonged to them."* Esau warned his people to get ready, for the *Crusaders* were almost upon them. This was the beginning of the last one thousand years - and *"Jacob's Trouble"* had already begun.

Jerusalem proved to be much more resilient than Nicaea had been. For over a month, Gentile Catholic's *Crusaders* besieged what appeared to be a completely fortified city. They made several futile assaults on the massive walls surrounding Jerusalem. But finally, they gathered enough ladders and siege engines, and then launched an all-out attack on the eastern section of the wall. The Muslim population fled away from that part of the city, hoping to use the al-Aqsa Mosque as a refuge.

The Fatimid governor, Iftikhar ad-Daulah, offered to hand over the city to Raymond of Saint Guilles in exchange for his life, and the lives of his family. It was agreed and they were escorted out of Jerusalem. The governor and his family were fortunate. The rest of the population, who had taken refuge in the Mosque, were dragged out and slaughtered. Judah Jacob's people, some of which were again living in Jerusalem, had sought refuge in the main synagogue. The *Crusaders* burned the synagogue down, with the Judah Jacobs still inside.

When the butchery was done, the temple area of the city

was piled high with bodies and blood. One *unbiased* eye witness said, "No one has ever seen or heard of such a slaughter of infidels..." Jerusalem had been taken back for the Gentile Catholic church, but at the most horrible cost to mankind. This was not a Godly win, but a brutal butchery.

This massacre was not sanctioned by God. It wasn't that God was behind these horrific crusades, as much as He was against the Muslims taking the world by storm. It wasn't time yet for them, so perhaps God *did* have a little to do with strengthening the worn-out *Crusaders*. But He never intended so much carnage to take place. These were supposed to be Godly people, and they were supposed to take prisoners, not butcher God's inheritance - and everyone else.

In *Old Covenant* times, many times God commanded Judah Jacob warriors to kill everyone of their enemies for a particular purpose, like with the Amalekites, but not in these *New Covenant* times. The *Crusaders* had seemingly botched this one, but Jerusalem was back in *Christian* hands. And the Muslims had been stopped - temporarily.

Esau's people, watching from afar now, could not believe what was happening. *"How could this happen?"* Esau said to himself. *"These crusaders aren't even Judah Jacobs, so why would they want Jerusalem?"* *"If we don't retreat now though, we will not be able to take Jerusalem back."* So they retreated, and began to regroup. Even if it took a thousand years, they would regroup, and they would return to take Jerusalem - and the world.

Esau's Muslims needed a plan that would eventually gain

them the world. So they began to come up with a new plan that would kill as many infidels as they could, to make room for al-Mahdi. al-Mahdi would take this world in whatever form he needed to. And first and foremost, he must remove the Judah Jacobs from this world!

><><

One group of the *soldiers of the Church,* called themselves the *Knights Templar.* The *Knights Templar* began as a group of nine secular knights, who already had been fighting in the crusades for several years. They joined together to dedicate their entire lives to the service of the Holy Land. The monastic-order-like vows they took were completely opposed to the life goals of the typical secular medieval knight. In a world that was cruel, and barbaric, taking these vows was remarkable. These men were not going to hide themselves behind the walls of a monastic cloister, safe from the outside world. These *Knights* planned to patrol the roads of Jerusalem fully armed, ready to fight any enemy in order to protect the Gentile Catholic pilgrims on their way to the holy cities and back.

Because one of their vows was poverty, the *Knights* were supported by the king of France. The *Knights* were given a portion of the al-Aqsa Mosque, which was built on the temple mount. The temple became the reason for their name, and was then shortened from *"Knights of the Temple"* to the *"Knights Templar."*

The *Knights Templar* were given much power by the king. They collected tithes, but they didn't have to pay tithes themselves, nor were they required to pay taxes. They were also given land in each of the countries, where they formed their bases. So they actually went from being poverty stricken to having a huge surplus of funds, even after their expenses.

Soon the *Knights* went from only nine men guarding Gentile Catholic pilgrims, to a whole *order* which consisted of thousands of secular recruits, taking the same vows as the *Knights*. The *Knights Templar* were definitely revolutionary men for their time, not only in their battle tactics and maneuvers, but in their finances, and also in the delegation of authority and departmentalization. They became an order where a soldier could hold his head high, no matter where he came from - converting from the angry, the independent, the aggressive and the resentful, to living a *holy life*. They were, after all, *Soldiers of the Church* now. To be a part of the *Knights Templar* order was a high honor.

For three hundred years they continued as a respected order for the Church, but then Jacques de Molay, the last *Grand Master* of the *Knights Templar*, was summoned to Europe, instigated by King Philip of France. King Philip wanted to get his hands on the *Templar* wealth, and though his plan was dangerous, if improperly handled he knew he could unleash forces that could easily turn on the French monarchy. King Philip knew there must be a charge of heresy, because this charge called for confiscation of property. He called for an Inquisition of the *Knights Templar* in order to find the order guilty of heresy.

It wasn't an easy task since the *Knights* were excluded from secular law and torture, but after much planning, infiltration and deceit, King Philip got his wish - eight years later. He found a way around the no-torture rule, and the *Knights* were in fact tortured until confessions were made. With over two thousand confessions, Pope Clement V decided their guilt could not possibly be open to question. Many did not believe the charges against the order, but in Paris in the year 1314, Jacques de Molay and Geoffrey de Charnay were burned at the stake. Pope Clement V died during the following month, and King Philip also died within seven months. A fitting end for a brutal act of greed.

>━━◆━━◆✕

The *Crusaders* really had no idea who God's enemies really were. As far as they knew, anyone outside Gentile Catholic's Church deserved to die. And so they continued for many years, killing *in the name of Jesus*. Because of these killings, it opened the door for Esau to take over future leaders, who would commit future *holocausts*.

The crusades continued for several hundred years. Although they went about it very wrongly, killing *in the name of Jesus*, there would have been not one Gentile Catholic left if it hadn't been for the *Crusaders* and the *Knights Templar*. It was because of this that these crusades were somewhat *justified*. For God calls those to do for Him, but because of free will He has to allow them to do His work however they see fit - even if it is brutal and wrong. They will ultimately have to answer to God for all the evil they have committed in His name.

The crusades paved the way for Gentile Catholic's people to stay alive and prosper - and hopefully, they will eventually find their way back to Him.

But they never really stopped this new false religion, Islam, to grow. For Esau would always find a way to continue his personal war against Jacob, no matter who he was disguised as. Esau didn't care, as long as all of them were eventually wiped off the face of the earth. That was Islam's, and Esau's, ultimate plan.

While history books will claim the crusades stopped after about two hundred years, nothing could be further from the truth. Wherever the Moors were conquering and taking lands, the *Crusaders* planned to attack to win the land back. Their goal was to push the Moors back to where they came from. For in the following seven hundred years or so, the crusades continued in the guise of wars of other names, such as *World War I*.

The wars against Muslims did in fact continue. But the crusaders never truly won, for the Muslims continued, and proved they were a force to be reckoned with for a very long time. This was proven at the *final crusade* in Portugal. Officially, the *battle of the Three Kings* was the last Gentile Catholic crusade - the last battle of the last crusade. On August 4, 1578, twenty-six thousand men were slaughtered, including three of Portugal's Kings.

But still, the Muslims were not completely stopped. In fact, they had only just begun.

*T*he city of Constantinople was really all that was left of the once-mighty Byzantine Empire, and was now a most treasured prize to be conquered by the Ottomans. The battle of Ankara allowed Constantinople to survive for another fifty years, but it was not the end of the Ottomans, for their losses only gave them incentive to consolidate. Esau's Ottomans made another attempt to seize Constantinople for Islam. The use of artillery had changed the rules of the game, making the old proven strategy of encircling a city no longer necessary. Constantinople was doomed, and would soon be in the hands of Esau's Muslims.

After finally breaking down the walls of the city, fierce fighting led to another victory, Esau's Mehmed II's army was allowed to pillage the city for three days. It wasn't a pretty victory, as none ever are, and many died that day, including civilians.

Constantinople now began its rapid transformation into *Istanbul*. A church built by Constantine was transformed into a mosque. The statue of Constantine, which was erected almost one thousand years earlier, was now taken down. Constantinople was now Esau's.

The Ottoman Empire was now the major power in the East, and the sultan was the self-appointed leader of the Islamic world - and empire. But they still wanted Rome - according to Islamic prophecy, Rome would also one day be theirs.

The capture of Constantinople, in the year 1453, marked the real *beginning* of the Turkish Ottoman Empire. There were many nationalities in the Empire now, and thus the whole position of the sultan and his army had changed. The absolute union of church and state developed into a system which governed in all Islamic states.

In order to keep Muslims and non-Muslims separate, and the different nationalities separate from each other as well, cities were divided into the various communities. The Sultan, who more or less had become an emperor, chose not to convert the non-Muslims because he collected taxes from them that were not paid by Muslims, thus adding to his Empire's revenue.

As a result of these separate communities, disturbing influences began to permeate this evil leader. Lands of the Greek families were confiscated and then transformed into "fiefs" - land held for feudal service. It left the Gentile Catholics at the mercy of the feudal lords, who were warriors of the Empire. This situation was one of increasing *oppression* for the Gentile Catholics, and their priesthood had been drastically altered. Gentile Catholic priests were now acting as civil representatives of their people in feudal matters, which actually gave them an advantage. But because of this position, even more apostasies developed and took hold within the Gentile Catholic church.

><><

The Spanish Inquisition had been instituted by Pope Innocent III to prevent conversos from engaging in Jewish practices - those who were Judah Jacobs who had been forcefully converted to *Christianity*.

But this was eventually deemed inadequate, and they began expelling all Judah Jacobs from Spain because of the "great harm suffered by Gentile Catholics from contact and communication with Judah Jacobs who had converted, who always attempted in various ways to seduce faithful Gentile Catholics from their Holy Catholic Faith." The Inquisitions lasted from about 1233 until the late eighteenth century - more than five hundred years.

About half of the eighty thousand Judah Jacobs who left Spain in 1492, chose emigration - to Portugal. But only five years later they were forced to leave Portugal in 1497. But most Judah Jacobs of any country chose to be baptized into the Gentile Catholic religion before the deadline, to avoid expulsion. But even this didn't protect the Judah Jacobs from the Inquisition, because they were still suspected of practicing Judaism.

It would be another two hundred years or so before the true nature of the Inquisitions was exposed, and then it continued for several hundred more years. The Inquisition not only hunted for Protestants and false converts from Judaism, the conversos, but also searched for false or relapsed converts among the Moriscos, converts from Islam. Officially, all Muslims in the Crown of Castile had been converted to *Christianity* in 1502. Muslims in the Crown of Aragon were obliged to convert by Charles I's decree of 1526, and most had been forcibly baptized during the *Revolt of the Brotherhoods*.

Many Moriscos were suspected of practicing Islam in secret, but the jealousy with which they guarded the privacy of their domestic life prevented the verification of this suspicion. Initially they were not severely persecuted by the Inquisition, but experienced evangelization without torture, a policy not followed with the conversos.

There were some Protestant Jacobs who were tried in these inquisitions, but none were executed. It was during the fifteenth and sixteenth centuries when the bulk of these trials took place, which often resulted in burning at the stake for the conversos. Although pretty much anything that could be constituted as sin could not avoid these Inquisitions, it was the Judah Jacobs who suffered the most. The Inquisition under Ferdinand and Isabella alone had several thousand conversos burned at the stake. Plus, there were about thirty two thousand *heretics* that were burned at the stake (most of these being conversos), another eighteen thousand were burned in effigy and about two hundred ninety-two thousand made reconciliations as a result of the Spanish Inquisition *trials*.

The Inquisition was abolished on July 15, 1834 by a Royal Decree signed by regent Maria Christina of the Two Sicilys. But it was temporarily reinstated during the First Carlist War, *to protect the Church*. The Church carried out these Inquisitions as much for taking the property from the conversos as for defending their faith. They were called *trials*, but they always ended up in execution.

Esau's Gentile Catholic church has definitely lived up to his expectations, being the bloodiest religion ever to exist so far. While the crusades and the inquisitions no longer exist, the Gentile Catholic church has been Esau's most dependent instrument of cruelty ever to exist. Who would have thought that a religion supposedly based on the Word of God, could do so much damage, supposedly *in the name of Jesus*.

><del>~</del>~<del>~</del>

Once the crusades appeared to be finally coming to an end, the Ottoman Empire flourished. Esau was proud of his latest Islamic empire, and it continued to grow and thrive for another six hundred years. The Ottomans moved steadily west, battling and conquering lands for their empire. Serbia, Albania, Poland and Macedonia were soon a part of the huge Ottoman Empire. For little more than half a century after the Ottomans had founded their dynasty, they formed one of the many bands of Turks who roamed over western Asia and southeastern Europe.

><del>~</del>~<del>~</del>

Not long after Islam began, there were constant disputes over religious and political leadership, which caused a schism much like the Gentile Catholic schism. The majority of the Muslims accepted the legitimacy of all the four caliphs, and became known as Sunnis. The minority disagreed and believed that Ali, who was one of the succession of three caliphs after Muhammad, was the only rightful successor. They became known as the *Shi'a*. Ali was assassinated not long after that, and a new caliph, Mu'awiyah, seized power and began the Umayyad dynasty.

There were five caliphs in less than fifty years since Muhammad's death. So even though they continued on as an Islam empire, there was much strife and conflict throughout the forty countries and territories. But in spite of all that, the Umayyad dynasty did manage to prevail for seventy years, and expanded Muslim territory into many more countries.

Then even another sect sprang up out of the devout Muslims, who questioned the piety of indulgence in a worldly life. This new sect emphasized poverty, humility and avoidance of sin based on renunciation of bodily desires. The Devout Muslim Hasan al-Basri inspired a minor movement called *Sufism*.

Esau was getting tired of these constant arguments between his own instruments. Esau had to find a better way to keep these guys in control. They were messing up his plan! He decided to concentrate on a different country, such as Arabia where his new religion had its beginnings. He caused Arabia to become a major region of the Islamic world. For nine hundred years the holy cities of Mecca, once called Quraysh, and Medina were under the control of the Sharif of

Mecca. But at most times the Sharif owed allegiance to the ruler of the present Islamic Empire, based in another region.

Esau thought he had finally gained some control over his Muslims, at least in Arabia, and the first Saudi state was established in 1744. Sheikh Muhammad ibn Abd al Wahhab and Prince Muhammad ibn Saud formed an alliance to establish a religious and political sovereignty determined to cleanse the Arabian peninsula of *perceived* deviations from the orthodox Islam and heretical practices. But this empire collapsed too, when the Ottomans came against the Sauds, a battle known as the Ottoman-Saudi war.

Islam had spread quite far by the nineteenth century. Esau's Ottomans had always been in control, to some extent, but now they had control over all the Islamic states. However, in Arabia there was a rebuilding period following this Ottoman-Saudi war and the House of Saud returned to power and established a second Saudi state in 1824. This state lasted for almost seventy years, when the Al Rashid dynasty of Ha'il, the rival family, captured the Al-Saud ancestral capital city Riyadh in 1891, calling his new state *Rashidi Arabia*. But it didn't last long before Abdul Aziz Ibn Saud recaptured Riyadh in 1902. His continued conquests eventually expanded Arabia to Nejd and the Hejaz.

><sup>
The Ottomans were not particular with whom they considered their enemies though, for there was supreme power to be considered. They plundered many a crusading Gentile Catholic, and they even fought each other in contests of

supremacy. But even with these little civil squabbles, there was an upward tendency. Not only were these Muslim Ottomans vigorous on the battlefield, but they showed shrewdness in their policies. They had become a terror to all.

Transylvania and Bosnia yielded their rules to the Muslims, and the war spread southward and westward against the Albanians and Venetians. Moldavia and the Crimea were next, then Hungary, Italy and Persia were also added to the Ottoman dynasty. The conquest of Syria and Egypt were the final additions to this vast empire.

✎~✎

The Ottoman Empire included forty governments and four tributary countries. And there were twenty kingdoms included in the forty governments. To these territories were added the lower part of Russia, held by the Cossacks of the Ukraine. They voluntarily submitted to the Sultan as protection against the Russians and Poland. Of course, this caused a war with Poland. This war developed into a war against the *"Holy Alliance"* of the Gentile Catholics, a league against the Turks, under the protection of the Pope - no doubt another *crusade*.

This league was formed by the Emperor of Austria, the King of Poland, and the Republic of Venice. The outcome of this war was a treaty signed, called the "Peace of Carlowitz" in 1699. This was the first great mistake the Ottoman Empire made. Esau's Ottoman Empire had ceased to be an object of dread in Europe.

This peace lasted for about a hundred years, until

aggressions against the Muslims commenced by Peter the Great. The Ottoman Empire seemed near its dismemberment since most of the kingdoms were now independent. Another defeat, another treaty, and the Ottomans of Turkey no longer had control of Esau's empire. Esau would need to switch gears and concentrate on his other false religion, *Christianity*, to inflict more damage. Esau's Muslims will have to wait until a later date - but they *will* rise again.

✂✂

In its last sixty years, Esau's Turkish Ottoman Empire had become known as *"The Sick Man of Europe."* This *illness* had been going on for quite some time. The defeat at Vienna, the humiliations thrown upon the empire by the Treaty of Carlowitz, the loss of the Crimea and Napoleon's invasion of Egypt and Syria, had all been only the first signs of the *disease*.

There were also conflicts with neighboring states due to the constant religious disagreements between Jordan, Iraq and Kuwait. But boundaries were eventually established through a series of treaties negotiated after World War I.

In 1926 Abdul Aziz Ibn Saud became King of Hejaz and King of Nejd. He later united these two kingdoms, and in 1932 this kingdom was called the Kingdom of Saudi Arabia.

In 1938 oil was discovered and it completely transformed Saudi Arabia. Eventually the Saudi economy and infrastructure was developed with help from overseas, particularly the United States, which created strong links between these two very different countries. This created a considerable American presence in the Saudi Kingdom. But those Muslims who were not of the Royal Family, considered this American presence extremely *problematic.*

There was a series of modernization of the Saudi government: the creation of ARAMCO, the petroleum company between Saudi Arabia and America, the building of the Saudi passenger airline service, and the development of Saudis defense industry. Saudi Arabia was no longer the pure Islamic country it had started out as.

Another series of events, including more wars between the Islamic countries, ended up with Saudi Arabia purchasing America's half of ARAMCO.

After several successions of family leaders, due to death from natural causes and one assassination, as of 2005 King Abdullah took over for his brother King Fahd, who died in July 2005. Many of the other Islamic countries are still in conflict with the worldly Arabians. There will soon be another war.

〜〜〜

The Egyptians, Assyrians, Babylonians, Medo-Persians, Greeks, and Romans didn't know anything about running an empire - not even the Ottomans at the end. But Esau's Islam will show them how its really done. *"We will infiltrate their lands, and absorb their culture and their language, and we will enforce Islam on them or they will die. We will thrive, because we will be disguised as the locals, but Islam will live on.*

By the time al-Mahdi has been ushered in, we will have conquered most of the world - Islam will be the ruling religion of the world," Esau mused, "*Islam will own the world. Allah will not fail. The Islamic Empire will not only rise again, it will survive and conquer - the whole world. The Islamic Empire is the eighth, and is of the seven.*"

*A*bout four hundred years earlier, over in Europe, many attempts had been made to question the false teachings of the Gentile Catholic church, but it all came to a head in the early sixteenth century. This one particular Gentile Catholic German Monk questioned why some of the things he was taught were done. The Church leaders just scoffed at him and told him that what was in the Canon Law was approved by the Church Fathers - and they were the final word on Church matters. It was not his place to question Canon Law and the Church Fathers.

But God had revealed something to the spirit of this Gentile Catholic German Monk named Martin Luther. He began wrestling with what he had been taught in the Church, but he had no access to the Scriptures, so he had never read them. He was finally sent to study in Wittenberg, Germany where the Scriptures were available to read. He did in fact read the Scriptures, and found what he thought he had been searching for. Most of the clergy had never read the

Scriptures either at that time, but nothing had *bothered* their spirits. The Gentile Catholics had always trusted what the Church told them. But many of the traditions of his Church just didn't seem right to Martin Luther. And now that he had read the Bible, he wondered, *"These things are not in the Bible, so how did the church fathers come up with these things?"*

After reading and studying the Scriptures, Martin Luther finally came to a conclusion, and disagreed with the Church leaders. So he sat down one night and wrote out all his complaints, that he based on Scripture - it was a very long list. Then he posted this list on the main church's door, in hopes that everyone would see it. *"He wasn't actually questioning the pope, was he?"* Martin Luther thought. He just wanted to point out certain things that were not in the Bible, and he wanted to know why these things were done and taught in the Church. Luther only wanted to bring reform to the church, but in reality Martin Luther, *was* indeed challenging the pope's authority.

Because they had never truly read the Scriptures and had lost everything Jewish that inspired the Scriptures, the Gentile Catholics really didn't know much about salvation, other than what the Gentile Catholic church leaders told them. They truly had no understanding of Judah Jacob's Law, which was the foundation for the Church Gentile Catholics claimed to be. Thinking that Jesus had destroyed the Law, because of translation errors in the Scriptures, they didn't want anything to do with Judah Jacob's ways or laws. They didn't need those laws anymore, so they thought. And so, Gentile Catholic ignorantly continued his church through *man's* humanistic, and very Gentile ways. They adopted Greek philosophy and tradition after tradition, and constantly argued with others about how the church should be run, and how to interpret the Scriptures of the *Final Covenant.*

Little did Gentile Catholic know, but the Scriptures were not to be interpreted by using the mind of man, or Greek philosophies. The Greek's used intellectualism, and the Gentile Catholics had adopted this Greek thought process. And so they interpreted the Scriptures in this manner.

Gentile Catholic's idea of living for God was limited to his humanity and intellectualism. They had no concept of God's ways and laws, and couldn't even conceive of being a follower of Jesus any other way than what they were told by the Gentile Catholic church leaders. They did not know that one must have a spiritual experience to know God. It wasn't just a choice, it was the rebirth of a dead spirit - a reconnection to God, through Jesus alone.

The Reformation of the sixteenth century was a movement to purge the Church of its many medieval abuses, and to restore the doctrines and practices that the reformers believed conformed with the Bible and the New Testament idea of the Church. This led to a breech, or rather *war,* between the Gentile Catholic church and the reformers. Because of the beliefs and practices of these reformers, these people eventually came to be known as Separatists, Puritans and Protestants. Some of these words were originally used in a derogatory sense by the Gentile Catholic church.

><><

Martin Luther was a thorn in the pope's side, and he was messing up Esau's Gentile Catholic religion, and was stirring up trouble among the people. The pope could not have this happening in *his* Church! So he summoned this Gentile Catholic monk, Martin Luther, to the Canon Court, to expose him as a heretic. But it backfired, and many of the other Church leaders backed Luther up. There was much chaos and unrest among the people, who stood behind this one Gentile Catholic, who was seemingly against the Gentile Catholic church. But Luther was not against the Gentile Catholic church, he simply wanted to reform it, and bring it back to the pure Word of God. It soon became evident that would not be happening any time soon. And now there were two *churches*.

Peasants joined Martin Luther's quest, much to the displeasure of the Gentile Catholic church. And many of these peasant people were killed for their rebellion against the Gentile Catholic church. But Martin Luther prevailed. The *Church* had split into two - there was Gentile Catholic church who clung to all the false teachings of the Catholic Church Fathers, and was predominantly still Gentile. And then there was Protestant Jacob, a part of Jacob who had reemerged and was trying to find his way back to the Truth. The Truth of the Bible was within Protestant Jacob's grasp now.

When the Gentile Roman Catholic church refused to heed Luther's call to reform and return to biblical doctrines and practices, the *Reformation* began. From this *Reformation* four major divisions or traditions of Protestantism would eventually emerge: Lutheran, Reformed, Anabaptist, and Anglican - making the Protestant Jacob church not much different than the Gentile Catholic church, with their many false doctrines.

><del>~~</del>><

It was hard to break old habits, so using the Greek mindset of trying to *figure out* Scripture instead of realizing that God is not to be *figured out*, Protestant Jacob originally had four basic questions that were the basis for the *Reformation*. How is a person saved? Where does religious authority lie? What is the Church? What is the essence of Christian living?

It would be these questions that Protestant Jacobs Martin Luther, Ulrich Zuringli, John Calvin and John Knox attempted to answer when they came up with these five things to measure a church by, which eventually came to be known as the "*Five Solas.*"

Sola Scriptura, or Scripture alone, was the establishment of Scripture alone as the sole authority for all matters of doctrine, faith and practice. *Sola Gratia*, or Grace alone, was the establishment of the belief that God's grace alone saves us. We are saved from His wrath by His grace alone. *Sola Fide*, or Faith alone, established that justification is by grace alone, through faith alone because of Messiah alone. *Solus Christos*, or Christ alone, was the establishment that salvation is found in Christ alone. His substitutionary atonement alone is sufficient for our justification and reconciliation to God the Father. *Soli Gloria*, or for the

Glory of God alone, is the establishment that salvation is of God, by God and is for His glory alone.

᠆᠆

Demanding the Truth had caused many more wars between the Gentile Catholics and the Protestant Jacobs. Many people died for their beliefs, whether they be for the Gentile Catholic church or the Protestant Jacobs.

There should never have been wars concerning the things of God. Although there were battles in the Old Testament of the Bible, these wars were against the enemies of God. There was never a war between God's people - and if there was, God would be the judge of them. But these wars of the *Reformation* were inevitable between those who did not truly know the Word, nor what it was all about.

The humanistic Gentile Catholic church could not see that they were wrong in their false teachings, and the Protestant Jacobs wouldn't stop trying to show them the *error of their ways*. These constant squabbles, that many times turned into all out wars, showed that neither of them truly knew God's ways.

But the Protestant Jacobs were open to learning more and they continued to learn more as they went along, for they were reading the Bible and truly wanted to know God in the way the Bible told them they could.

᠆᠆

Five hundred years before Luther rocked the boat, there was a split between the Gentile Eastern Orthodoxy Catholic church and the Gentile Roman Catholic church that became known as the "Great Schism" of 1054 - so God was already intervening at this point. Their argument was over political and doctrinal differences, as they always are.

There were other theological disputes as well, such as whether leavened or unleavened bread should be used in the *eucharist* - which was a false doctrine and teaching in itself. And then there was the biggest dispute of all: Roman legates traveled to where Cerularius was, to insist that he recognize the Church of Rome's claim to be the head and *mother* of the churches - claiming succession to the *chair of Peter*.

Cerularius refused. Cardinal Humbert, the leader of the Roman group, was so angry he excommunicated Cerularius from the Gentile Catholic Church of Rome. In return, Cerularius excommunicated Cardinal Humbert from *his* church. This fundamental breach has never been healed.

Protestant Jacob also tried to claim succession. Some groups tried to establish a *"Trail of Blood"* that can be traced back through the centuries to the first century church, and the apostles themselves. But most of these churches are simply trying to establish a connection to the early church in some small degree, to establish the authority of their *own* doctrines and practices - and ultimately, the authority of *their* church.

Just another little ploy of Esau's, for he still had his hand in everything. Little did they know that no one can ever have a claim to succession, except Jesus Himself. The churches fall very short of having *any* authority to establish doctrines and practices, yet they continue to do so.

The Word itself, is its own authority. But of course, Esau

will go to any length to keep this truth hidden from the churches, both Gentile Catholic and Protestant Jacob. Without the Jewish element to show them what the Scriptures were really all about, these doctrinal confusions would always continue.

✵∼✶

Protestant Jacob trudged on. He read and studied the Bible for he wanted to know the true ways of God. He knew that the Gentile Catholic church way was very wrong Biblically, in their beliefs and practices. But even so, Protestant Jacob kept some of Gentile Catholic's heretical practices, for he didn't know any other way.

But soon, even Protestant Jacob would have schisms within himself. Still arguing over how to interpret the scriptures resulted in many churches who did not agree with each other. And even though there were many disagreements between them, they still all called themselves Protestant Jacobs. Surely this couldn't be what God wanted?

Many of the Protestant Jacobs had formed churches - many churches that all claimed to be the *only* church of God, with the *only* true doctrine and the *only* true interpretation of the Scriptures. But these churches were all the same, yet different, because while each based salvation on a different Scripture, they were still the same in their basic meetings and operations. And they each thought they were the *only* true church! And so, these humanistic practices that were not in the Bible and should never have been a part of any church, continued even within Protestant Jacob's churches, too.

God's true ways were still hidden from them. It would be over five hundred years before Protestant Jacob would even begin to see the real truth of the Bible. But once he grasps the initial truth, God will pour the rest into Protestant Jacob's spirit.

><><

In the seventeenth century, many of the Protestant Jacobs of England, who called themselves *Separatists*, because they separated themselves from the Church of England, left England and ventured over to the new land so they could practice their religion safely, for the wars between them and the Gentile Catholics were still going on. It seemed that whenever the Queen of England would change, so would the preferred religion of their country. So they went in search of a new country for *freedom of religion.*

The Puritans stayed in England a bit longer, thinking they could still reform the Church of England from within. They did this at great risk to their lives. If they were caught, they were branded and an ear was cut off, as a warning to others. And some were killed. But eventually, they too would find their way to the new land - forced to live in the colonies of a new land, because life had become too unbearable in England.

But Separatists and Puritans found that it was no different in this new place called Boston, because they weren't free of England. And the founders had their own ideas of what religion should really be, and they wanted a town where only one religion would be acceptable - *their* version of the Scriptures. Anyone who had any differing idea to what the

Protestant Jacob church leaders thought the Scriptures meant, were imprisoned as heretics. This new land proved to be the same as the old.

Unfortunately, this would also be another part of the *Falling Away*. For as families lived and grew in these new colonies, their faith waned. About every hundred years, a colony would find itself completely along another path. But then someone would rediscover the Word, and try to pray his colony back to God. It wasn't that these people were not going to church, for they were. But they had completely strayed from the truth of the Word of God, because these churches eventually became full of unbelievers.

In some cases, a colony did in fact experience some kind of a revival. But once the colonists separated completely from England, and formed their own country, they were in danger of traveling too far from the Word - too wrapped up in patriotism instead.

While their original motives might have been good, original motives always get lost in the shuffle of life, when the focus of the people is off of God. Forgetting why they came to the new country completely, their minds were more on what was going on in their new country than it was on God.

This new country was supposedly founded on principles of freedom, and of God, but these *principles* were rooted deep within the minds of the affluent, right from the very beginning. Hiding behind the supposed idea that this country was founded on Godly principles, the ultimate bluff was only beginning - the lie of the *American Dream* had just begun.

While the original leaders of the colonies were *men of the cloth*, by the early eighteenth century, rich merchants were now leading. And it was these leaders who eventually triggered the Revolution against England. The first President of this new nation was one of these rich merchants. Except for maybe Abraham Lincoln, this new country's leaders have been corrupt from day one - none were truly Godly men; but they did the best they could.

After only two hundred thirty-five years, this new country has completely lost touch with God. It is destined for ruin. America will succumb to her greed - and ultimately, her enemies.

><rr>⌒⌒rr><

Supreme authority for all matters of faith and practice God had given in His holy Word, the Bible. Jesus warned us in the New Testament, almost from the beginning, that false teachings have been invading the Church and leading people astray. Most Protestant Jacobs think they have left all false teachings behind, but they are blind to the real truth of this matter.

When the time comes, the Truth of the Word will win, and the false teachings will finally be abandoned - and Protestant Jacob, and maybe even a few Gentile Catholics, will find what was stolen from them, as adopted sons of God. Esau will not win in this.

*E*sau's Ottoman Empire wasn't doing too well, but they were still in power when the first World War began in the summer of 1914. It all started when someone assassinated Archduke Franz Ferdinand of Austria, an ally to Germany. A Bosnian-Serb student and member of *Young Bosnia*, was accused of assassinating the heir to the Austria-Hungary throne while he was in Bosnia, so Austria-Hungary invaded Serbia one month later. As is always implied in assassinations, only *one* person was involved.

Esau couldn't be happier, but this war eventually got totally out of hand, leaving his beloved Ottomans without a Caliph - and without an empire. It seems that there were two groups of countries that were the main characters in this battle. There were the *Central Powers*: Germany, Austria-Hungary, Ottoman Empire and Bulgaria; and the *Allied Powers*: France, Britain, Russia, United States, Italy, Japan, Belgium, Serbia, Romania, Greece, Portugal, Montenegro and Brazil.

◥◤◥◣

Austria-Hungary invaded Serbia, Germany invaded Belgium, Luxembourg and France; and then Russia attacked Germany, and so on, and so on. It was all to maintain a balance of power throughout Europe, or rather it was because they *couldn't* maintain it.

The German Chancellor of Bismarck had negotiated the *League of the Three Emperors* between the monarchs of Austria-Hungary, Russia and Germany back in 1873. But the agreement failed because Austria-Hungary and Russia could not agree over Balkan policy, so Russia bowed out of the agreement, leaving Austria-Hungary and Germany with the *Dual Alliance* formed in 1879. Later, Italy was added and it became the *Triple Alliance*.

Of course, Esau had a hand in just about every nation at this time. He had to make sure these treaties did not stick, and they didn't for very long. This so-called *balance of power* was not working, and Europe was simmering.

Meanwhile, Esau's Ottoman Empire was warring with the Balkan League, which eventually created an independent Albanian State, and enlarged the territorial holdings of Bulgaria, Serbia, Montenegro and Greece. Another Ottoman battle lost.

The *Battle of Mecca* was instigated by the Arab bureau of the British Foreign and Commonwealth Office, and ended with the Ottoman surrender. The Ottoman commander of Medina held out for more than two and half years during the *Siege of Medina*, but it finally ended with the Ottomans surrendering.

This *Great War* ended on November 11, 1918, when a ceasefire came into effect. All in all, the result of this war was the end of the German, Russian, Ottoman and Austria-Hungary empires; the formation of new countries in Europe and the Middle East; the transfer of German colonies and regions of the former Ottoman Empire to other powers; and the establishment of the *League of Nations*.

The first national creation by the British, was a homeland for the Judah Jacobs in 1917, which centered around Jerusalem. The *Versailles Treaty* was signed in 1919, and combined with another treaty, the *Treaty of Lausanne*, the Allied forces released Constantinople in August 1923, and the nation of Turkey was formed, and although they had already transformed the city, *Constantinople* officially became *Istanbul*.

Shari'a Law was repealed and the office and role of *caliph* was eliminated. The *last caliphate* of Islam was the *Ottoman caliphate* - it was the *end* of the great Ottoman Empire, and the caliphate - for now.

Although this was a beginning for Turkey as a country, under the new leadership of Mustafa Kemal Ataturk, a radical *secular revolution* set the course for Turkey for the rest of the 20th century. Most of the rest of the Middle East countries were also created, or recognized, by the British authority, such as Iran, Iraq, Jordan, Kuwait, Arabia and the United Arab Emirates. Syria's borders were also drawn up by the British in 1923, but was administered by France, and was not granted independence until 1946. And thus were the majority of the Middle East nations formed, giving homelands to *all* peoples who lived in the region once called *Syria Palaestina* about a thousand years ago - a name given to Israel by the Roman Emperor Hadrian.

⟩⟨⟩⟨

A young Adolf Hitler volunteered for the German Army, enlisting in a Bavarian regiment. His part in the first World War wasn't much though, since he never actually saw any fighting. But shortly after the war, in 1919, he was sent to investigate the *German Workers' Party*. He discovered it wasn't much of a party, but decided it had potential, and at the age of thirty, Hitler joined the party.

The party grew mostly because of Hitler's newfound ability to speak. He had become a highly effective, and visible speaker in front of ever larger crowds. He gained notoriety outside of the Nazi Party for his rowdy, highly emotional, and at times hysterical manner of speech making. Hitler's tirades were mostly against the *Treaty of Versailles*, and for anti-semitism and anti-Marxism. It wasn't long before the *German Workers' Party* had over three thousand members. Once again, Esau had found another perfect puppet.

Adolf Hitler had begun his political career as a street brawling revolutionary, and was already a totally deranged, and unstable human being. A bipolar, narcissistic, sociopathic maniac, Hitler chose the swastika symbol to identify his *movement*. This movement now had a new name: the *National Socialist German Workers Party* or "*Nazi*," short for "Nationalsozialistische Deutsche Arbeiterpartei."

The swastika was nothing new, for Hitler had seen it often as a boy while attending the Benedictine monastery school in Lambach, Austria. But when it was placed inside a white circle on a red background, it became quite powerful and instantly recognizable, plus it helped Hitler's party gain popularity.

By July 29, 1921, Adolf Hitler was the *Fuhrer* of the *Nazi Party*. Over the next several years, Hitler tried to overthrow the Bavarian government, was on trial for treason, went to jail for nine months, dictated a book to Rudolph Hess while in prison, was banned from speaking in several countries and dreamed of future glory for himself and *his* German Reich. Those dreams centered around asserting the supremacy of the Germanic race, acquiring more living space for the German people, or *Lebensraum* as Hitler called it, and dealing harshly with Marxists and the Judah Jacobs. The ban against Hitler speaking was lifted in 1927.

Meanwhile, in New York, Esau decided to *play* the market. On October 29, 1929, the Wall Street stock market crashed with disastrous worldwide effects. Happening first in America, it soon spread to the rest of the world. Companies went bankrupt, banks failed and people instantly lost their life's savings. Unemployment soon soared, and poverty and starvation became real possibilities for everyone around the globe. A depression had been born.

At the outset of the depression, Hitler knew his opportunity had arrived. His *Nazi Party* was ready to spring into action. The economic pressures of the depression had begun to cause the German democratic government to unravel.

The people of Germany were now desperate enough to listen to a crazy Adolf Hitler. Governments seemed powerless against the worldwide economic collapse. Esau engineered the next move of Hitler and thought it was ingenious. A series of events within the German government led to the dissolvement of the Reichstag and a call for new elections, which resulted in Hitler's rise to absolute dictator of Germany.

It was 1933, and political independence was over for Germany. Political enemies were arrested by the thousands and placed into old army barracks, or abandoned factories. Using them as prisons, the prisoners were often beaten and even tortured to death - the beginnings of the Nazi concentration camps.

Ten days after the election, Esau's Hitler managed to coerce the government into passing the *Enabling Act*, which in effect voted democracy out of existence in Germany, and established legal dictatorship of Adolf Hitler. Shortly after the *Enabling Act* was in place, the Nazi's boycotted Jewish shops. The following month Nazis burned Jewish books in Germany, and they opened the Dachau concentration camp in June 1933.

Austria was the first nation Hitler targeted for German occupation. Schuschnigg, the Austrian Chancellor, was given a long list of terms to be met within three days, or Austria would be invaded. Schuschnigg reluctantly agreed. Germany met no resistance, and in most cities, German soldiers were welcomed like heroes. Many of Austria's seven million Germans had longed to attach themselves to its dynamic Fuhrer - a son of Austria.

The Nazi occupation of Austria was marked by an outbreak of anti-Jewish violence. Such violence had not been seen in Germany or Austria before. Throughout Vienna, Jewish men and women were grabbed at random by Nazis, and thousands were jailed for no reason at all while police allowed open looting of Jewish homes and businesses.

><><

Nazi Propaganda against Judah Jacob's people had flooded Germany with a six-year ceaseless stream of leaflets, posters, newspaper articles, cartoons, newsreels, slides, movies, speeches, records, exhibits and radio announcements. Included in this propaganda was accusations, denunciations and opinions such as the claim that the Judah Jacobs were engaged in an international conspiracy to achieve world domination.

In his speech on January 30, 1939, Hitler added a stark new warning: "If the international Jewish financiers in and outside Europe should succeed in plunging the nations once more into a world war...." - insinuating that the Judah Jacobs would be to blame if there was another world war.

Hitler also believed that the very presence of Judah Jacobs in Germany and Nazi-occupied neighboring countries posed a threat to a victory in the war for Germany. Hitler was now beyond insane.

Neighboring political leaders came to Hitler to help

resolve the ongoing *crisis* of unrest (propaganda campaigns of *wrongs* committed against local Germans waged inside their boundaries). They would then be offered *help* in the form of a German Army occupation to "*restore order.*"

Russia tried to align with England and France, but they and Poland wanted nothing to do with Russia - they did not trust Stalin. This outright rejection caused Stalin to negotiate with the Nazis. A pact was signed, with Hitler making plans to destroy Soviet Russia in the future. Hitler broke every single pact or treaty he ever signed - a practice that the treaty-signers seemed to be completely ignorant of, until too late.

Hitler was threatening war now, but so were Poland, Britain and France. Hitler's bloated ego caused him to slowly succumb to the belief that he was infallible. The *Fuhrer-god* of Germany was suffering from a megalomania that was blinding him to reality.

War was now inevitable. Hitler wanted war, but not with England. Poland and England had now signed a pact to join forces. Hitler was now pretending to want to negotiate for Danzig and the Polish Corridor. He wanted it to appear as if Germany was willing to discuss a peaceful solution with Poland, but that the Poles were being entirely uncooperative.

On September 1, 1939 the Nazi troops roared across the border into Poland. The Polish Army, who were hopelessly outdated, had put up a brave resistance but were crushed without mercy by the German Army in only eighteen days. Hitler had plunged the German people into what would become a new world war in the not too distant future, simply to fulfill his own mad ambitions - *Lebensraum*.

>>~~~<<

Hitler's first goal was to round up and deport the Judah Jacobs to the already-established ghettos in Lodz, Cracow and Warsaw, Poland. Inside these walled-in ghettos, the Judah Jacobs were cut off from the outside world and were squeezed into overcrowded areas where malnutrition and disease would naturally diminish their numbers. These ghettos brought a slow death to those inside their walls, which is exactly what the Nazis planned.

Then at Auschwitz, a nearby city, a much larger concentration complex was constructed. Auschwitz was chosen by Himmler, one of Hitler's partners in crime, to carry out Hitler's order of the *Final Solution*.

Hitler's Nazi army next invaded Denmark. His troops marched into Denmark and simply informed the Danish King that his country was now under Hitler's protection and that resistance was futile. To protect his people from Hitler's wrath, the King and his government surrendered.

The German army also tried the same tactics on the Norwegians, as they did with Denmark. However, Norway refused to submit. The British army aided the Norwegians, but they were outnumbered and were unable to hold out against the German tanks and attack planes. They held out for over a month, but a Norwegian Nazi sympathizer helped to topple his own country for Hitler, and Norway was taken.

The invasion of France was mistakenly thought to begin with their northern neighbors, Belgium, Holland and

Luxembourg. But as the French, British and Belgian troops rushed into position to confront the invaders, German troops came from the south, through the Ardennes Forest, roaring northward through France. At the same time, the Germans also crushed Holland.

With the French army on the verge of collapse, the French government was in a state of panic and fled Paris, hoping Hitler would spare its destruction. Hitler's German army freely rolled into France, and the French meekly asked for armistice terms.

Hitler's gangster diplomacy would gain him *Lebensraum* in many surrounding countries, some without a single shot fired. His primary goal of *Lebensraum* was being achieved step by step, and with very little bloodshed. Drunk with power, the Nazis thought they could do anything, maybe even conquer the world!

These were German victories almost beyond belief. Austria, Czechoslovakia, Poland, Norway, Denmark, Belgium, Luxembourg, Holland and now France, were now all under German control. Spain and Italy had already signed political alliances with Hitler, but Great Britain was the only European major power who still remained free.

Winston Churchill, who openly admitted to being anti-Nazi, was the man in charge of Britain now. Churchill flatly refused to discuss anything with Hitler or any of his Nazi representatives, and much to Hitler's egocentric surprise, Britain would not fall for his games either.

Britain was ready to stand against this evil maniac, who

would plunge Europe into a new *Dark Age* if the war was lost. Almost every European leader who Hitler had challenged, had either backed down or been conquered. But the British Empire would stand against Hitler - there would be no negotiations.

For fifty-seven days Hitler bombed England, but he still lost this battle. Hitler then decided to turn on Russia. Hitler's war had always been more of a racial war, than anything. And so, when he attacked Russia, whom he considered one of the lower forms of humans, he planned for senseless murders of even civilians.

The Russians were not prepared and not ready, despite intelligence reports warning that a Nazi invasion was imminent. The fate of the Russians seemed inevitable - they were surrounded by German soldiers. The Russians kept fighting though, and the Red Army sent four hundred divisions to push the Nazis out of Russia.

Russia's size alone was to their advantage. Stalin regained his bearings and appealed to the public for a *"Great Patriotic War"* against the Nazis. Stalin's "fight to the death" strategy kicked in for the Russian soldiers and eventually the Nazis began to lose momentum.

Hitler's generals now wanted to scrap their original plans and stage an all-out attack on Moscow, but Hitler stuck with his original plan. It would mean German forces would be attacking simultaneously on three major fronts over a two thousand mile long stretch of land, causing their manpower and resources to be stretched to the limit.

Millions more Judah Jacobs came under Nazi control as

Hitler's armies swept through Russia when they first invaded. The existence of so many of these *unwanted* people in the tracts of newly acquired *Lebensraum* was presenting a dilemma. The Nazis had to rethink what to do.

One school of thought was to first rid themselves of those in their path: the Nazi field commanders, following behind the German Army, shot Russian political officials on sight, then they targeted all Judah Jacobs, including Jewish families living in the countryside of Russia. Nazi troops would arrive unannounced and inform the residents they were to be immediately resettled. The Judah Jacobs were taken to a different locale and ordered to hand over their valuables and their clothing. Then they were executed by shooting them while they stood next to a ditch. They were then thrown into the ditch after they were shot.

>━━━◅

At this point, Japan was already engaged in a war with China. In efforts to stretch their borders even further, they had tried to invade parts of Russia, too. These clashes, which ended in defeat, convinced the Japanese government that they should focus on pacifying the Russian government to avoid their interference in the war against China. So they turned their military attention southward, toward the United States and European holdings in the Pacific. This was when the two wars merged. These holdings were spread across several continents, and so caused this huge war to cover most of the entire globe.

The United States tried to stay neutral, but assisted China

and the Western Allied countries. The American Neutrality Act was amended to allow cash purchases by the Allies. But directly following Germany's capture of Paris, the size of the United States Navy seemed to significantly increase in size.

The United States further agreed to a trade of American destroyers for British bases, and they also protected British convoys. Because of this, the United States soon found themselves engaged in naval warfare with Germany, yet still remained *officially* neutral.

Japan had seized French Indochina, and had occupied it. As a result of this, the United States, United Kingdom and other Western governments froze Japanese assets. The United States - which supplied eighty percent of Japan's oil - responded by placing a complete oil embargo against Japan. Iron, steel and mechanical parts were also embargoed against Japan. Many Japanese officers considered the oil embargo an unspoken declaration of war.

Although the United States knew Japan was canvassing their Pacific fleet in Pearl Harbor, they thought they were untouchable there. But on December 7, 1941 Japan attacked British and American holdings with near-simultaneous offensives on the American fleet at Pearl Harbor, landings in Thailand and Malaysia, and Hong Kong. They thought they had neutralized the whole United States fleet.

But the United States, Britain, Australia and other Allies formerly declared war on Japan. Then Germany, Italy and Japan declared war on the United States.

With every attack the Japanese Navy tried, the American

Navy planned counter-attacks. With every loss, the Japanese Navy tried other attacks. Following the Guadalcanal Campaign, the Allies initiated several operations against Japan in the Pacific. They were successful in pushing Japan out of every country they tried to invade.

><><

The weather changed in Russia. It was now winter - a Russian winter the Germans were not prepared for. The once-mighty German military machine had all but come to a halt in Russia, and Russians noticed the change. By mid-December 1941, German forces were battered, cold and fatigued, and were in retreat. They were facing the possibility of being rounded up by the Russians. Only six short months before, the Germans were ready and able to achieve the greatest victory of all time. But Hitler's army would never be the same. They had lost their illusion of invincibility that had caused the world to shudder in the face of Nazi Germany.

*M*uch to Esau's joy, the propaganda had worked in Germany, and many locals participated, including police and governmental officials. They issued specially marked identity cards and then compiled lists so that by the time of the *Final Solution*, Hitler's answer to *"the Jewish Question,"* no European village, town, city, state or nation had been left uncatalogued as to the number of Judah Jacobs and where they could be found. Around the clock, seven days a week, trains arrived at Auschwitz from all over Europe, to deliver the Judah Jacobs.

When they arrived, they were inspected to see who was fit enough to work in the Nazi slave labor program that Hitler put into effect - the rest went to the gas chambers. The gas chambers were horrific. People were marched to rooms that looked like locker rooms at a gym and told to remove their clothes, then they were ushered into nearby *shower* rooms. The doors were closed behind them, and locked. Then Zyklon-B pellets were dropped through hollow shafts that extended to the floor of the shower room. The burnt almond-like odor the cyanide gas gave off, caused the people to gasp for air, rendering them unconscious - then death came from oxygen deprivation.

Meanwhile, unbeknownst to Hitler, Winston Churchill had just allied himself with Russia, and the United States. Better late than never? By the summer of 1944 almost two million Allied soldiers were assembled in England, to fight against Hitler's *empire of death*.

One year later, the war was ending. Heydrich had been killed, but Hitler, Goring, Goebbels and Himmler were in Hitler's Fuhrerbunker almost to the very end. Himmler and Goring did eventually flee to Berchtesgaden, but they were caught in the end. Goebbels couldn't stand the thought of living without Hitler, so he and his wife poisoned their six youngest children, and then themselves.

All of Hitler's *disciples* had committed suicide at one point or another - even Hitler. Hitler and his long time companion Eva Braun stayed in the bunker, and committed suicide together. Their bodies were burned by the remaining troopers who were ordered by Hitler to do just that. Goring then took command, but by this time it was too late. Himmler had already surrendered all German troops in the West to General Eisenhower, but continued the fighting against the Russians in the East.

Himmler had planned to play a key role in the new German-American-British alliance, and thus be the leader of post-Hitler Germany. But things did not quite work out like he planned. Around the world his name was already synonymous with mass murder.

Russia bombed Berlin and the Fuhrerbunker, making direct hits on the Reich Chancellery buildings and the bunker. Russian ground troops were making their way through Berlin next. On May 7, 1945 an unconditional surrender of all German forces to Allies was signed by General Jodl, with authorization from Donitz, whom Hitler had named successor in his will - not Himmler. Nazi Germany was finished, and the war with Germany was over.

>━━━◇━━━━<

Japan wasn't ready to give up just yet. In May 1945, Australian troops landed on Borneo, overrunning the oil fields there. British, American and Chinese troops defeated the Japanese in northern Burma, and the British pushed on to reach Rangoon shortly thereafter. American forces moved toward Japan, taking Iwo Jima and Okinawa by the end of June. American bombers destroyed other Japanese cities, and their submarines cut off Japanese imports.

On July 11, 1945, Allied leaders met in Potsdam, Germany. They confirmed earlier agreements about Germany, and reiterated the demand for the unconditional surrender of all Japanese forces. They specifically stated that "the alternative for Japan is prompt and utter destruction."

When Japan continued to reject Potsdam terms, the United States dropped atomic bombs on Hiroshima and Nagasaki in August. Russia also invaded Japanese-held Manchuria, and quickly defeated the Kwantung Army, which was the primary Japanese fighting force. The Russians also captured Sakhalin Island and the Kuril Islands. On August 15, 1945 Japan surrendered.

><++~~<

Esau was the catalyst behind World War II. It was essentially two wars that merged. There was Japan's war against China, and there was Germany's war against everyone else. Italy and Soviet Russia signed non-aggression pacts with Germany, but eventually Russia switched to the other side when Germany invaded them. It was with the help of the Russians that drove German troops out of their country and neighboring countries. It was with their help that Japan was also driven out of the territories it had captured.

These were wars of aggression on Germany's and Japan's parts. Their leaders were power-hungry, and their goals were to take as much territory as they could - each for different reasons. The other countries were simply trying to win back the territories Germany and Japan had taken. Which they did, but not until after mass deaths of civilians, which included the Holocaust and the only use of nuclear weapons in warfare to date. This war has been the deadliest conflict in human history, with losses of seventy million lives.

Eisenhower insisted a filmed record be made about the atrocities against the Judah Jacobs, because he believed people would someday deny that such things ever happened. German boys and girls were required to attend local theaters and watch the Allied educational films concerning the concentration camps. Only six months later, the trial of all trials took place at Nuremberg, lasting three hundred fifteen days. The evidence against the German leaders was overwhelming and horrifying, and convicting. Their sentences were handed out on October 1, 1946.

><del>~</del><del>~</del><

Even though he lost the war, Esau still felt he had gained points against the Judah Jacobs. Through Hitler, Esau had taken the lives of six million Judah Jacobs. Those Judah Jacobs who *did* survive World War II were still no longer wanted in their homelands. Many of their homes had been occupied by their neighbors, wishing the Judah Jacobs had never returned. Others lashed out at the returning Judah Jacobs and hundreds were killed. The displaced Judah Jacobs headed back to Germany and took refuge in American DP camps. While there, they considered leaving Europe to relocate to the historic Jewish homeland in the Middle East.

><del>~</del><del>~</del><

Zephaniah prophesied, *"For then I will restore to the peoples a pure language, that they all may call on the name of the Lord, to serve Him with one accord."*

The Hebrews had long lost their language as a people. Rabbis and scholars still used it in the synagogues, but it was no longer the language of the people. But about the year 1881, a young man named Eliezer Elyanof, and his wife Deborah, decided to move to the land that had been designated for the Jewish people. He changed his surname to his Hebrew surname, Ben-Yehudah, and began to write articles for the rebirth of Israel and her native language.

Eliezer Ben-Yehudah knew this Hebrew language would not be the same as the Hebrew of the rabbis and scholars. It would be a Hebrew language in which the people could conduct the business of life. He also knew it would not be easy to revive a language that had been dead for a very long time.

Eliezer's family spoke only Hebrew in their household, thus making them the first household in nearly two thousand years to speak Hebrew. His son was born a year later, and he was raised speaking Hebrew exclusively.

Hebrew soon became the language of the courts, the theatre, business, and society. And then when Israel became a nation again, Hebrew was adopted as the language of their new state. Hebrew, God's pure language, had been brought back to life - just like He said He would do.

><>~<><

The push for a Jewish state began as early as the late nineteenth century. Those Judah Jacobs that remained in the Palestine region, were a part of the *Zionist* movement, that was organized by Theodor Herzl in 1897. This movement united forces seeking the creation of a Jewish homeland.

At the time of World War I, the Ottoman Empire controlled the Palestine region, and they had supported Germany. But after the war, Britain was given control over the Palestinian regions and territories.

The *British Balfour Declaration* of 1917, and the *League of Nations Mandate* of 1922, provided Britain with the power to mandate the creation of a "National Home" for the Judah Jacobs of Palestine. Judah Jacob and Israel Jacob's people from around the world began to immigrate to the new homeland. Almost four hundred thousand of both Judah Jacob and Israel Jacob's people moved to their new homeland in the period from 1920 to 1945, and have been doing so ever since. From the time Judah Jacob and Israel Jacob's people entered Israel they became one people again.

The Arab population there grew restless and began attacking and killing Jew Jacob settlers. Arab marauders caused the Jew Jacobs mayhem, and hindered the attempts of the new settlers in making their new homes into settlements.

But the events of World War II strengthened worldwide support for a Jewish state. The United Nations proposed splitting the British Palestine region into a Jewish state and an Arab one. The plan was fragile, but it could perhaps have worked had it been any other two groups of people. The Jew Jacobs greeted the news of partition with joy, but the Arab representatives at the United Nations immediately rejected this proposal - causing the Arabs who lived in the Israel region to be without a home in the Middle East.

Fulfilling several prophecies, May 14, 1948 was the date the British officially gave the Jew Jacobs their own homeland. Although the Arabs had not been a big problem in recent times, needless to say, they were not happy when the Jew Jacobs were given their own nation - right in the center of all Islam! And Islam's third holiest city was right in the middle of Israel - not *Palestine*! "This cannot be," said Esau. "I will put an end to this abomination and stir up my people to do what is right!"

On May 15, 1948, the very next day, the first of many Arab and Israeli conflicts began immediately after the nation of Israel was created. Five Arab countries – Egypt, Syria, Jordan, Lebanon and Iraq attacked Israel.

Even though they too were granted nations with borders - seven nations in all - the Arabs did not recognize Israel as a state. They felt that the little patch of land now called Israel, belonged to them too. All the armies of the Arab states had entered areas that had been designated as part of the Jewish state. The Arabs attacked Israel from all sides, and even inside Israel's own borders!

The Arabs began bombing sections of the old city of Jerusalem. The Jew Jacobs retaliated with their own bombs. There were small truce periods, but not a day passed during these *truces* without one or more people being killed. The regular armies obeyed the truces, but the Arab *irregulars*, which included the Arabs from the *Palestine* region and the Arab Liberation Army, generally disregarded the *truces*.

Though Israel was a new nation and new militarily, they were able to organize their resources and add a growing number of Jew Jacob immigrants into their society as active parts of their military - forming a united people. The Jew Jacobs sustained many losses, but *against all odds*, they won the war - and with this victory, even more land!

By the end of the war, Jew Jacob's borders had expanded beyond those the British had first outlined. These borders were not recognized by the Arab states, but then they didn't recognize *any* borders of Jew Jacob's new nation. The two wars eventually created three hundred sixty thousand Arab refugees and seven thousand Jew Jacob refugees.

During this war, although Jew Jacob won additional land, his nation lost control of the eastern part of Jerusalem to the Arabs. Western Jerusalem became Israel's capital city, while Eastern Jerusalem, including the temple mount, was occupied by Transjordan. The city was divided between two armed camps separated by barbed wire, concrete walls, minefields and bunkers.

The Arabs continued to refuse to recognize Israel as a state. Though hostilities ceased, the refugee problem was still there. Many of the Arabs had fled voluntarily to other Arab countries, but were not received. The Jew Jacobs absorbed the Jewish refugees, but the Arab refugees still had no home. The Arab leaders had rejected the creation of a Jewish state - and a Palestinian state - causing their own people to become refugees with no where to go.

This action by Arab leaders converted the refugees into a human tragedy and a real disaster for Jew Jacob's nation. The Arab's continuing obsession with wiping out the *"Zionist entity"* is the driving force behind this problem.

Esau now put all his concentration into the Muslims. The Muslim states were not willing to accept in their defeat, or in the decree of the UN that there should be a Jewish state in a part of Palestine. The Palestine issue, which had been a part of the motivation for the creation of the *Arab League*, now moved front and center into Islamic politics, and became the locomotive of a rising Arab nationalist movement.

There were two more periods of fighting between the Jew Jacobs and the Islamic nations during this time, with the next one lasting from July 9 until July 18, 1948. Then after that, the third period of fighting between the two peoples was from October 15, 1948 to January 7, 1949. There were a couple truce periods, but even during those times there was once again constant small scale fighting. Jew Jacob's nation was out-manned and out-gunned, but still they held their own, and eventually won these little battles.

More wars, or broken peace treaties, all started by the Muslim nations surrounding Jew Jacob's nation, continued for the next sixty years, with the last *official* war in 2006.

The Sinai Campaign, the Six-day War, the War of Attrition, the Yom Kippur War, the Lebanon War, the Gulf War and the second Lebanon War, were all wars between Jew Jacob's nation and the surrounding Muslim nations. And all were based on the *false fact* that there is a *Palestinian people*, without a home. Esau's lies were proving to be great propaganda.

The testimony of the founder of the PLO, Ahmed Shukari, already proclaimed in 1956 at the UN, that, "Such a creature as *Palestine* does not exist. This land is nothing but the southern portion of Greater Syria..." So if Ahmed Shukari says that *Palestine* does not exist, the logical deduction is that "*Palestinians*" do not exist either. But in 1964, Egyptian president Gamal Abdel Nasser hired Shukari to found the "*Palestine Liberation Organization,*" the PLO, an organization dedicated to the liberation of a country that, in his own words, *does not exist.*

All the prominent spokesmen of that *poor, homeless people* say openly: "The Arabs who live in Israel are precisely the same Arabs who live in Syria, Jordan and Lebanon. They are not a separate country or people, but a fragment of the enormous Arab nation divided amongst many Arab countries. In their identity, they are Arabs and the invention of *Palestine* is just a transparent bluff: *'a means for continuing our struggle against the State of Israel for our Arab unity.'*"

No one could have imagined that anyone would use the name *"Palestine"* to create a monstrous, hostile, false identity for propaganda purposes, and would engrave on their flag the destruction of Jew Jacob's nation and people. But that is the reality for today and for the future of Jew Jacob's nation, and in 2011 the issue was still on the table.

Since their inception in the seventh century, the Islamic people have become Esau's newest, and last *puppet of evil.* The war that Germany waged unleashed an evil that seemed like it could not be stopped. Although it *was* stopped, that evil just transferred to another people, and it is surfacing once again. It will be an evil no one would ever imagine.

This evil will be much like Hitler, for these people think of Hitler as a hero. The war against Jew Jacob is far from over. But this time, Jew Jacobs and Protestant Jacobs alike, will need to prepare for the most deadliest evil they have ever encountered. They must be ready, and strong in their Lord.

Part V

The end of the age

E sau's people are a misunderstood people. Because of the limited, and one-sided news coverage of the *Palestinian problem*, Muslims across the globe are fuming with a rage with only one outlet. A once peaceful (or rather, *dormant*) people, more and more Muslims are joining the *Fundamentalists*, feeling victims of the *Palestinian tragedy*.

With many young Muslims out of work and hungry, they blame only two nations - Judah Jacob's nation and America. And they are ripe for a war, with plenty of hatred toward these two *corrupt, boastful* and *condescending* countries. While some are sympathetic with these people, God has chosen the Islamic religion to be the *false religion* behind the AntiChrist's *one world system*. Everything that is happening, is being orchestrated or allowed by God.

>✒︎✒︎<

On September 11, 2001 people all over the world saw the most horrific, and unimaginable, scene they had ever encountered in America. At first it appeared to be an accident, but when the second commercial airplane crashed into the second of the Twin Towers of the World Trade Center, the horrible truth began to creep into everyone's minds. And then they heard the TV announcer say another airplane had struck the Pentagon building in Washington DC. Some people were stunned and stared at their TVs in disbelief. But others, those in the Middle Eastern nations, seemed to be dancing around and cheering - both reactions to the same events.

While it was a horrible and tragic thing, especially when the Twin Towers came tumbling down, the powers that be knew something like this was soon to happen. The United States government did their best to stop terrorists attempts in America, they just couldn't be everywhere at once. And it really didn't matter that America's borders were virtually unprotected, the terrorists had been living in the United States for some time now. Many terrorists are born and raised in the United States. And it hasn't taken long to convert many of America's citizens over to their cause.

><<

After almost ten years, and thousands of lives later, Osama bin Laden, leader of the *famed* al-Queda group, who master-minded the attacks of that fateful day on September 11, 2001, was shot and killed. And then the natives of America celebrated the death of this unarmed man, much in the same way the Muslims celebrated the September 11, 2001 attacks. American's condemned those Muslims who celebrated, but they appear to be no different.

Bin-Laden was an evil man, and killed many people on September 11, 2001. But he was unarmed when shot, and should have been taken prisoner. And, he was only a pawn in this great terrorist war anyway. Another leader will rise up, and then what will America do?

On June 22, 2011 America announced it would begin removing troops from Afghanistan. So what would happen if all troops were removed from Islamic countries? It would set America up for a fall. The war against terror is not over - but then, it will never be over. But with no American presence in Muslim nations, America makes herself to appear weak and vulnerable - bringing the war onto American soil.

Iran has been threatening to annihilate America for some time now - and America might be the first to go so they won't be able to help Israel. Although America has already pulled away from Israel, Iran does not care and won't take the chance that America will help them. But the missiles won't be coming from Iran - there are other Muslim nations who already have nuclear bombs.

The *Falling Away* is happening, and has been happening for a long time now. America's citizens are searching for God, but those that are there when they *end* their search, are *not* the children of God. They are the children of Islam - the children of Satan. Many of these *searchers* call themselves Christians, but if they were truly children of the Most High God, born from above, Spirit-filled believers in Jesus, grounded in God's Word and their Jewish heritage, they would not have been swayed so easily, nor would they have continued to search for God in the first place. But of course, Esau is always there for anyone searching for some new thing.

Esau is spreading Islam everywhere. Much of the United Kingdom is now Muslim. Most of Europe is Muslim. America has been infiltrated and will also soon be mostly all Muslim. Islam is the fastest growing religion in the world, mostly due to their high rates of birth. Much like the Gentile Catholics, simply by being born into a Muslim family, that child is a Muslim.

Everything that has been written in the Bible has come true except for the end of the age events; and those events are lining up fast. So it is only a matter of time until these final events come to pass.

><>

Esau's Ottoman Empire was replaced by the Western-oriented *Republic of Turkey*. The former Ottoman general, Kemal Ataturk, founded and dominated this new state. Over the next fifteen years, he imposed a Westernization program so stringent that at one point he had rugs in mosques replaced by church-like pews. Although Turkey is nearly one hundred percent Muslim, Ataturk insisted on a purely secular state.

Ataturk never won the entire Turkish population to his secular vision. In time, his secular republic increasingly had to accommodate pious Muslim attitudes. But Ataturk's military officer corps kept his memory alive into the 1990s, which made secularism established so firmly it couldn't be changed - or so they thought.

Esau was adamant, the secularization of Turkey had to go - it was not the way of Islam. Muslims acquired parliamentary representation in the early 1970s when their leader, Necmettin Erbakan, served three times as his country's Deputy Prime Minister. And then Erbakan went on to become Prime Minister for the years 1996-97, becoming the first devout Muslim to hold the office in modern Turkey. As Prime Minister he attempted to further Turkey's relations with the Arab nations. But only one year into office, the Turkish military asserted itself and pressured him to step down. He was later banned from politics by the Constitutional Court for promoting Islamic fundamentalism in the state. The military corps saw him as a threat to Turkey's secular nature.

But Esau could not see defeat. He pushed Tayyip Erdogan, an ambitious lieutenant of Erbakan, to form a new Islamist political party called the AKP in August 2001. Just over a year later, the AKP won an emphatic thirty-four percent of the votes and, due to the unexpected changes of Turkish electoral regulations, dominated with sixty-six percent of the seats of Turkey's parliament. Islamism was making a comeback in Turkey, and as time went on, became more and more obvious. Erdogan was using *democracy* to gain control of Turkey's government.

According to Islamic prophecy, the Turkish government would fall to Islam - and it did in 2007, when Esau's Erdogan went on to become Prime Minister. With a renewed mandate, Esau could go further with his aggressive plan for

AKP to pursue elaborately false conspiracy theories. Such as a political media critic was fined $2.5 billion, over two hundred political opponents were charged with conspiracy, and now Esau's leader was altering the constitution.

But Esau's people have an even better plan than simply altering their constitution. His Foreign policy overreached even more blatantly. Erdogan's Turks have been at the forefront of developing propaganda for a new Islamism – a popular, *legitimate* and *nonviolent* version of what Ayatollah Khomeini and Osama bin Laden tried to achieve with brutality. Esau's new form of Islamism is destined to threaten civilized life even more than did the original form.

The violence that is ingrained in Islamism must eventually emerge, and then Esau's new form of Islamism must revert to its origins. But all in good time. At this moment Turkey hosts the most sophisticated Islamist movement in the world. But no one is watching Turkey.

Esau has installed a *propaganda machine* to smooth the way for this ultimate plan - Abdul Odnan. He would pave the way for the "*Islam is a peaceful religion*" motto, and with it the ushering-in of al-Mahdi.

Plus, Esau's AKP party has caused dissension within the government - a ploy to win the internal battle. Revamping Turkey's Islamist outlook was free sailing from here on out.

><>~~<><

When the United State's spoke of a *new world order*, the idea turned out to be a mobilizing idea invoked for a *particular* situation. But they did not want to create expectations that the United States would always be available to lead a coalition against would-be breakers of *world peace*. So the whole undertaking of a *'new world order'* seemingly disappeared from any political conversations right after the Gulf War.

But the *new world order* is not one conjured up out of American imaginations. While the conspiracy theorists claim there is a hidden agenda for a *New World Order* behind the economic collapse around the world, it is only a smoke screen. Those who think they are going to be in power, are in for a sad awakening - reality will prove otherwise, and they will have to submit to those who are truly in power.

It is something that has *always* been part of the agenda of Islamists. It *will* emerge - just not in the way that America thinks or wants. The *new world order*, otherwise known as *Shari'a Law*, is in the process of emerging all over the world, and will completely be in place when Islam's al-Mahdi returns.

⤞⤝

While some wondered and accused Israel for the so-called *unprovoked* Israeli commando raid on a Turkish flotilla in May 2010 and again in June 2011, Esau's influence, and this event, had caused Turkey's change in policy to burst into public view. Taking a closer look though, it was obvious that both these incidents were definitely provoked raids, but had worked their magic in almost severing relations with Israel, Turkey's longtime *ally*.

Esau's Turkish people set out to "Free Gaza" using these flotilla guises in a typical dramatic act to cause Jew Jacob's nation to lose favor with other nations. It was a *statement* of

Turkey's *future* policies, and a *prediction* of the Islamist movement's future. Esau planned to win this one, using whatever means he had at the moment.

In another strategic maneuver, Turkey appeared to go behind America's back when it announced that along with Brazil, it had struck a deal with Iran to ease a nuclear standoff. The Brazilian-Turkish initiative bore fruit in Tehran. Iran agreed to an arrangement designed to defuse the mounting confrontation with America and Jew Jacob's nation, concerning its enrichment facilities.

The agreement reaffirmed support for the *Nonproliferation Treaty*, as well as acknowledged Iran's right under the treaty to develop nuclear energy for peaceful purposes, which meant the entire fuel cycle, including the enrichment phase.

This *new* bargain closely resembled an arrangement reached some months earlier. Iran had agreed to turn over a similar amount of low enriched uranium to France and Russia in exchange for their promise of providing fuel rods that could be used in the same medical research reactor. That earlier deal floundered as Iran raised political objections, and then withdrew. The United States had welcomed this earlier arrangement as a desirable confidence-building step toward resolving the underlying conflict. But the United States wasted no time in refusing to accept the Turkish agreement, which seemed so similar.

✖∼✖

Esau's Turkey has definitely been making changes. It is

no longer a secular nation, as its parliament is now a full blown Islamic government. Its shifting foreign policy has made its prime minister, Tayyip Erdogan a hero in the Muslim world. And Esau's influence on Erdogan is working according to plan. Also, Turkey is openly challenging the way America manages its two most pressing issues in the region, Iran's nuclear program and the Israeli-Palestinian peace process.

The American Secretary of State branded the Brazilian-Turkish initiative as an *amateurish irrelevance*. He immediately rallied China, Russia, France and the United Kingdom to support a *fifth* round of punitive sanctions that were to be presented to the UN Security Council. It seems the prideful America wants things only one way - their way. While it may seem that America is suspicious of Turkey's manipulations of the situation, this opposition to the Brazilian-Turkish agreement speaks suspiciously of "*but we suggested it first!*"

Esau's strategy for Turkey to move forward as the leading Islamist nation, and his plans for Iran and Syria to also move forward, are the catapults needed for his *whole* Islamic Empire to gain momentum.

>⟶⟍⟋⟶<

On May 19, 2011 the American President once again took the reigns away from Turkey, and in so doing, showed his true colors in being against Israel. Although Jew Jacob's nation's Prime Minister pleaded with United States Congress to back their concessions, which included security issues, it was to no avail. America has taken her stance in this imminent battle. America's stance to split Israel to create a *Palestinian* state will have dire results, for anyone who attempts to divide or go up against Jew Jacob's nation, will be cursed. Once again, the United States was battered with storms and earthquakes.

><><

The tension in the Middle East is at an all time high and war is rumored to soon break out - wars and rumors of wars have been in the news for almost one hundred years now - well, actually war has always been "*in the news.*" When Jesus spoke of "*wars and rumors of wars*," He referred to them as happening in the "*last hour.*"

In Biblical times Jesus spoke of the "*last hour*" often in referring to the *end of the age* - but He was also referring to those present times, too. There is a theory concerning the "*one day is as a thousand years, and a thousand years is as one day*": it is highly likely that Jesus considered these last two thousand years as "two days," in which case, yes those times, two thousand years ago, would also be considered the beginnings of the *end of the age* - as in the *last hour.*

><><

The economies of the whole world are in trouble. But Turkey's Abdul Odnan seems to have all the people's admiration. He has promised to fix this economic problem and bring peace to our countries.

More than two-thirds of the world is Islam now, due mostly to culture decline in the European Union nations the past several years. It appears as if Islam is taking over the world. But Jesus's followers have been growing, too. Sadly, though, too many of His followers have fallen for the propaganda being thrown around by the Turkish and Jordanian governments, which is now so prevalent even in America. Islam is indeed on its way to becoming the dominant religion - even in America. It is only a matter of time.

Turkey's Abdul Odnan is looking more and more like he will be Turkey's - or even the world's - new leader. He has laid out a legitimate plan that will help every single nation on earth to restore their economies to a normal status. And unemployment will no longer be an issue, according to his plan. This plan, however, is also propaganda, for it is designed to usher in the new revived Islamic Empire, and its *Shari'a Law.*

✖～✖

Meanwhile, Saudi Arabia has its own problems. Their stockpile of weapons purchased from the United States is actually for use against their own people. Their increasing attachment to Western culture is an abomination to most Muslims. And while the Royal Family continues to become richer and richer, living in extreme extravagance, their own people live in extreme poverty throughout the rest of the country. Their youth have numerous degrees in Islamism, but there are no jobs for them. The *natives are becoming restless*, to say the least. They are a country just waiting to implode.

March 11, 2011 began the *Day of Rage* by Saudi Arabia's

youth. They want a new government and leader. The days of the Royal Family are numbered, but they don't plan to go easily. Of course, al-Queda and the Muslim Brotherhood will be there to pick up the pieces.

While they have always been at odds with each other, it will only be a matter of time before the Sunnis and the Shi'ites come together, fighting as one, to bring about the coming of their savior, al-Mahdi. It might seem an impossible thing to come to pass, but in actuality they aren't exactly going to come together *fighting as one*. While neither the Sunnis or the Shi'ites would ever submit to one another, they *would* submit to a dominant nation - such as Turkey.

But this can only be done if they come into agreement, leaving their differences behind - which they can do under Turkey's United Muslim flag. Esau's Muslims are his primary focus right now. He wants Turkey back on the radar, but they are Sunnis. He needs everyone to be on the same page, if his plan is to work. They all must be *Fundamentalist* Muslims, fighting for the same cause.

Since Muslims think all unbelievers are *Christians*, they also think all wars against them are *crusades*. The final *crusade* will happen - and Esau's Islam plans to win this time!

The miscellaneous riots breaking out in Muslim countries will only usher in the leadership needed to pull off Esau's *Fundamentalist* regime - and ultimately the revived Islamic Empire. It is his plan to invoke these riots everywhere to bring this end result.

God began shaking things up early in 2011. With earthquakes occurring all over the world more rapidly, and with more intensity, than ever before, Japan took the hardest hit to date. The 9.1 earthquake, triggered by the Pacific plate and the Asian plates grating against each other, the tension building until something finally snapped on March 14, 2011 in the Pacific Ocean just off the coast of Japan. While dealing with the thousands of huge aftershocks, the initial quake triggered several tsunami waves that devastated several cities, and damaged the Fukushima Dai-ichi nuclear plant.

In the weeks that followed, the four nuclear stacks each took a turn, with the hydrogen blowing up and exposing the nuclear rods. The fallout from the radiation slowly became an every day nightmare for Japan. Several years later, they are still dealing with the aftermath of this disaster. But they weren't the only ones. Ever since, earthquakes have become part of everyday life on this earth - each leaving devastation behind in its wake.

*A*merica is definitely in trouble, and there doesn't seem to be a way out. But, then again, they have been in trouble for a very long time. The budget deficit has gained momentum, and because money needed had to be borrowed from large global banks and corporations, notably Chinese and Japanese banks, anything in the trillion dollars range will never be paid - a debt for future generations. And don't forget the interest on all the international loans, which has to be paid off eventually with taxes. Depending on the type of taxes and how it effects America's working class, tax increases could significantly lag the American economy - *indefinitely*.

A series of so-called crises led to increased government control over financial institutions, and the auto industry. Government takeovers were abounding, which only added to the national debt. And lets not forget government intervention, or *solutions*, in the so-called healthcare crisis, which just added to this growing economic problem.

><del></del><

The mainstream population probably doesn't realize that America and all other nations, already have a *global economy*, so it wouldn't take much to make a *global currency*. In fact, up until recently, the world's trade economy has been based on the United States dollar. Back in 1944, right after World War II, the world's trade economy was in trouble. So seven hundred thirty of the world's leading politicians from all forty-four allied nations convened at the Mount Washington Hotel in Bretton Woods, New Hampshire. Their main goal was to stabilize and reorganize the world economy. And that they did, and for over seventy years it has worked. A few glitches along the way, but there was some kind of order.

The National Debt of the United States was topping fourteen trillion dollars in 2011 - and that didn't even include private debt or Social Security debt. But some of this debt is due partially because America's currency is also the International Reserve Currency. One must maintain a certain amount of trade debt, if they are also the country hosting the International Reserve currency - which really causes many disasters in the constant balancing act.

><

But the end of America's struggles is not quite what everyone expects. More than thirty countries have a piece of America's National Debt, with China holding the largest percentage. China was one of the leading nations who pushed for the new Reserve currency.

For several years the stock market went up and down. In

some years it went down more often than it went up. But no one paid it any mind, because it had happened before and America survived. In fact, after the last depression of 1929, the economy seemed to bounce back better than ever - but we cannot forget why it bounced back: World War II and the fact that America still manufactured its own products, and of course the Bretton Woods meeting.

≻┉╭┉≺

One of the earliest triggers of financial instability in the United States was when the Social Security Act was passed in 1935. According to the creators of this scheme, America would be rid of all the evils associated with "old age" and make it possible for every American to have some kind of retirement income in their old age. And it would have worked, if all the money that was being deducted from America's paychecks would have actually been put into an account to be used only for Social Security checks. But it wasn't.

Contrary to popular belief, today Social Security functions as an *unfunded* entitlement program. Money is deducted from American citizen's paychecks, and then instead of being deposited into an account that can later be used to fund retirements, the money actually goes right into the government's main account - to be used to pay for other unneeded programs and grants. This money is simply not protected in a trust fund, as most people are led to believe.

The 2011 so-called *changes* to the Social Security *Trust Fund* was a joke, for Social Security operates exactly like the schemes of Charles Ponzi and Bernard Madoff - a *Ponzi scheme*, or more literally, a *Pyramid scam*. New contributors to the program fund the promises made to the earlier contributors. There is no end to this madness.

><del style="font-style:normal">᳇᳇᳇</del>᳇<

Of the military expenditures of the entire world, 41.5% in 2008 belonged to the United States, and has grown exponentially since then. The United States spends more on defense than China, Russia, Japan and Europe combined. War is expensive, but apparently more expensive for America.

America's government's constant spending above and beyond the gold supply, the Social Security Ponzi schemes of borrowing from the future to pay for the present, borrowing from citizens to bail out banks and car dealerships, the blatant health care scam, defense spending, the growth of big government, national debt and personal debt, and borrowing from other countries to buy oil instead of dipping into our own reserves, were all finally about to blow up in the American leaders' faces.

And now it has been rumored that China is about to call in its loans. The White House is frantic. "What do you mean China is calling in their loans?" asked an aid to the President. "I thought all they did was cut us off from borrowing any more money."

"No," said the Secretary of Finance, "Word just came in that China has issued an ultimatum; in other words, a deadline for America to payoff what they owe them, or they will push to change the trade monetary reserve to another currency. It seems they too are in a financial crisis, and need money. Even if the international currency changes, we may collapse anyway. Maybe its just a rumor?"

The President's aid answered, "There was that rumor last year that the Republicans started about a debt default for a few days. It was an effort to force the White House to slash spending. So I suppose this loan thing could be a rumor, too."

Conversations of this sort were flying throughout the whole White House back in 2012 - and beyond. Somehow this information leaked out to the public, in other words, the media. The media was cutting into TV programs with *"Special Reports"* on almost every single channel. And now those watching wondered what exactly this meant.

As soon as the President heard about these leaks, he too went on TV to give a Press Conference. He tried his best to counteract what the media was stating, but it was too late. The damage had been done, and there was nationwide panic.

The President knew the only way the United States could possibly even make a dent in the deficit, was to call in America's loans too. But how could he do that? He knew they would not be able to repay either. No, he knew there was no possible way out.

It is now way beyond everything being too expensive for consumers. The US government is about to default on its promise to pay its debt on loans it obtained from China. The economy is about to plunge into a level of chaos no one has ever seen, nor can they possibly comprehend what happens next. There simply is not enough money for America to buy their way out of debt. Instead of paying back everything it owes, it will simply have to go bankrupt and default on every international loan - which will snowball around the world.

Since the value of the world's money is based on the value of the United States dollar, which virtually has no value, the United States government is contemplating the idea to reset the value of their currency. Yes, rumors were definitely flying around.

$\sim\!\!\sim\!\!\sim\!\!\sim$

Taxes will have to be raised to a rate of more than 60% of income. Social Security is already gone forever. The Stock market was on the verge of crashing for good this time, and will also soon be no more. The practice of making money on *future* profits simply cannot exist anymore. Many, many more new policies to help the government to recover will be put in place - of course, all these new policies and programs will come out of *someone's* pockets - the peoples' pockets, meaning even higher taxes.

The United States has been reduced to a country of eroding wealth. The wealth of America was obtained through sinful acquisitions. Big business got rich by deliberately paying lower wages, less benefits and piling more work on less people. Justifying deals that ruin mom-and-pop companies, using the cold-blooded phrase, "Its just good business," will not hold water when those who put these deals together will one day find themselves standing before the throne of God.

The government just keeps getting bigger and bigger. And their salaries just keep getting bigger and bigger. Once upon a time, delegates of America's government were not paid exorbitant salaries, and they certainly didn't continue to receive those salaries after they left office - a practice that goes on today.

The ever-growing programs to fund handouts, or this and that grant, demand the additional employees to administer them - which means more salaries - and more taxes. At some point, the people will not be able to afford their own government anymore.

But this can't go on forever - God will intervene soon. You cannot continue to treat employees and God's people badly without consequences. Companies will fail, people will be arrested for embezzling, companies will be fined for illegal practices, and much, much more. Many who pursue wealth disdain honest labor or service in favor of manipulation and ruthless power - but in the end these means cannot be justified.

The Third Seal in Revelation tells of a time when people cannot afford to buy a loaf of bread, for it will cost a days wages. The world is just about at this point now. But the book of Revelation does not say whether or not this situation lingers until the end of this age.

>✦✦✦✦<

Back on April 8, 2011, Gregorio Soroson funded a major economic conference in order to establish new international rules concerning the reserve currency. His plan was wildly accepted by a two thirds poll of this group before they even entered the building. Although this gathering generated less publicity than a barn raising, it was attended by more than two hundred academic business and government policy thought leaders, and their goal was to repeat the famed 1944 Bretton Woods gathering. Some of the two hundred complained that the United States government intervention in the fiscal crisis hasn't been enough and wanted "restructuring," including asking for letters of resignation from the top executives of all the major banks. But the main subject that was discussed, and was also the introductory video subtitled: "*How currency issues and tension between the US and China are renewing calls for a global financial overhaul.*"

In 1944, the Bretton Woods meeting helped to create the World Bank and International Monetary Fund. But now Soroson was calling for a new "multilateral system" or an economic system where America wasn't so dominant. And it worked.

When they came out of the meeting, decisions had been made to convert the International Trade Reserve Currency to what is now called the *"Bancor Note,"* which is definitely multilateral and universal. Soroson was happy that solutions had been reached to create this new monetary system.

⚬⚬⚬

The only thing that temporarily saved America from impending doom, was a new president - and the *Bancor Note*. Against all odds, in 2012, Daniel Trimble was elected President. And the last couple of years, his economic policies have turned things around tremendously. But, apparently, not quite enough, and not quick enough, for America is still in trouble. Although the trade deficit has been reduced because of the adoption of the *Bancor Note* as the International Reserve Currency, the early Baby Boomers had completely tapped out Social Security in previous months. Many seniors have moved in with their children, or are homeless. Its a wonder the revolutions have not happened in America.

Trimble did his best to try and get oil prices down, but it was pointless dealing with OPEC. He turned to the oil sands of America to try and persuade the environmentalists that this was the only solution to America's never-ending oil thirst. Saving a few acres was not in America's best interest at this time.

Democrats disagreed, and still tried to get unnecessary programs passed, but Trimble was in their way. He continually tried to reason with them, showing that America's economy simply could not afford the luxuries of federally-funded programs anymore, especially when it came to creating crude oil from the Oil Shale and Tar Sands in Colorado, Wyoming, Utah, and Southeast Idaho. The Green River Basins seemed to be an answer to America's prayers - but for the environmentalists, it was a nightmare. Trimble continually tried to reason with them to focus only on what were the country's most basic needs. And oil was a basic need - just not quite the amount that America is used to consuming.

But the United States government will operate as it always has - self interest, with little to no interest in actually helping the people; and spending way beyond its means. There will eventually be a revolution by the people in America too -

most likely spurred on by the Muslim Brotherhood. The Bible has predicted this monetary meltdown several times. There doesn't seem to be a way out of this mess.

America was only a threat as long as it was an economic superpower. But not so anymore. The American dream no longer exists and will never be possible again. It never really was possible to begin with, but many bought into the lie. Those who attained it are now a part of the group who have just lost everything because of the fall of the Stock Market and Social Security, and/or had money in a failing bank. America is no longer a threat - it can no longer afford its own military.

>~~~<

The Muslim revolutions of 2011 just added to the chaos of the world's economy. Even though the United States did not export oil from those first few countries who rebelled against their corrupt governments, oil prices went up all around the world anyway. And if oil prices go up, so does everything else. It is a round and round cycle of panic that never ends.

These revolutions were taken over by the Muslim Brotherhood, at first slowly and they pretended to want to simply help the rebelling groups stand up against their governments. But not long after they arrived on each scene, it became obvious why they were there. Their presence helped overthrow the governments and then they moved in their own people into power. They wanted Islamic power and *Shari'a Law* where there was none. It has already been happening in America for several years now, but no one seems to notice. The Muslim population is growing in America - beyond anyone's comprehension.

><del>∼</del>∼<del>∼</del>

Economies failing in almost every country, Muslim revolutions, people losing their homes, no food that anyone can afford anymore, and of course why bother going anywhere since no one can afford gas anymore. Unemployment has continued to skyrocket, despite the bogus reports stating that unemployment is down - all based on claims filed, but they neglected to mention those who can no longer file a claim because their benefits ran out - but still are not working.

Unemployment benefit accounts, that everyone thought the companies paid into, the states had borrowed from these accounts until there was not enough to go around any longer. Many states in America could not pay the benefits that should have been there for the unemployed. In the past, they borrowed federal money, but the government simply no longer has the funds to loan to them.

The stock markets of New York, Moscow, London, Frankfurt and Hong Kong finally collapsed in 2012. It seemed as if *plagues* and *locusts* had been loosed on the world. The United States stock market fell hard, Japan, a nation already deep in earthquake, tsunami and nuclear contamination woes, is sinking into a sea of no rescue economically, and unemployment was even further on the rise. Consumer spending has been steadily falling, and house prices are plunging into darkness - all across the globe.

When the economies of every country on earth are affected and a crisis looms large, we must expect it to have long-term implications. And those implications are a globalized and organized progression of changes. Esau was preparing the world for the coming centralized government of the *final world order* and its global economy - and not necessarily a recognizable one.

>∼∽∼✕

There was an emergency European Union meeting called and all heads of state of the General Assembly members were called to attend. The whole world was in a crisis. Most nations had now become members, so it was, more or less, the whole world. Only two nations had not chosen to join yet, but that was because they did not have a Muslim majority population - yet. The EU now consisted of all Muslim member states.

The members began to argue about where the fault lay, then brain-stormed for a bit, then they sat in silence as they all realized there was nothing to do - but start over. And then Abdul Odnan of Turkey walked in, a little late, but some thought just in time to "save the day." But he didn't actually "save the day" today - it isn't time yet. Those that had thought he would have the *saving-day* economic plan, had relied on rumor and were very disappointed when he said nothing.

Turkey had been admitted as a member of the European Union a few years ago. But Odnan had other plans for the head of the EU, but it wasn't time yet to reveal them. He did, however, mention something about a *possible* plan - and left it at that. He still had a few things to work out before he could go ahead with his plans. Besides, he was only present at this meeting to observe, and then report back to his parliament the status of the European Union's economy - and of course, the world's economies, too. There will be plenty of time to reveal and implement his strategy for overhauling the economies of the world - and everything else.

><del>~</del><del>~</del>×

Esau's plan was working great. Turkey had completely moved away from its secular roots under its Islamic government, and it has become a vibrant, and competitive *democracy* with a thriving economy whose influence in its region has grown tremendously.

Turkey has a core of internationally competitive companies that turned the nation into an entrepreneurial hub, tapping cash-rich export markets in Russia and the Middle East, while attracting billions of investment dollars in return.

For decades, Esau had given America the deceptive appearance that Turkey was one of its most reliable allies. Since Turkey is a strategic border state on the edge of the Middle East, and supposedly followed American policy, the deception had worked out nicely. But recently, Esau has asserted a new approach in the region. Turkey's words and methods seem now to be designed to provoke those in Washington at every turn, as well as to advance its own agenda.

><del>~</del><del>~</del>×

Esau's pawn, Abdul Odnan, took a moment to ponder Turkey's past. Modern Turkey had its beginnings in 1923, under the leadership of Mustafa Kemal Ataturk, a Turkish army commander-turned-statesman, whose radical secular revolution set the course for the rest of the 20th century. Although this was a beginning for Turkey as a country, it was the end of the great Ottoman Empire. But even Ataturk's regime came to an abrupt end when top military officers were detained in connection with an alleged coup plot.

In recent history, around 2009, the struggle in Turkey had been between politicians from the traditional, religious middle class, and the elite bureaucracy that has steered the state since its beginnings. In September 2010, voters by a wide margin approved a set of sweeping constitutional changes. The changes were intended to bring Turkey's military-imposed Constitution in line with European standards of law and democracy, but were widely viewed by voters and politicians as a referendum on the government of Prime Minister Tayyip Erdogan.

Although it was gradual at first, Esau's Turkey is seen in America as at cross-purposes with it continually. But from Turkey's perspective, it is simply finding its footing in its own backyard. A troubled region that has been in turmoil for years, some of Turkey's leaders view this to be in part, as a result of America's interfering with Turkey's policy making. At least that's what Esau has led Turkey's new government and the infidels in America to think - using both as pawns in his devious plots.

$\mathcal{J}$ust a few years after Israel won back control of Jerusalem in 1967, something interesting began to happen. Jew Jacobs all over the world began to discover who Jesus really is. They began to discover that they didn't have to convert after all - this Jesus that everyone was talking about was a Jew Jacob, too. He was their long-awaited Messiah - they could believe in Jesus and still be Jew Jacobs!

Messianic Jacob had emerged again - he was back! It was so exciting he wanted to share this news with Protestant Jacob. Messianic Jacob tried to tell Protestant Jacob about what was missing from his walk with Jesus, but he wouldn't listen. And so, a two thousand year old deception continued a little longer. Esau thought he had won this round.

But the seeds were planted, and it was only a matter of time before God would release this information to Protestant Jacob Himself. About the Gregorian year of 2005, God began to do just that. The seeds began to grow in a few Protestant Jacobs around the world, and at first they knew they were stumbling onto something new, but they weren't sure what exactly it was. Those few Protestant Jacobs had been reading their Bibles - about Jesus's last Passover. They were reading it over and over again, hoping to find what they were looking for - only they didn't know what they were looking for!

And then, all of a sudden they saw it! The Protestant Jacobs looked it up in each of the books of Matthew, Mark, Luke and John and discovered they all said the same thing about three of *God's Feasts*. They had always had a feeling that Jesus never did *institute* what was known today as *communion*, and now they had proof! In each case, Jesus and his disciples were celebrating the *Passover* season, which included *Unleavened* Bread and the day of *Firstfruits*! In the Bible it is called "*Unleavened Bread*," but that was how the whole season had become to be referred to by the Jew Jacobs. Jesus *is* the New Covenant, but He did *not* abolish the Old Covenant - *He fulfilled it*!

And when Jesus said, "*....as often as you come together, remember me....*" He was speaking about the *Passover season*, the other Spring feasts, and of course the *cup* He picked up was the infamous *third* cup, known to the Jew Jacobs as the *Cup of Redemption*. By saying "*as often as you come together*" Jesus was stating that God's Feasts were always to be a part of their lives - whenever they came together each year to celebrate them. So when God said to celebrate His Feasts forever, He meant *forever*!

John the Immerser had called Jesus the *Lamb of God*, and

Paul called Him *our Passover* in First Corinthians. So Protestant Jacob contacted some Messianic Jacobs who believed in Jesus, to ask them what they thought about this - and they did indeed confirm it. Jesus died on the *cross* on Passover, becoming the *Passover Lamb*! It was these festivals that Christians were supposed to be celebrating once a year, as commanded by God. And they were supposed to be remembering Jesus at the Passover celebration week, rather than having Communion *every* week. Communion was just a derivative of the Gentile Catholic church's *eucharist* that had been carried over at the Reformation.

Protestant Jacob discovered that Jesus died on *Passover*, was buried on the first day of *Unleavened Bread* and then was raised from the dead on the third day, which was the *Feast of Firstfruits*. Protestant Jacob was ecstatic now, for he knew that each and every one of God's Feasts meant much more than he had ever thought before!

><><

And then Protestant Jacob discovered what the day of Pentecost really was. The word *Pentecost* was the Greek word for *Shavu'ot*, the last *Spring Feast* of God. It was called Pentecost because it happened fifty days after the *Feast of Firstfruits*. And on that day, Jesus gave His disciples a gift - the gift of His Holy Spirit!

When that happened, all the Spring Feasts had been fulfilled by Jesus, at His first coming. He had fulfilled Joel's prophecy, "'*And it shall come to pass in the last days,*' says the Lord, '*that I will pour out My Spirit on all flesh. Your sons and your daughters shall prophesy, your young men shall see visions, your old men shall dream dreams...'"* Protestant Jacob was on his way to becoming Gentile Messianic Jacob again!

Protestant Jacob went back to the book of Leviticus to see what more he could find out. First of all, the Protestant Jacobs discovered that God had put in motion His plan of salvation *through* His Feasts. Protestant Jacob also discovered that God had put these same prophetic meanings in His *Tabernacle,* too. Protestant Jacob was beside himself with excitement now. He began to see things throughout the whole Bible that he had never noticed before!

"If Jesus fulfilled the Spring Feasts, then that must mean that His second coming will fulfill the Fall Feasts! But how?" he said out loud. He began to research this online to see what he could find out, for he just knew there was much more to these Fall Feasts.

Protestant Jacob's searching led him to some of the Jewish writings of tradition. Jewish tradition stated that on Shavu'ot, what was known as the *First Shofar* would be blown, and then there were a series of shofars that were to be blown afterward, at the *Feast of Trumpets,* in the Fall. Although, as with all *traditions of man,* they were a *little* off.

The first Fall Feast is called the *Feast of Trumpets,* or the *Feast of the Shofars.* They also believed that on this day the *Last Trumpet* would be blown and the dead would be resurrected.

Then Protestant Jacob discovered that Jew Jacob believed

that on the *Day of Atonement*, the sun would be darkened and the moon would turn red, and they would be judged that day by God. In times past, also on this day, the High Priest would sacrifice the unblemished lamb for the sins of the Jew Jacob's for the previous year. But without the temple, they could no longer do sacrifices. So the Rabbis invented the present celebrations surrounding the first two Fall Feasts, in hopes that somehow God would honor *their* own traditions.

Since they are also unaware of what happened on what they call the *torture stake (*cross*)*, when Jesus died for their sins, they have no idea that what they have been doing for the last two thousand years to atone for their sins, means nothing to God. Their sins are not forgiven, and won't be until they accept Jesus as their Messiah.

The last feast of the fall is the *Feast of Tabernacles*, but is also known as the *Ingathering*, or the *last harvest* of the year. So Protestant Jacob determined that this feast must be the *Wedding Feast of the Lord*! And most likely, the rapture will happen then, too! Protestant Jacob was beyond excited. "Then it's all true!" shouted Protestant Jacob, after he had been online for several hours reading everything he could find on the *Feasts of God*. He knew he had found something wonderful - and perhaps the key to opening up the Scriptures!

And so he began to search even further. *"What else had he been missing all this time?"* Protestant Jacob wondered. *"And why did we miss out on these wonderful Feasts of God? When did we stop celebrating them?"*

The following night Protestant Jacob turned on the TV to

watch a Christian channel, and he stumbled across a couple of shows that were very different than the station's regular programming. Both the teachers were Jew Jacobs, and they were talking as if they were believers in Jesus! They also talked about being called *Messianics*, which was the Hebrew word for *Christians*, or for the followers of *Yeshua*, also a Hebrew word, for *Jesus*. Protestant Jacob sat there mesmerized. These guys were saying the same things he had just found out about the Feasts - and much, much more!

This was all so exciting to Protestant Jacob. He began to think, "*This must be what I've been searching for!*" He had been unhappy in the churches he was visiting, unable to find a true church for a very long time. But Protestant Jacob wasn't sure what a "true church" was, or what he was looking for. He just knew he would know it when he found it.

He had just been on a long journey, searching for what was about to be revealed to him. Protestant Jacob remembered the scripture in Daniel where it said knowledge would increase at the end of the age. "*Could the end of the age be here soon?!*" he wondered. "*Could this be the knowledge that will be revealed?*"

So Protestant Jacob continued to search the Scriptures and prayed for them to be opened up to him. Bit by bit, Protestant Jacob began to discover many more new things in God's Word. He was so hungry to learn more, he gave all his attention to studying the Bible. The Holy Spirit led him to study the *Feasts of God* even further. Then he was led to study the *Sacrificial System of the Tabernacle*, and the

Tabernacle itself - what it all meant, what the spiritual meaning was in all the furniture, and much, much more. Books, online articles, and Messianic TV shows brought more and more information to Protestant Jacob. The more he studied, the more things just began to fall into place, and Protestant Jacob's eyes began to be opened even more. He would never be the same again!

Protestant Jacob also soon discovered some things that Esau had obviously inspired the translators to put in the Bible - that were very far from the actual meaning of the words that were written by the apostles. Jesus brought with Him the equality that Adam and Eve shared. Those who believed in Him, were equal *in Him* - men and women alike. But the translators had translated a few words incorrectly, causing the Bible to appear to be contradicting itself. But worst of all, these few little wrong words caused God's people to continue the bondage on women that Jesus had so clearly removed.

The Greek word that was translated *"head"* in First Corinthians, First Timothy and Colossians, actually meant *"source of life"* rather than *"authority"* or *"leadership"* - changing the whole meaning of the Scripture passage. While it *can* mean "leadership" in some instances, the subject of these chapters was clearly *"origins."* Protestant Jacob was delighted to be finding the answers to all these errors in the Church. He wanted to do the things of God as correctly as he could, and he was determined to do things right from this point on. There had always been things that nagged on his spirit before, but Protestant Jacob could never put his finger on what was wrong - until now.

><><

Protestant Jacob was excited, but still full of questions. He suddenly had an insatiable need to know the true history of the Church. He wanted to know how he had gotten separated from Messianic Jacob, and how did Gentile Catholic fit into all this? So Protestant Jacob went to the library and he also went online to search for more information on how the Gentile Catholic church began, and what had happened to the first church. He wanted to know everything he could on how the church had gotten so messed up!

Protestant Jacob searched and tried to find any and all information on who had supposedly ruined the Church. He wanted to know how the Messianic Jacobs and Gentile Messianic Jacobs had gotten separated. And he wanted to know why the Gentile Catholic church thought they were the first church.

He discovered that the Roman Emperor Constantine I was not entirely responsible for the changes within the Gentile Catholic Church, as many had thought. The Gentile Catholic church had swayed far into Greek philosophy, and false teachings and doctrines since about the late first century. They also had begun to call themselves the Gentile Catholic Church shortly thereafter. So when Constantine came along, he just put into law all the practices and celebrations the Gentile Catholic church had already put into practice - making them a part of the law of the land, and easier to enforce.

Protestant Jacob also found out how new things were

added to the Church that were not in God's Word, such as *Christmas* and *Communion*, and worshiping on Sunday instead of the true Sabbath, Saturday. And also how the Gentile Catholic church continued to add more and more *traditions of men*, and other false teachings through their *Canons*, and never-ending councils. He also discovered that it was the Gentile Catholics who insisted that a law be passed to rid the church of any and all Jewish influences - completely ignoring the warning in Romans: *And if some of the branches were broken off, and you being a wild olive tree, were grafted in among them, and with them became a partaker of the root and fatness of the olive tree, do not boast against the branches. But if you boast, remember that you do not support the root, but the root supports you. Therefore consider the goodness and severity of God: on those who fell, severity; but toward you, goodness, if you continue in His goodness. Otherwise you also will be cut off.*

Protestant Jacob realized that many of these practices are still being carried on today - even in the Protestant Jacob churches. Protestant Jacob was convinced that most of his questions had now been answered. He believed it would be a good thing to celebrate God's Feasts, even if only to replace all the unbiblical practices and doctrines.

And so, Protestant Jacob discovered that the Church celebrated the Jewish God, but did absolutely nothing Jewish for the last two thousand years! Which meant that they did not celebrate *God's Feasts* any longer, thinking they had been eliminated. They also knew nothing of *Old Covenant* Jewish tradition, or practices. The Church had been operating completely without the most crucial element - their Jewish heritage! Their Jewish heritage had been stolen from them by the early Church fathers of the Gentile Catholic church - and then Constantine sealed the deal!

Without knowing their Jewish heritage, they did not understand the Jewishness of God's Word. Because God's Word is full of Jewish phrases and idioms, this caused Protestant Jacob to misunderstand many things in God's Word. So now that he had found what was missing all this time, Protestant Jacob was happy. But he was sad, too, for as far as he could tell, many churches had not discovered these wonderful things yet.

Protestant Jacob paced back and forth for a very long time, saying, "Oh my, oh my, oh my..." over and over again. He would stop and ponder a bit, and then begin pacing again, and saying again, "Oh my, oh my, oh my..." "Whatever can be done?" he asked himself out loud.

And then Protestant Jacob knew. It was then that he realized that not every church would find, or accept this new revelation. The *Falling Away* had already begun with the Gentile Catholics, and also with the wayward Protestant Jacob preachers who were pulling away from the truth of the Word. But this was going to be the *straw that breaks the camel's back*. This would truly separate the *wheat* from the *tares*. "*Oh, this is all so sad*," thought Protestant Jacob.

For a long time after finding this wonderful news, Protestant Jacob spent a lot of time alone because no one would listen to him. He couldn't understand why they didn't want to hear this wonderful news.

But the churches were comfortable in their deception. They didn't want to give up their rituals, even though they now knew those things had nothing to do with Jesus. Plus, they simply didn't like change.

And the Gentile Catholic's churches didn't want to listen at all either. They already thought Protestant Jacob was a heretic, and now here he was presenting all these *Jewish* things to them - things they had gotten rid of many centuries ago! They didn't accept him five hundred years ago during the *Reformation*, so why should they accept what he was saying now? But there were a *few* true worshipers even within Gentile Catholic's churches. And they would soon embrace their Jewish heritage too, along with a *few* from each of Protestant Jacob's churches.

>⤜⤛⤛<

Those few from Protestant Jacobs' churches and from Gentile Catholic churches, formed what today are called Messianic *churches*, or synagogues. They had been spreading for several years now, and were thriving. Many of them were really the Protestant churches that had embraced their Jewish heritage and had become Messianic churches or synagogues. They did things a little differently in their churches now.

They no longer celebrate Easter - in its place, they celebrate all the Spring Feasts: Passover, Unleavened Bread, Firstfruits and Shavu'ot. And they celebrate all the Fall Feasts: *Feast of the Shofars* and the *Feast of Tabernacles*.

They weren't quite sure how to celebrate the *Day of Atonement* yet, but had begun to celebrate it just like the Jew Jacobs, only instead of afflicting themselves for their sins, they afflicted themselves in fasting and prayer for the Jew Jacobs to know their Messiah.

They also began to celebrate Purim and Hanukah, also. Because the actual event happened a couple hundred years after Malachi was written, Hanukah was only mentioned once in the Bible - it was called the *Feast of Dedication*. But it was mentioned in the apocrhypa, which has many of the Jewish histories. Hanukah is also known as the *Festival of Lights*, because of the lighting of the Menorah.

This *Festival of Lights* was celebrated because a miracle had occurred. After Jew Jacob had finally won many battles against the tyrant Antiochus IV Epiphanes, the priests had to cleanse the temple before they could rededicate it. They first tore down the statue of the Greek god Zeus that Antiochus had placed in the temple - a *pattern* for what is to come at the end of the age. He had also sacrificed a pig on the altar in the Holy of Holies, which defiled it, so the priests had to remove the stones from the altar in the Holy of Holies. Because they were holy, they didn't want them removed from the temple, so they set them outside in the area that was known as Solomon's Porch.

They also had to relight the temple Menorah, but they only found one small jug of oil, which was only enough to burn for one day. The Menorah was to be lit continuously, but it would take eight days to prepare more oil. They filled the Menorah with the oil they had, and lit it. Miraculously, the Menorah stayed lit for eight days! The priests declared a holiday to celebrate the Rededication and the miracle of the oil!

The Feast of Purim was indeed in the Bible, for it was the story of how Esther and Mordecai had saved their people, the Jew Jacobs. It was a feast celebrated by the Jew Jacobs, and it was now a feast celebrated by the Messianics, the followers of Jesus. Plus, in a way it replaced Christmas for it was the only feast where people gave gifts to one another.

Protestant Jacob felt very happy now. He had found what he had been searching for, and in doing so had discovered his Jewish heritage. Protestant Jacob was happy to embrace his Jewish heritage, and in doing so had discovered something even more wonderful - God was blessing him and the Scriptures were now opening up to him like they never had before. And he began calling himself Messianic Gentile Jacob again - just as the first believing Gentiles in the first church did.

Messianic Gentile Jacob had been studying the Book of Revelation - at first from a Gentile perspective. But now he had come to realize that he had been wrong about a lot of things. He knew now he had to see the Bible through *Jewish eyes*, and try to see it with a *Jewish mindset*.

He soon found that Revelation should not only be looked at through the Jewish Passover, it must also be looked at in relation to an ancient Jewish Wedding.

Messianic Gentile Jacob knew he had much more studying ahead of him, and planned to learn all the Jewish meanings behind everything Jesus was trying to show mankind in His Word.

Some of the first things Messianic Gentile Jacob found was about Revelation Chapter Twenty. There had always been the *argument* that a literal period of one thousand years would occur, and then Satan would be released on the saints again.

But Messianic Gentile Jacob found that the first three verses of Revelation Chapter Twenty were really speaking of when Jesus first came. His death and resurrection caused Satan to definitely be bound, yet not incapacitated. While he still has access to the people, to harass them day and night, he no longer has access to heaven - where he used to accuse God's people before Him.

Messianic Gentile Jacob found that the literal one thousand years couldn't be true, based on a Scripture passage in Matthew. Since God is the God of the living, then everyone who goes to heaven is alive already. The only thing that happens at the rapture, is bodies being raised to join with their spirits - living and reigning with Jesus in heaven.

It could also be determined that the one thousand year period is most likely referring to the church age - not the end of this age. There was so much more that Messianic Gentile Jacob needed to learn about the mysterious Revelation, but he knew now that God would show him the truths of the secrets it held.

><>

When the Jew Jacobs heard about the Protestant Jacobs now calling themselves Gentile Messianic Jacobs, they were provoked to jealousy. They began to wonder about these people who would dare to call themselves Messianics. They wanted to prove these *Messianics* were imposters, so they infiltrated these churches of the Messianics - and just the opposite happened. Many discovered that their Messiah had already come!

Both Gentile Messianic Jacobs and Messianic Jacobs were now attending these Messianic gatherings. They attended them on Friday nights, or Saturday mornings, but no longer were they meeting on Sundays because they wanted to honor God's true Sabbath day, according to the Fourth Commandment.

Going to these gatherings had become so much more pleasurable now. They no longer went to church to get God to do something *for them*, to have God bless *them* and have others pray for *them*. They now went simply to worship *God*, to bless and praise *Him*. These gatherings became what they were originally intended to be - worship to their creator, the Lord God Almighty Jesus! Their focus was no longer on themselves, it was on Jesus!

Jew and Gentile had joined together, and now began calling themselves *Messianics*. They began praying in Hebrew, for they discovered it is a spiritual language - the same language God spoke when He created this world! They also began speaking Scripture in Hebrew, for they had discovered that this pure language was revived by God so perhaps He would be pleased if they spoke His Word in Hebrew.

God honored them with the *power* He had given the first church. While many in Protestant Jacob's churches thought they had God's *power* in *their* churches, they truly had no idea what God's *power* truly felt like or what it could actually do - until now!

They reached out to Jew Jacobs first, then to all the nations of the world, as God commanded them in His Word. And everywhere they went, people were healed, and many accepted salvation - more than had ever accepted Jesus into their lives in the past two thousand years!

God blessed the Messianic congregations from this point on. His power was so strong among the people, that more and more Jew Jacobs were finding their Messiah! And many Gentiles were finding Jesus too - and learning what a true Messianic really was. They were going from city to city, healing everyone in their path - physically and emotionally. There wasn't much they really had to do - it wasn't the songs they sang or the sermons they preached - for it was the *power of God* coming through them because they had joined together as Jew and Gentile - making them *One New Man*. They were truly *One* in Jesus.

They now knew that this is what they had been waiting for all their lives! By bringing the Jew Jacobs into the kingdom first, a revival was unleashed on the Gentiles! It was nothing like the revivals of old - there was so much more power, anyone who came near where God had sent His Messianics, His Spirit dropped on everyone there and they could not stand for the power!

Some believed that you must be baptized in the name of Jesus, or do all kinds of works in addition to believing in Jesus, and some believed you must ask Jesus to come live inside your heart, or you must be *born again* to be saved. And still many other churches had their own ideas of what it took to be saved from God's wrath at the end of this age.

But Scripture states it very simply: *He who believes in the Son has everlasting life. For God did not send His Son into the world to condemn the world, but that the world through Him might be saved,* and the Messianics found this to be true over and over again, for they were witnessing the Spirit of God pouring out on everyone they came in contact with!

But they also knew about what Jesus said: *Strive to enter through the narrow gate, for many, I say to you, will seek to enter and will not be able. When once the Master of the house has risen up and shut the door, and you begin to stand outside and knock at the door, saying, 'Lord, Lord, open for us,' and He will answer and say to you, 'I do not know you, where you are from,' then you begin to say, 'We ate and drank in Your presence, and You taught in our streets,'"* so they knew that if those were saved did nothing else and learned nothing else from this point on, they would only have the "milk of the Word" and they would always be babes in Messiah. To be mature in Messiah one must read the Word in order for their minds to be renewed. So they also encouraged all those who had been saved to continue searching for more truth in God's Word, and they would in fact be very blessed. And they would be strong in the Lord when the time came.

*T*urkey's rise as a regional power has been evolving for years, and things have definitely taken a turn in the past twenty years or so. A popular Prime Minister in the nineteen eighties, and President in the early nineteen nineties, Turgut Ozal freed the Turkish stagnant economy. It had been largely centrally controlled, but the Prime Minister transformed Turkey's economy by paving the way for the privatization of many state enterprises.

This shift created a manufacturing boom. Turks from the rural regions flocked to cities for work, which in turn caused a major population shift. Together with the growing wealth among the traditional Muslim middle classes, it strengthened democracy and reduced the forces for radicalism.

Esau's Erdogan caused a *new* shift by *his* rise to power. He represents a rising underclass of religious Turks. Although he was despised by the secular establishment, he won a national election in a landslide in 2007.

Turkey's economy has taken on an astonishing transformation since then. Just twenty years ago it had a budget deficit of sixteen percent of gross domestic product and inflation of seventy-two percent.

But this transformation has its roots in the rise to power of Erdogan. He has successfully combined social conservatism with fiscally cautious economic policies to make AKP the most dominant political movement in Turkey since the early days of the state. While the rest of the world's economy struggles, Turkey seems to be thriving.

So complete has this evolution been that Turkey fulfilled the criteria for adopting the Euro in 2012. This made Turkey an excellent candidate for EU membership, and at this point it will be wise to sign the necessary treaty so Esau's man can rise to power - first within the EU, and then the world.

A few years ago, Turkey's foreign minister said in an interview, ".....economics is at the heart of the new policy." But his party, AKP, has now taken a turn toward advancing Islamic solidarity. Turkey's vision of economic interdependence has led to friction with America, particularly over Iran, which happens to be Turkey's only alternative energy source, after Russia.

For years Erdogan encouraged closer ties with Jew Jacob's nation, but their relationship had deteriorated badly in a few years ago. Although the flotilla incidents of 2010 and 2011 seemed to be signs that Erdogan had abandoned his quest to join the European Union, he backed up, at Odnan's request, and gave the impression they were at *peace* with Israel again.

Tayyip Erdogan, while keeping his religious views low key for awhile, is also a devout Muslim, with all the hotheadedness and zeal of Iran's Ahmadinijad.

Turkish and American officials play down their differences, saying they share the goal of *peace* in the Middle East. But their differing viewpoints seem to be ignoring the realities of Jew Jacob's security concerns. The reality is, at the right time, al-Mahdi will indeed come - and the temporary illusion of *peace* will disappear completely.

Although "*the last Ottoman*" died in 2009, Esau still continued with his plans to revive an *Islamic Empire*. He wasn't raising the dead Ottomans anyway - just the legacy of the Turks. In his mind, Islam will be the *Last Empire*, and *final* Empire. When al-Mahdi returns, Islam will be the only, and true, religion on this earth, and then there will truly be *peace*. *Shari'a Law* will be upon every nation, bringing them into complete unity with Islam and all that it is.

Islam already rules the Middle East, but it is Odnan's plan to take the Empire even further. But it must be done slowly so no one will notice until it is too late. Turkey is strategically becoming a true leader again. Saudi Arabia is about ready to implode, and Iran and Syria are still fuming and bellowing threats to Jew Jacob's nation and America. The world economy is getting weaker and weaker, making it vulnerable to a new *emerging regime*. The scene is just about set. All of Esau's pawns are in place - it will be time soon.

Abdul Odnan again reminisced on a more recent development. Erdogan's appointment of him has given

Odnan the power he needed. Odnan now had the *signal* to go ahead with his plans. He would replace Erdogan very soon, and then make sure he became head of the European Union.

The spirit of Esau had long ago possessed Abdul Odnan, so Esau knowingly looked on Odnan with pride, knowing he will do his bidding. In a slow, but calculated effort, Odnan's plan of bringing the Islamic Empire back to its peak is just on the brink of happening.

The barbaric ways of the first rising of the Ottoman Empire just won't do this time. Abdul Odnan thought of himself as much more *civilized*. But he definitely would not allow *his* Islamic Empire to go the way of the famous Kupruli Mustapha Pasha. Odnan was convinced that Kupruli was the beginning of the end of the great Islamic power the first time around.

This time will be different. Odnan is leading his empire with the guise of the finesse of Kupruli, but once he has everyone's full alliance and admiration, he will change his tactics. There will only be *peace* treaties in order to regroup and then to conquer, just as Muhammad had written was the law of Allah - the *Hudaibiyah* treaty, the ultimate false treaty. And there will be no strife among those within the Empire, for there will be only one ruler - al-Mahdi. Esau's plans for Odnan will take him far beyond his own human limits.

Although the Islamic Empire began in 1299, it didn't really begin as the true Turkish, or Ottoman Empire until 1453, after the Turks took Constantinople. Odnan's plan was to take his Empire in an entirely different direction. But of course, taking large cities was tantamount to growing his Islamic Empire. But he will not take these cities by force, like his predecessors did. He will use more sophisticated and modern tactics, much like Hitler. Muslims had already infiltrated the American states, so Odnan would take advantage of these *new Americans*. America will belong to Islam soon, and they won't know what hit them. Being so careful and politically correct all the time, has blinded them to reality.

In 2010 Iran was too much of a powder keg just waiting to erupt. Ahmadinijad of Iran, and Assad of Syria, were way too obvious and will ruin Odnan's plans. They will need to be subdued and persuaded to back off and be more low key, in order for them to truly take over. Odnan will assure Ahmadinijad and Assad that it is only a matter of time for al-Mahdi to return, but it will take strategy, not threats, to usher Him in. Iran and Syria would just have to step aside and be absorbed into the soon-to-come Islamic Empire.

But knowing Ahmadinijad, Odnan took another way to slow him down. "A computer virus will be just the thing to slow down Iran's nuclear program - and then I will blame it on Jew Jacob's people," Odnan said out loud to no one in particular. Just a couple days later, a mysterious computer virus did in fact turn up in Iran's nuclear program's computers. And rumor had it, that this virus originated in Israel. It was a five-year setback to Ahmadinijad's plans. Plus, the Ayatollah Ali Khamenei wasn't pleased with

Ahmadinijad's behavior lately - he was now pushing to have him impeached. As for Assad, he constantly used devious plans such as staging a protest against Israel, not only to provoke Jew Jacob's nation, but to draw attention away from the fact he was killing his own people. These uprisings in Syria, and those on Israel's borders, kept him busy for awhile.

Now, almost five years later, Turkey was almost in position to take over. Odnan plans to announce his new position as head of the EU, and ultimately as Imam of not only Turkey, but of all Islam very soon. He wants all to know that he is the new caliph of Islam, and that Islam will take over the European Union. The ceremony to swear him in as a part of Turkey's Parliament would be taking place tomorrow evening, and then the rest of Odnan's plans will fall into place. Odnan has plans to turn this ceremony into much more than it was supposed to be.

><<><

Abdul Odnan was on the stage now, and stepped up to the podium, straightened his tie and smoothed out his suit before going on the air. The applause went on for a full five minutes. Odnan had an economic plan that he was sure would save the whole world from it's financial troubles.

The swearing-in ceremony took place without incident. Odnan raised his right hand, and had his left hand on the Qur'an. Erdogan shook his hand, and then motioned him toward the podium.

Erdogan had no idea what Odnan was about to announce. "This country, as well as the rest of the world, is taking on a new transformation. And there are meetings of our world's leaders coming together to form a *Global Government* from the nations of the European Union. Eventually, all nations will be a part of the European Union, and thus the new acronym, *Global Government*. At some point in time, of course we will come up with a more appropriate name for our new unionized nations - perhaps *World Union*?

In uniting our nations together, the world's economic problems will have a much better chance of being resolved," Odnan waited for the response. There was only silence. The people liked Abdul Odnan, in fact, who didn't. He had made friends all around the world. But the world was unaware of his *global* plans. He had a great poker face, even if his actions didn't.

Odnan could hear the murmurs among the crowd, "Global Government?" "I didn't even know we had a Global Government?" "What Global Government?" "Does anyone know what this guy is talking about?" "What's he talking about, 'Global Government?" "Is this going to be that *One World Order* thingy those Christian wackos have been talking about?" "And what does the EU have to do with this?"

After the murmurers calmed down, Odnan again began speaking, "Let me explain," he began, "the world is in an economic crisis and governmental chaos, and it has been decided by the world's leaders that we need to band together, as one group of many nations. This will be for the good of the people. Trust me."

The crowd stood still this time and remained quiet. They

were waiting for the other *shoe* to drop. They weren't sure what to think - they had heard those two little words before - *trust me* - and they weren't followed by anything good. Odnan knew even if they wouldn't agree to what he was about to say, they had no choice at this point. Most nations were at a point of no return. "As you have just seen, I have just been sworn in as the Prime Minister of the parliament of Turkey, but now I am in a position to help our world move toward a *Global Government.* Better yet, *Global Parliament!*"

Most of the crowd could not believe their ears. "What has just happened?" they began murmuring again. "We can't become a 'Global Parliament'!" one guy shouted. And the rest soon joined him as he raised his fist in protest. Chaos was beginning to take over the crowd.

Odnan put his arms in the air, palms down, in an attempt to quiet the crowd so he could continue to speak. The crowd finally calmed down after ten minutes or so, "But I have a plan for this world. Much like what happened after World War II, we must regroup. We must reorganize the world economy. But this time we will need more than what the IMF or the GATT can offer us.

We must provide good leadership to these nations whose leaders fell in the revolutions. In fact, the measures they brought to the reorganization in 1944 is what brought us to today's chaos.

No, we need something better. My good friend, Gregorio Soroson, started the ball rolling a few years ago, but now its time to make lasting economic decisions for our world."

The crowd was now listening, as well as everyone online around the world. No one else had come up with a working plan, so they wanted to hear what this guy had to say. Someone at the back of the crowd said, "Who *is* this guy?"

Odnan began speaking again after a moment, "As you know, the United States dollar is no longer the reserve currency of the world," Odnan stated so matter of factly. "Ever since American President Richard Nixon eliminated the gold basis for the United States currency in 1971, the rest of the world has not been bound to a gold fixed rate. But unknowingly, it began the demise of the dollar and all the other currencies around the world," Odnan paused, took a drink from the glass of water sitting on the podium.

"A vote was taken a few years ago, and the new International currency, for trade purposes only, came from a neutral source. So no country will carry the burden of a steep trade deficit ever again. With that out of the way, we have been concentrating on the more important parts of our economies," Odnan took another breath, then continued.

"I won't keep you much longer. I just wanted you to know that we plan to fix this economic mess. And I think you will all be pleasantly surprised. I will be giving another Press Conference in a couple of weeks. At that time I will lay out our plans, which will be in several phases. I will explain these phases at that time. Tune back in two weeks from tomorrow night! I'll see you all then!" Odnan shouted as he waved, a huge smile on his face, and disappeared into the waiting, black SUV with blackened windows. *"Two weeks should give me plenty of time to get the ball rolling to organize my Global Parliament,"* Odnan thought to himself.

The world did not know of Odnan's *first phase* of the plan, and that it had already taken place. He had instigated riots in and near Saudi Arabia, in order to change their governments - or at least, that was one of the reasons. Another purpose of these riots was simply to remove the infidels from their nations, and to move in fundamentalist leaders through *democracy*. The infidels would leave for safety reasons. It would also cause the oil of the Middle East to seem untouchable - raising prices.

Although President Trimble was doing his best to get them back on track, the greed of America was going to blow up in his face - within the next two weeks. Trimble was not happy about this "Global meeting" he was supposed to attend in a couple weeks.

✂━━✄

Odnan felt the time was right to present his plan to the newly revived Islamic Empire and the world. This plan will eventually make Abdul Odnan seem to appear as the world's Savior. But it is not time yet to unveil who he really is. *"There are still pawns to maneuver into place. And there is also my prophet to arrive,"* Odnan mused to himself.

The Global meeting of all the world's leaders took place in the European Union headquarters building. All the usual things were said at the beginning, as with other European Union meetings, and then Odnan was recognized to speak.

Odnan walked up to the speaker's podium and set the papers he had been carrying under his arm, onto the podium before him. "Ladies and gentleman, and World Leaders," he began, "I am here today to present to you my plan to *save* our world from economic disaster."

Other than a few chuckles throughout the room, everyone was listening. They liked Odnan and wanted to hear what he had to say, they just didn't believe he could solve this world economic dilemma. His plan couldn't be any worse than any other plan up to this point, so they gave him their full attention.

"First, we will eliminate all the world's currencies. Although it took a couple years before the Euro came out as a paper currency, Europe survived without actual paper currency for those two years - so it can be done. Most everyone uses an ATM card of sorts anyway - paper currency has already been on its way out for some time now," Odnan took a drink from his water glass sitting below the podium, while pausing for effect.

"The banks will work with us, as they have already been way ahead of the world when it comes to a *paperless society*. We will have them average the value of the world's currencies, and base the value of people's bank accounts on this average.

The Trade Reserve Currency is the *Bancor Note*, as you have all been aware of for several years now, and we will introduce something similar to the *Bancor Note*, which will be the *one-value* currency for the economic world. There will no longer be a stock market - which was the biggest culprit in bringing our economies to an almost complete end.

Our new *Global Parliament* will create an international *one-value* currency, and there will be no paper currency. We will announce this *one-value* currency plan soon. This plan will save the world's economies and all the world will applaud us and thank us." Odnan's egotistical mind told him it was *him* they would love and applaud.

During the past two weeks, Odnan had been in overdrive in getting himself appointed head of the European Union. His next phase, that none of the other leaders knew about, was to dissolve the EU without them knowing. He would rename it under the guise of needing a new name now that new Asian and South American nations had joined. He had already planted the seed for this new name - hardly anyone was aware of it.

>~~~~<

The Islamic Empire had just conducted a census and they were just about ready. Every single nation now had a Muslim majority, and the *Islamic World Order* would be able to move in and pronounce *Shari'a Law* on the world. *"They won't know what hit them,"* Odnan sat there smiling as this thought came to him.

On the night of the second conference, Odnan walked up to the microphone, which was strategically placed on the podium. Or rather, under the podium. Odnan wanted his voice to carry over the crowds, and to appear as if his own voice had the power itself. He knew the people would not fall for this child's magic trick, but it would still give the desired effect he wanted.

Odnan began with his plan to save the world economy, "The first phase is to eliminate all the currencies of all the nations." He was just about to continue, but the crowds burst out in angry shouts. Odnan quickly put his hands up, to quiet the crowd, "Don't worry," he shouted over the crowd's own shouts, "None of you will lose what you have in the bank. If you have cash, you will simply put that cash into your bank account, as cash will no longer be used. Your money may not have the same value, but we will work that all out. Again, whatever you have in the bank, and any cash you have, which you will need to put into your bank, will be your actual *cash-value account*. Your bank will then give you a printout of how much money you have, based on the new value of the global currency - which is yet to be determined. It will be an average of all currencies, to be fair. You will also be issued a *World Union* ATM card.

The *World Union* will have accountants in each nation's capital, and they will give you the bottom line. By the way, we had to change the name of the European Union, since our union is no longer only European nations.

The value of your money shouldn't be much different than it is now. Just be patient. Your bank will issue you a date that you can go in to take care of your accounts.

Phase II will be the elimination of the stock market. Phase III will be the elimination of all federally, or state funded programs, and replaced with *World Union* funded programs for just about everything you can think of, which will not only produce more jobs; those who cannot work, will be taken care of also!

There are many more details, concerning complete peace throughout the world and complete access to Islam oil reserves, but this is only the beginning for our *Global* economy and will mean better prices, and better quality products, as well as the means to purchase them. There will also be changes to the governments of each nation, so those changes need to be implemented also before we can release the rest of the details. But rest assured, we are now on our way out of this economic suicide, terror-ridden life. There *is* light at the end of the proverbial tunnel!"

Odnan stood there for a few moments, while the applause peaked and died down to just a few claps. Then he waved to the crowds and the cameras, and walked off the stage into a waiting limo. The smile on his face was bigger than anyone could have possibly have known, or understood. In fact, he just laughed out loud, after the car doors were closed. "This is only the beginning," Odnan remarked as his secretary sat there stunned, wondering why he was laughing. He had just announced his plan to "save" the world from their own economic nightmares, setting them up for the *ultimate fall*.

To the community of Islam, Esau's Odnan had one plan, but for the rest of the world, he had another. He quickly had a state email memorandum sent to every Muslim leader, so they would know what was really going on. The information was quite different for the public than it was for

Muslims. Odnan made sure all Muslims knew his plans for the future of Islam.

>⚬⚬

After several months, it was apparent the Islamic Empire had risen again. Everyone thought the empire was dead, but it only appeared to be so. The Islamic Empire was the seventh, but then was not, and is now the eighth. It has risen as if from the death of a mortal wound.

Esau's Odnan was now running the *World Union*, which now boasts almost all nations as General Assembly members. Only Israel and the United States were not in this World Union. The US because of their failed economy, and would soon become the Western part of the Republic of China. And Israel for obvious reasons - Odnan believed they will soon no longer be on this globe.

What is really frightening, is that no one has a clue as to what is really happening. The majority of Protestant Jacobs think they can pray it away, and don't really believe anything the Bible says. And most Protestant Jacobs also don't believe the end will come in their lifetime, or maybe it won't come at all. Nonbelievers in Jesus don't really care, one way or the other. And most Gentile Catholics don't have a clue about anything that is going on. Those few Gentile Catholics who do actually read their Bibles and know about the end of the age, are praying to the wrong person.

Jew Jacob's nation's peace treaties with Jordan and Egypt were dissolved with the collapse of their governments. With Turkey, Jew Jacob's nation thought they had an ally. But these treaties, which Jew Jacob has always been warned by God not to engage in, were only a disguise to regroup. And that Egypt and Jordan did - regroup to attack again. Their biggest concern was their immediate neighbors, the *Palestinians*. After the fiasco of September 2011, Jew Jacob's nation had become smaller, and still there were daily threats.

But still, Turkey and Jordan, and a few other Islamic nations, were still crying "peace, peace," where there was no peace. Turkey and Jordan stepped up the propaganda to promote the "peaceful" Islam.

━━━

No one realized what kind of evil had just been released on the earth. It will be Hitler's "*Final Solution*" all over again - only this time Messianics, Christians and Gentile Catholics will join the Jew Jacob's in this nightmare. And it will be more evil than anyone has ever seen before, or could ever have imagined.

December 2016

Islamic Empire

Memorandum

Salam,

Our goal for these next several years, is that we will not only continue with the current propaganda that Islam is *peaceful*, we will step up our efforts. There will be an all out, no expenses spared, campaign to spread the *peace* of Islam.

What is happening to the world is one of the fastest demographic evolutions in history. Even if we have no more converts to Islam, the population growth of Muslims far surpasses any other religion on earth. Non-Muslim nations are simply not having enough children to maintain their populations. But Muslims are having far more children than any other group on earth. It is only a matter of time before all nations are overrun by Muslim immigrants.

The spread of Islam will happen even if we do nothing, and the earth will be under *Shari'a Law* within twenty years. But it will spread much faster if we convince the rest of the world that we are a *peaceful* people, and convince unbelievers to convert to Islam.

We must stop terrorizing these nations, for there will be plenty of time for that when the time comes. Band together, my brothers, and we will win the earth for Allah!

The future of this earth is Islam!

Inshallah!

Abdul Odnan

In an article back in April 2011, Jew Jacob's nation was reported as stating that *diplomatic corps* conveyed the message that support for international recognition by the European Union, encouraged Palestinians to forgo negotiations with them. Such a move violates the Oslo Accords and will not lead to a Palestinian state even if the General Assembly grants recognition, but could lead to violence.

In light of the 2011 deadlock in negotiations, international recognition of Palestinian statehood appeared unavoidable. Many times, over the previous fifty years, negotiations had been tried, and failed, between Jew Jacob's nation and the so-called *Palestinian* people. What most of the outside negotiators didn't seem to realize is that there were already several Arab states that surround Israel, and they could have absorbed the Palestinian refugees at any time - but had continually refused to do just that.

Palestinian leaders had reminded the UN Security

Council of UNGA Resolution 377, also known as the *"Uniting for Peace"* resolution, which states that should the five permanent members of the UN Security Council find themselves at odds, rendering the council incapable of exercising its "primary responsibility for the maintenance of international peace and security," the General Assembly can step into the breach.

If the Security Council's permanent members cannot reach unanimity, it elaborates, and "if there appears to be a threat to the peace, a breach of the peace, or act of aggression," the General Assembly can fill the vacuum by issuing its own *"appropriate recommendations"* for "collective measures" to be taken by individual states – right up to and including "the use of armed force when necessary, to maintain or restore international peace and security."

The *Palestinians* did in fact, invoke the UN's *"Uniting for Peace"* resolution in September 2011, during the EU meeting. The *Palestinian* leadership pushed for the necessary two-thirds General Assembly support for a recognized *"Palestine,"* along the pre-1967 borders. However, they were not given a "right of return" for refugees, under the *"Uniting for Peace"* resolution to ensure global action. Concessions on behalf of Jew Jacob's nation had been made in order to obtain "statehood" status for *Palestine* - concessions they had to agree with or there would be no state.

By taking their quest to the EU and trying to bypass any negotiations with Jew Jacob's nation, *Palestinian* leaders finally coerced Jew Jacob's nation into giving them more land for the establishment of statehood for *Palestine*. *Palestine* was indeed recognized and given a portion of the land of Israel, and they were recognized by the UN Security Council, the European Union and all other nations, shortly after the meeting attended by Jew Jacob's nation's leaders, and Palestinian leaders in September 2011.

Israel had now been divided, as well as Jerusalem. From the West Bank to the northern tip of Gaza, a boundary line had been drawn, and *Palestine* would officially have a state where the refugees could actually return to live.

And so, Jew Jacob's people were forced to give up land that was rightfully theirs. Israel halted any building projects within the borders of the West Bank, which had been divided according to the treaty agreement.

At this point, Scripture states clearly that Israel will indeed be divided. But Scripture is also clear about what happens to those who cause and support this move. Just look at the natural disasters the United States has endured for their part in this disastrous plot, and the devastating, daily earthquakes over the whole earth. And they are still coming!

A state that should never have been recognized, is now being forced upon the world. It is also a state that is run by Hamas, Hezbollah and the Muslim Brotherhood. The *Palestinians* who think they have just won a battle, are in for a sad awakening. Although, at first it will appear like they have also won the world, God has other plans for these enemies of Jew Jacob.

For the past several years, Jew Jacob has still been at war

with its new neighbors, the *Palestinians*. Statehood meant absolutely nothing to them, for they want all of Israel. They have never recognized Jew Jacob's borders, and they still don't.

Jew Jacobs own the land that the *Palestinians* claim belongs to them. Jew Jacob's people were given this piece of land, not only by England at the end of World War II, but by God over four thousand years ago. And they won the extra land in the Gaza strip and the West Bank back in 1967, which was also given to them by God. Any other country who had won land in a battle, has every right to that land. But now, the whole world had turned against Judah Jacob's right to their own land.

The Arabs were given much more land by England at the end of World War II and should have been satisfied with all that was given to them. But alas, God and His Word will win out in the end.

><

The *"abomination of desolation"* has long been thought to be the Anti-Messiah's act of enthroning himself in the place of deity to display himself as God - literally. Abdul Odnan's thoughts have gone in this direction many times: *"I shall raise my throne above the stars of God," "I will make myself like the Most High," "I am a god, and I sit in the seat of the gods."*

But it wasn't Odnan's time yet. He would reveal himself in due time. He hadn't yet won enough people to Islam, and he needed them to complete his plan. But then again, Odnan knew that once al-Mahdi and Isa appeared on the scene, even those in America would see who the real *Jesus* is, and he would convince them to turn to Islam.

What most Biblical scholars don't realize, is that the "*abomination of desolation*" already took place twice, as is the norm for Biblical prophecies - first for the pattern, and then for the fulfillment. The first time was when Antiochus IV Epiphanes desecrated the temple in the year 175 BC. And then again when the Muslims took Jerusalem in 638, and then built the shrine on the *Temple Mount,* which still stands today - the *Dome of the Rock.* This happened in 688. If you add the "*....one thousand two hundred and sixty days...*" from Revelation, you get 1948 - the year Israel became a nation again. And as Scripture states in Daniel, "*And from the time that the daily sacrifice is taken away...there shall be one thousand two hundred and ninety days,*" which brings us to the year 1978, which was when Israel signed a peace treaty with Egypt.

But then if the next verse in Daniel is read: "*Blessed is he who waits, and comes to the one thousand three hundred and thirty-five days,*" which brings us to the year 2023 - the end of almost fourteen hundred years of Islamic presence on the earth. God has timed this event right from the beginning of time itself, and He will not forget His inheritance. Jesus was born in a Jubilee year and He will return in a Jubilee year. But because the Jew Jacob's did not always obey God, no one really knows what year Jesus was born or what year it really is today. So, like that *pattern* of the ancient Jewish Wedding ceremony states that the bridegroom, in this case Jesus, will come *as a thief in the night.*

✕✕✕

The Islamic *peace* propaganda and the so-called *peace* with the *Palestinians,* was now pretty much accepted worldwide, even though the Qur'an preached otherwise. This *trojan horse* of peace was exactly what Odnan had planned on. The people of the world were now accepting Islam as a peaceful religion - the propaganda claiming the word '*Islam*' actually meant '*peace.*' And the gullible ones bought it all, hook, line and sinker!

Thirty years ago, the infiltration of America began - possibly even before that. Incidents such as the one in a California department store, where an Iranian manager was hired. Shortly thereafter, several Iranian employees were also hired and scattered throughout the store. One by one, longtime American employees began to be fired. They had been set-up for the silliest of transgressions, but store policy violations just the same.

Another incident where two *Persian* men were hired as salesmen at a big city Car Dealership. They not only sold cars, but also spent time making friends of the ignorant Americans. Ignorant, because they didn't know Persians were really Iranians. But that business was taken over too.

Similar incidents throughout the United States have been happening over these past thirty years. And Americans have been none the wiser.

✕✕✕

Many Protestant Jacobs have always believed there will be a peace treaty, and besides the false peace with the Palestinians, there has already been a false *peace* message that Islamic leaders had been already spreading for many years now.

This *peace* propaganda had been going on for almost ten years now, and most people fell for it. The *peace* will be over soon, surrounded by Muslim countries on all sides, Jew Jacobs were pretty much the only holdouts, other than the *few* Messianics around the world, to turn to Islam. Most already did believe the lie of the propaganda in America, but there were some who claimed to be followers of Jesus that were still holding out. Odnan must sway them, for he must have full and complete worship of the people. But Esau's man, Odnan, took a deep breath, closed his eyes, and calmed himself. He was not worried. He had another plan that would reign in those holdouts, and then he would have the whole world under his rule.

><

No one called it by its true name, but *socialism* had definitely taken over every country in the world, and there is chaos everywhere. Funny how the leaders promised that this way of life would be better for everyone. Abdul Odnan had promised that the world would be a *utopia* after his plan to save this world from economic ruin went into action. But history shows that an earthly government will never take care of the people. Their agenda is to always take care of themselves. And this *utopian government* was finally taking its toll on the people.

After five years of this *utopian world*, many no longer had jobs. Their paper money was gone. Their homes were being taken away, and their cities were in ruins. Abdul Odnan, the leader of the whole world now, was beginning to look very evil.

How did the world come to this? They just wanted their old, normal lives back. But there was no way this new economic system could reverse itself - at least, not without *government intervention*. But the government had become the enemy!

The people were doomed to follow this Odnan guy. The only ones who *seemed* to be thriving in this economic hell were those who worked for the Islamic government or were non-government Muslims. And no one was immune to the effects of this evil system - even Saudi Arabia's Royal Family was being governed by the *World Union*. Although the high price of oil had given them even more wealth than they could ever imagine, they were forced to give most of it to the government - all in the name of Allah.

*H*e had not revealed his true identity yet, but Abdul Odnan had appeared on the scene and had been ruling over the earth for about five years or so now. His three-phase economic package was working great for some people, but for others it wasn't going too well. By all appearances, Muslims seemed to be much better off than most others - which was actually quite true. "And now it is time to introduce *Phase 666*," Odnan chuckled quietly as he talked to himself while waiting, and had been lost in his own little world for the last few minutes, but then he saw Isa walking toward him.

Isa had just arrived, and he joined Abdul Odnan on the stage. Odnan asked him to lead the prayer, but Isa insisted that Odnan take the honors, and then stepped behind him. Abdul Odnan led the prayer before all the world. When he had finished, he looked up and announced, to every single person present, and those watching on TV and the internet had their eyes glued to the man on the screen, and then Odnan raised his arms in the air, as if embracing the people, and said, "I am your awaited savior! I am al-Mahdi! I am Allah come in the flesh!" Many had claimed to be al-Mahdi over the years, but not one of them had ever said he was Allah! al-Mahdi was claiming to be Allah himself!

Muslims all over the world were stunned. They did not know al-Mahdi was Allah, but now they knew who he was! They had wondered about why Abu'l-Kasim Muhammad al-Mahdi was kept hidden and alive all these many years, but now it all made sense! al-Mahdi was Allah, come to save the world and bring peace!

But those who did not believe yet, didn't understand. But they would soon. Isa now stepped forward and stood beside al-Mahdi, and introduced himself, "I am Isa. In English, that is *Jesus*. I have come to tell you that I am Muslim and you are to believe in Allah!" he finished with a slow, but dramatic motion with his arm toward al-Mahdi. Isa was very charismatic, and he had the crowds mesmerized in no time. Then he turned toward al-Mahdi and prostrated himself before him. He waited until he heard that telltale sound of all Muslims prostrating themselves. He then stood and continued his speech while they all still remained down on the ground. "I have come to tell all you unbelievers that Islam is the way, the truth and the life! You must renounce your Christian falsehoods, and come to Allah! We all worship the same god, so come to the truth of Allah, and praise our long-awaited al-Mahdi!" Again he motioned his arm toward al-Mahdi.

Those unbelievers who had falsely called themselves *Christians* joined in with the partying Muslims. They had no idea that Isa was not the real *Jesus*. He seemed like an angel, glowing with the glory of God, like an *angel of light*. They just knew what he was telling them was true! Those who knew who the al-Mahdi was were ecstatic. The al-Mahdi and Isa had come at last! Now *peace* would come over the whole world! They shouted with glee and danced around, with their arms in the air. They worshiped the al-Mahdi, and they cried with happiness.

The al-Mahdi began his speech right away, "Now, let's get down to business. Oil business. The oil in Saudi Arabia is almost gone, but we still have plenty to go around. Iran and Turkey are our leading oil producers now. Production in all other oil producing countries will also be stepped up. We will, however, need to tighten our belts on our own consumption, for it has developed to a level that is abominable."

The al-Mahdi looked around at the crowds, smiling as big and as real as he could muster up. He had to convince them that all would be well with the oil. He needed the people to trust him, if he was to win all to himself and to Islam. The unbelievers will either bow down to him, or they will forfeit their lives.

Of course, he was lying about the oil. It wasn't all that readily available anymore. The reserves reported by the different OPEC countries were over estimated at best. Their reserves were dwindling fast. *"But no matter, soon there would be a lot less population consuming the oil,"* thought Odnan.

al-Mahdi once again raised his arms up to quiet the crowds,

then began to speak again, "Within the next few weeks, we will be introducing the final two phases of our economic plan, Phase IV and Phase V. First, *Shari'a Law* is now in all nations, and all must submit to this Law. Any other laws in effect before today, are no longer valid.

Second, there will be a new system put into place, that will make it much easier to buy and sell goods and services. Unfortunately for some, this will only be for Muslims. You will all be *contacted* and given the opportunity to convert to Islam, so you will be able to buy and sell. This is the new way, and it is the way of Islam!"

Again the crowds went crazy with shouts of glee. Islam would finally be in all the world! It was finally here! Some could not believe it. They had heard it all their lives, yet their lives had been riddled with poverty and want - until now! Muslims all over the world celebrated all night!

><><

Many Christians will fall for this Isa, this false Jesus, and will *fall away* from the true faith, even though the true Jesus warned us many, many times not to fall for the false Messiahs. For Islam's Jesus is not the same as the Christian Jesus. Islam's Jesus will say he is a Muslim, and he will convince many to convert to Islam. And they will be completely unaware of what was really happening here today.

The real believers in the real Jesus, knew what was happening. They couldn't believe it was here already! Knowing their destiny, they slowly backed away, and stealthily left the areas, whether it be in the crowds or in an office or home watching TV or on the internet. There wasn't much time now - they wouldn't be able to purchase anything very soon, but they needed supplies to get through these next few years. And where to hide?!

They couldn't use their cars for very much longer, for they could only use what was already in their gas tanks, plus maybe one more fillup before they couldn't buy anymore. They couldn't go to their homes, because those would soon be confiscated in the Islamic raids on their cities if they hadn't already lost them. Some were unsure of what to do. Most were not prepared for this, because they didn't truly believe it would ever happen - at least not in *their* lifetime. They should have been better prepared. But they knew they had to head for the hills!

The Messianics had discovered that not only did they have the power to heal people like in the first church, they also had the power to translate. So that they did, to hiding places in the mountains!

And the rest of the Christians, who refused to embrace their Jewish heritage, so were not rooted in Jesus either, willingly converted to Islam, falling for the false Jesus, who was Isa.

>~~~<

It always seems like *someone* is trying to *correct* the believers of Messiah Jesus in their beliefs, and much like Diocletian in the third and fourth centuries, Odnan, too, was now trying to correct these *wrong* notions and beliefs of the *Messianics.* al-Mahdi believed they would renounce their false god and accept Allah, peacefully. He would send Isa in among them, and he would be the one who would make this happen.

They were not only not converting to Islam, they were making things happen all over the earth - miraculous things...and their message had to be stopped!

⋙⋘

al-Mahdi had put into law, and Isa was to enforce it, an order for only those who could prove they were Muslim, usually with the headband or right armband that stated, "*There is no god, but Allah*," only those could be allowed to buy or sell anything. But these headbands or armbands were not really necessary, for all the stores and companies had been slowly bought out by al-Mahdi over the past five years, and the employees were replaced with Muslims. If someone came through their line to purchase something, it was very simple to find out if they were Muslims or not. And there were even some who didn't mind having the *Bismillah* tattooed on their foreheads. Many chose to also wear the tattoo on their right arms or hands, instead of the armbands and headbands.

Those who had thought this *mark of the beast* would be something very sophisticated, involving technology, were surprised by the ingeniousness of it. In its simplicity, the name and the symbol have the same meaning - in other words, it is a creed and a literal name, that represents the *image of the beast*. For many years it has been common among

Muslims to wear these badges of the *Bismillah*, or some form of it, to identify that they are Muslims. Muslims are taught that a *beast* will come out *of the earth* and he would mark the foreheads of all true Muslims. And so, for a Muslim, the *Bismillah* is an honor, a *"badge of servitude,"* that they wear with pride.

But no matter what, those who do not believe in the Muslim god, Allah, still cannot buy or sell, and in most cases will be arrested on sight if they try. And they cannot wear the bands or tattoos, or even say the *Bismillah* just to buy something, for Jesus would surely see them or hear them. He wanted them to completely trust Him for all their needs - especially now.

And of course, the Jew Jacobs would definitely never compromise their faith. Unfortunately, they did not trust enough in their God, and they did not yet believe in Jesus. They were hungry, and a lot of them were executed when they were arrested and would not convert to Islam.

〉〈

Isa was in charge of the conversions, and they were going great. He had masses of unbelievers arrested and brought before Him. His police would line the unbelievers up in front of him, and then he had them kneel before him.

He proceeded to tell them he was *Jesus*, and that he was a Muslim. He at first encouraged them to believe in him and to convert to Islam and worship al-Mahdi. Isa told them they must confess the Islamic creed *Shahadatan, a* declaration to demonstrate allegiance and servitude to Allah and Muhammad.

This creed has two elements: *"Allah is the only One True Supreme god* and *Muhammad (The Praised One) is the seal and final messenger of Allah."*

It is not only to be stated, but can also be worn. While being perfection for Islam, both statements within this creed, perfectly fulfill both dimensions of the definition of *blasphemy* of the One true God.

But those who were belligerent, Isa then used force to make them convert. When even that would not work, he had their heads chopped off. Those who managed to avoid being arrested, had turned to raiding gardens and fields for something to eat. They could not buy, or even sell anything anymore, for they had to prove they were Muslims first. There were many Messianics in hiding, who had stored away food items that they thought would be needed in a crisis, plus they had gardens where they were hiding, and anything else needed they would depend on Jesus to provide for them.

Those *Christians* who did not live holy lives, did not know what was going on - they were not prepared. Those who avoided being arrested, still would not have renounced Jesus even if they were caught. And fortunately, they had found a couple websites where they could still purchase items through PayPal.

Those lukewarm Protestant Jacobs sought out the Messianics, not only to find refuge and food, but also to find out what was going on. Most of them did not have Bibles, which would have answered most of their questions. So they continued in their ignorance, trying to stay warm and to find food. This was not the life their church leaders had promised them. They were supposed to go up in that rapture thingy, weren't they? But not even the Messianics had gone up, or had they? They couldn't seem to find them.

These Protestant Jacobs were few in number, for most of them had already converted to Islam. They had believed in the false Messiah, Isa. But others had been swayed to believe in Isa, too - those who had church leaders who had already turned far from the truth, believing and teaching that their god was the same as the Muslim god, or simply preaching *another* gospel.

They had allowed that evil to infiltrate their churches and people, and now they were converting to Islam. Although they still had their lives now, they had chosen the wrong god. Their lives would ultimately end up in the lake of fire - burning for all eternity. They had been taught that evil did not exist and that there was no lake of fire. But believing something doesn't exist, doesn't make the threat any less real. Their lives were literally doomed for all eternity.

And the Gentile Catholics didn't know what to do either. Since they believed they were *Christians*, but did not know the Bible, they too didn't know what was going on. There was a handful of Gentile Catholics that truly believed in Jesus, and did not pray to Mary or any other saint, and had joined the Messianics.

But those who would not let go of their idols, and still prayed to Mary, and believed in all the other false doctrines of the Gentile Catholic faith, they would succumb to the false

Messiah. They would turn to Isa, believing he was the real *Jesus*. All of these events are the climax of the *Falling Away*.

⚡︎

It was now about seven years later and al-Mahdi must implement his final plans to rid this earth of Israel. The Jew Jacobs simply cannot be allowed to live on an Islamic planet. Those Messianics were making a menace of themselves by their constant chattering online about who the *"real"* Jesus was. They were all over the internet, but that won't last long. al-Mahdi had a team working on how to take down all those websites all at the same time. Once that happened, they would be quiet, or they would convert, or they would die. He needed them all gone before he could start his war. This war was to be against Israel only - against those infidels, the Jew Jacobs.

al-Mahdi was a bit puzzled about the infidels, *"Why can't they see what most of the Christians had seen when Isa told them who he was? It seems as if they don't care one way or the other. Very puzzling. And what about the ones who hadn't decided one way or the other yet, and they weren't even calling themselves Christians or Messianics. But that will soon be remedied."*

Esau whispered in al-Mahdi's ear an evil plan. This plan was for all the Islamic nations, which surrounded Jew Jacob's nation, to come together in spirit and come against Israel with all that their armies had. Right within Israel's borders was this plan unfolding, for Israel's enemies were in Jerusalem, in the al-Aqsa mosque. Five different regions of Turkey, and

Iran, Afghanistan, Pakistan, Libya and Sudan had representatives at this meeting. Representatives for Syria and Lebanon were there too. It had happened in 1948 for the *pattern*, and was now about to happen again.

They finished their meeting and it was decided that next week, during one of Jew Jacob's feast days, would also be their doomsday - and would also be Islam's triumph. September 30, 2023 would be the day Islam would invade Israel and take it for themselves - it would be made their new holy state. Jew Jacob's nation would replace the traitorous Saudi Arabia, and of course would be renamed. Jerusalem would replace Mecca as the most holiest city of Islam.

al-Mahdi wanted Iran and Turkey to be the ruling nations, but Saudi Arabia would not yield to them. It was an unspoken rule that the nation with the oil and the money is the ruling Islamic nation, but Saudi Reserves were getting seriously low, and soon everyone would be looking to Iran for their oil. Besides that, many radical Muslims thought Saudi Arabia was too westernized, and they were an embarrassment to Muslims, and to Islam.

*A*s they made their way into the city to see what they were up against, the Muslim spies passed the main cemetery just outside Jerusalem. On the first day of Tishrei, it was still just before daybreak and dark, but the Muslims thought they saw something floating upward into the sky. Actually, several *things*, that appeared to be coming out of the ground of the cemetery. The Muslim spies blinked their eyes several times trying to focus, but chalked it up to optical illusions in the pitch darkness.

But then as they began to enter Jerusalem, it appeared that the city lights were on, it was so bright, and they saw them! The dead had heard the *last trumpet* first. The Muslims saw angels descending down to earth, just above the cemeteries. This very thing was also happening all over the world, over every cemetery. Just as quickly, the angels took the awaiting dead, who had risen, and took them by the hands and then disappeared right before their eyes - the eyes of those who were watching!

The Muslims wondered about this, for there was nothing in their holy book about this occurrence. *"So who had done this?"* they pondered. But then they snapped out of their daydreams and decided that was exactly what they had just witnessed, a daydream.

><del></del><del></del>

Meanwhile, coming out of another part of the inner sanctuary of the temple of God in heaven, seven angels came flying down to earth. Each one had something in his hands, but if one could see them they would not be able to describe what the angels had.

Six days before Sukkot, the first angel appeared to be pouring out a bowl, but to earth it was a plague. First there was dust everywhere, but then a plague of sores came upon all who wore the *Bismillah*, physically and spiritually. And they were painful. Boils broke out on every one who had converted to Islam, at one time or another. Those boils blistered and then just turned into festering sores.

Covered with these festering sores, al-Mahdi just grew angrier and angrier. It never occurred to him that it was the God of the Jew Jacobs who had sent this plague upon the Muslims - even though he knew the story of how the Jew Jacobs came out of Egypt. So he did not turn to the One true God.

><del></del><del></del>

On earth, the Jews heard what sounded like the *last shofar* in their spirits, which was rather like God's voice - it was time. The sky seemed dark and eerie, but there wasn't a cloud in the sky. Yet it was darker than any night normally was. By midday it seemed like the total lunar eclipse that happened last November, was again happening today. The sun was almost completely blocked by three o'clock in the afternoon, and then the moon began to show, normally just a few short hours later, but it was now a blood-red color, as in a full lunar eclipse.

Today is the tenth day of Tishrei, the *Day of Atonement*, or *Yom Kippur*, and the air feels different - almost as if it is full of electricity. The Jew Jacobs turned to watch the people on the streets, and saw only a few people scattered, but only the Jews were looking up at the sky and cowering, crouched low to the ground. The Jews wanted to see if anyone else could tell if this day was affecting anyone like it was them, but it appeared it was only the Jewish people. This very same thing was happening all over the earth.

Jewish tradition had it that on the *Day of Atonement*, after the *last shofar* was blown, God would come to judge the inhabitants of the earth - the Jew Jacobs from the twelve tribes were convinced it was them alone that would be judged. For this dark day to happen on the *Day of Atonement* meant something to them - the final judgment of God, and the last day to convince Him of their repentance. But it was more than that. Something much more was happening today.

All the Jew Jacobs looked up to the sky and noticed that the clouds were moving faster than normal. Even the sky seemed to be excited. Something frightening happened next, for the sky opened up to show the temple of God in heaven.

There were no clouds to part, but still the sky seemed to part itself open, and there before all the Jew Jacobs was the God of Abraham, Isaac and Jacob - sitting on a white horse!

He was clothed with a garment down to His feet and about His chest was a golden band. His head and hair were white as snow, and His eyes were like a flame of fire. His feet had the appearance of fine brass, as if refined in a furnace, and His voice was mighty and loud, as the sound of many waters. His countenance was like the sun shining in its strength - bright and bold beyond any human comprehension.

As they stood there just staring up into the sky, stunned and mesmerized by what they saw, and Jesus waved His hand over all the Jew Jacobs, and His Spirit fell on them all! Jesus then spoke, *"Turn to Me with all your heart, with fasting, with weeping, and with mourning. I am the First and the Last. I am He who lives, and was dead, and behold, I am alive forevermore."*

Then something came over all the tribes of Jacob's sons, for their bodies were shaking and tears filled their eyes. There was *power* all around those Jews from the twelve tribes, and all of them were forced by the *power* to fall to their knees. The *power* seemed to be opening up the minds of all those Jews from the twelve tribes. They began to see things in their minds like they had never seen them before. Scriptures were being brought to the forefront of their memories. It was as if flashing images of the things concerning Messiah in the Torah were in their minds and all around them. And then they knew!

At first they were not jubilant for they were ashamed - they had rejected Jesus for over two thousand years! But now they understood why they had been suffering all this time - it was the longest of their captivities. They rended their hearts, and mourned their God with weeping and fasting. They mourned for the Messiah they had rejected, but then it became very real - their Messiah had revealed Himself to His people and He did indeed come to save them! They had just been freed! Their Savior had finally come!

><

Five days before Sukkot, the second angel did as the first angel, and poured out his bowl of a plague. The oceans turned to blood, but only wherever Muslims were. The Muslims were not only angry, they were scared. They did not understand where the blood came from. But al-Mahdi and Isa finally caught on. It still didn't matter though, for God had allowed their hearts to be hardened. Esau had already turned their hearts to Satan a long time ago, and God knew there was no turning them back.

The Messianic Jacobs were not affected by these plagues, so did not understand why the Muslims were angrier than usual - which isn't saying much, since they seem to be in perpetual hate-mode toward the Messianic Jacobs. This was the day they had discovered their Messiah, so they were concerned with *other things*. Whatever was happening to the Muslims didn't concern them at the moment.

Four days before Sukkot, the third angel came to pour out his bowl. He poured out his plague on the rivers and all the springs all over the world. Now there was no drinking water, and suddenly the Muslims became very thirsty. Some of them saw some Jew Jacobs taking a drink from a spring, but when they came to this same spring, the water had turned to blood. The Jews would see water, but the Muslims would see blood.

Because of the water being blood, anything that was a living creature in the oceans, rivers and springs had now died. So now the supply of fish for food had completely died out. al-Mahdi was now wondering how much longer this would go on, *"What else could the God of the people of the book bring upon us?"*

Three days before Sukkot, the fourth angel did as the others. His plague was to cause the sun to become hotter than it had ever been before. He caused solar flares all over the sun. These flares were not the normal kind though, and they were causing the earth to heat up. And because there was more than one solar flare, the heat kept climbing. Many Muslims died from their burns - burns they received from the scorching sun.

The Messianic Jacobs just watched as these strange things happened to everyone around them, except the other Messianics. To them it seemed like Moses was somewhere near causing these plagues!

Two days before Sukkot, the fifth angel came upon the earth. With him he brought a plague of darkness, for no sooner had the sun burst all over with solar flares, it appeared as if a solar eclipse was in its final stages. But it wasn't a solar eclipse, for the moon and earth were still in their normal positions for this time of year. Just the same, the sun was dark. No light at all shown on any area where there were Muslims trying to plan for their attack on the Messianic Jacobs.

They were in pain too, still from their sores from three days earlier. They were thirsty too, since there was no drinking water anywhere. Muslims everywhere knew there was some kind of *magic* going on, because al-Mahdi explained to them what was happening - although what he said didn't make much sense. But they fell for his lies once again, and so they suffered while trying to get ready for a war.

The day before Sukkot, the sixth angel poured out his bowl of plague on the Euphrates river. It wouldn't matter much anyway, since it had been turned to blood. But now al-Mahdi had an idea. The Euphrates, once a river, was now dried up and would be the perfect pathway for the Eastern armies to meet up with the other armies.

The seventh angel waited until he heard the *last trumpet*, for it wasn't time yet for him to pour out his bowl.

><del>></del>`````

Jesus signaled to His angels, the seventh angel, actually. For the first six angels had already done their deeds. The seventh angel was just about ready to blow his shofar any moment, which precedes the retrieving of the harvest of God. But he had something else to do. There were the *tares* of *Mystery Babylon* to deal with first; and then the tares of the beast.

Jesus had an agenda, and He would start with the land that

was once known as *Greater Edom* - the land between Teman and Dedan - the western coast of Saudi Arabia and all the way up to southern Jordan. Jesus would land in Bozrah first, but then He would go on to Jerusalem. It was time to destroy *Babylon*, the center of Islam. Jesus determined to bring the calamity of Esau upon himself. As prophesied in Jeremiah, it was time to punish him - again, the first time being a *mikrah* - the *pattern* in prophecy. The Dedanites and the inhabitants of Teman, those Edomites of Arabia, will all fall today, as also Isaiah prophesied. In one hour it will all be over. Jesus planned to crush Esau's plans. Jesus Himself, will see to it that the *desert by the sea* will become desolate.

>━━◄

Saudi Arabia has continually reported the highest reserves of oil in the world, which meant they had all nations in the palm of their hands. But these reports have been inflated a bit. In the past, the oil companies had continually raised prices by way of the futures market of the Stock Market, but Saudi Arabia had always had a hand in the price of oil, too - and for reasons beyond the consumer's knowledge. And now they have reduced their production of oil - which also raises the price of oil.

Saudi's Royal Family loves to flaunt their wealth, even as their people suffer in extreme unemployment and poverty. They are a nation who buys weapons from those nations who buy their oil. But these weapons are not for the use against these oil-hungry nations - they are to defend themselves against their *own* people. It is only a matter of time before the people of Saudi Arabia, and also the members of al-Queda, who are slowly taking over Arabia, will turn against the Royal Family. And then the oil will be in the hands of the radicals.

Esau has spread the idea that *"Mystery Babylon"* could be Babylon itself, in order to confuse those studying the Bible. Iraq's ruler, of many years past, had begun to rebuild the city of Babylon, so many Christians think it is the actual city that the Bible speaks of. And some think it is the Catholic Church, since the words *"harlot"* and *"whore"* usually only apply to God's people who have gone astray.

But "Babylon" is only a code name in the Book of Revelation - the code name for the present-day satanic regime at any given time. Today, the center of *Babylon* is the city of Mecca, Saudi Arabia, the capital of Islam - *the beast religion.*

⋙⌒⋘

Jesus mounted His magnificent white steed, and sat there so majestically for a moment. He wanted to savor this moment, for His time had finally come. He headed down to earth in a fury, gusting up clouds around Him and behind Him. As He descended on *Edom*, He yelled out a battle cry like nothing that had ever been heard on the earth before. It came as the sound of thunder, louder than the loudest thunder in an American midwest tornadic storm. All who dwelled in the land from Teman to Dedan looked up into the sky, for not only did they hear this thunder that was holy, but at the same time, perhaps it was the *sound* of the end of the world? They saw *Him* coming toward them with a vengeance!

Abdul Odnan sat in his favorite chair, contemplating his next move. At prayers this evening he would know, for Allah would show him what he should do next. Odnan did not want to reveal the rest of his plan too soon. All of a sudden, all of Odnan's phones began ringing, and his secretary ran into his office telling him to turn on the TV or the internet. Odnan was upset with her for her unsummoned interruption, but he would let it pass - for now. Ignoring the phones, he quickly shook the mouse of his computer to wake it up.

Saudi Arabia was smack dab in the middle of an all out war! But not against anyone who was counted as an enemy - they were at war with their own brothers! Odnan sat up straight, astonished at what he was witnessing. Odnan stood, while still staring at the computer screen. They were fighting in Mecca! "How could they desecrate our *Holy City* like that? Those fools!" Odnan cried out.

Blast after blast went off in Mecca, and all around Saudi Arabia - wherever there was an oil well, there was an out-of-control fire. It had started as simply as the 2011 riots of other Islamic countries, but then there were guns - everywhere, like the revolutions of Libya and Syria. The fighting erupted in violence against fellow Muslims. Those who were behind the Royal Family fought fiercely against those who rebelled against them. And then the fighting broke out in other Saudi cities, and the whole country was ablaze in gunfire, and blazing oil wells that were totally out of control.

Odnan just stood there looking on in disbelief. "Makka, Makka, how can they do this to her?!" He mumbled, and cried over and over again. Mecca was the first and most holiest city, and now Medina and Riyadh, too, were also in the news. Odnan began to grow angrier and angrier. If these holy cities were destroyed, there was still one more - the third holiest city in Islam - Jerusalem. He had already vowed to make Jerusalem the new, and most holiest city of Islam, should anything happen to his beloved Mecca.

While still in Turkey, Odnan was watching it all on his computer, and then he saw *Him*. The Man on the flying white horse. al-Mahdi was supposed to arrive on a white horse, so this enraged him. "Who is that?" he asked no one in particular. "That cannot be al-Mahdi, for *I* am al-Mahdi!" Odnan said in anger, as he watched this imposter dive into his city. And then he watched his people in Arabia - they saw something, too.

They were still fighting, but something caught their attention in the sky. "What is that?" someone said, as he saw a bright light in the sky coming right toward them.

Then they also saw *Him,* and what He was doing. And they all stood still, stunned at the sight of the Man on the flying horse! "Who is that?" yet another yelled. But it was too late, the Man had moved so fast and was upon them before they knew what hit them.

With one swoop of His arm, fire rained down on Mecca, and all the land from Teman and all the way north up to Edom, and southern Jordan. Jesus spoke one word and it was as if He swung a threshing scythe, and harvested those who had harbored those demons, foul spirits and unclean evil powers. Those that had clung to the false religion, and used it to kill the Lord's prophets, and His people, were destroyed and immediately scooped up and then thrown into the lake of fire. Death, mourning and famine came in one day - an hour to be exact. And the cities were left to burn to the ground. And, just like that, Saudi Arabia, or *Greater Edom*, was no more.

Just as the first Babylon was permanently destroyed, so was this *Babylon*. The Arabians will never again pitch their tents there. The Royal Family of Saudi Arabia had been brought down to *Sheol*, to the lowest depths of the *Pit*. His name and his descendants are no more. His city, his country and all that he had known in his life is now gone.

God had sent His wrath on Mecca, and it had happened as when He overthrew Sodom and Gomorrah. You could almost hear the angels singing, "Babylon has fallen, fallen." Arabia is never mentioned again in Scripture after the announcement that Babylon has fallen. Arabia does not have a part in the last war, for this abominable country no longer exists.

Those who had done business with the Royal Family mourned, not for the Royal Family or the Arab people, but for the loss of their fortunes that just went up in smoke - literally. Ships on their way to deliver goods to the Royal Family could see the flames from where they sat in the sea. They mourned the loss, because it appeared as if there would be no more business for awhile, if at all anymore. Many of these merchants made their living off the Royal Family, and now it was plain to see, they were gone.

Merchants stood at a distance, watching her burn, that great city of the Kaaba. Mecca, and all the cities along the Arabian western coast were on fire, with no hope of being saved from their torment. Those who were in the cities did not escape, for Jesus took every one of them down with His Word - His two-edged *Sword*. And then He cast their spirits and souls into the eternal lake of fire.

*T*heir clothes had been transformed into white battle clothes with white armor, and they were given *swords* - Scripture written on their hearts. Those who had gone up from the cemeteries were already in their saddles, their horses snorting, and dancing around anxiously. Now the angels had come to join them and were getting ready to get up on their horses.

Then there was the sound of a stallion, snorting and galloping toward them, and the sound of millions of chariots, it was so loud and unexplainable, but they couldn't see anything. It was a frightening sound, but then they saw him, the huge white horse that was restless, as were the horses he was coming upon. He had come out of the clouds above them, and prepared to land in front of all the waiting armies of God, this great white stallion with the glorious Rider, His robe seemingly splattered in blood.

He had swooped down to land in front of His army of all

the dead who had believed in Him, and His angel army. He had just come from a battle and was still ready for more. The armies standing before this great white horse with the Man sitting on him, said, "Who is this who comes from Edom, with dyed garments from Bozrah?" for somehow they knew He had just come from *Greater Edom*.

And then they will see that it is the One who is glorious in His apparel, traveling in the greatness of His strength, who says, "I who speak in righteousness, mighty to save."

They asked Him then, "Why is your apparel splattered red, and Your garments like One who treads in the winepress?"

Jesus jumped off His horse and responded, "I have just come from destroying *Babylon*, that Great Edom, the center of Islam, Saudi Arabia. It is burning, and it is gone. And now, together we will save Jerusalem, and My inheritance!" The waiting army then realized that it was Jesus!

Once He had everyone there and mounted on their steeds, Jesus focused on what still had to be done. He mounted His white horse again, and headed down to earth - with everyone on white horses following Him. They were going to save Jerusalem - and the Jew Jacobs!

⤙⤚

To the Jews it was Saturday, the 15th of Tishrei, in the year 5783. To the rest of the world it was September 30, 2023. It was a relatively quiet morning, despite the tension in the air from every side of Messianic Jacob's tiny little nation, Israel. From the north came armies from Turkey and Syria; from the east the armies of Iran and all the "stans;" from the west Libya sent their armies; and bringing up the south was Sudan. From the four corners of the earth, north, south, east and west, they came to surround Israel. These kings and al-Mahdi as their leader, together have plans to wipe Israel off the face of this earth, for they do not believe the Messianic Jacobs have a right to exist.

Syria's forces came by way of the ocean, from the port of Haifa, and there were planes, helicopters and tanks, carrying rockets and nuclear missiles. From the ocean there were troop carriers and aircraft carriers - all armed and ready to fight, just off the coast of Gaza. Eastern forces had just crossed the Euphrates - a much easier task since it had dried up the day before.

They came from all sides, and gathered at Har Meggido - some know it as Armageddon. There had been many battles on this very hill, but there would be no battle here today. Har Meggido, as a symbol of the ages-old struggle between God and Satan, good and evil, will only be the gathering place for Israel's enemies today. After all the armies of all the nations from the four corners of the earth had finally arrived at Har Meggido, al-Mahdi gathered his generals together to discuss the plan of attack; and then he led the way from there to Jerusalem. He wanted to be a part of this battle - the battle that would finally win him the world! So they traveled the sixty or so miles south, beginning on Highway 65, and then on down to the outskirts of Jerusalem, where all the armies would meet up again and regroup for their attack. The battle would take place in Jerusalem, near the Mount of

Olives, for that is where Jesus will step foot first.

While most believers in Jesus have their eyes on the European Union to reveal itself as the beast of the risen Roman Empire, instead, the European Union had in fact become the risen *Islamic Empire*, led by Turkey - and no one noticed, until it was almost too late. Some didn't notice at all.

For the past decade, Muslims have been spreading the message of the "peaceful" religion of Islam. They have been saying, "Peace, peace...," where there is no peace. Truly, most have overlooked the one obvious element in Islam - only if the *infidels* convert to Islam will there be peace with Muslims.

Isaiah told us what would happen to Egypt, and it did - thirty years ago, but once again it happened for the fulfillment of the *pattern*, for the new ruler is far crueler than the one they had before. Isaiah said, *"I will set Egyptians against Egyptians; everyone will fight against his brother, and everyone against his neighbor, city against city, kingdom against kingdom. The spirit of Egypt will fail in its midst; I will destroy their counsel, and they will consult the idols and the charmers, the mediums and the sorcerers. And the Egyptians I will give into the hand of a cruel master, and a fierce king will rule over them,' says the Lord of hosts."*

The rebellions in Egypt several years ago revealed that it had already had a cruel ruler over them for the past thirty years, causing them to live in poverty, with no jobs. When the new ruler came into power, the peace between Israel and Egypt was no more; and the peace between Israel and Jordan was no more, because they too rebelled. One by one, all the countries who had been *oppressed* by cruel, rich rulers, rebelled and their then present governments fell right before the whole world's eyes. And these countries gained new rulers, who at first seemed to be good and generous people, but these past few years have shed light on their true colors. Plus, the new ruler over all the world, al-Mahdi, is more evil than anyone could ever imagine.

><r><

The Israelite armies were ready to defend Jerusalem. They had been there for quite awhile now, then all of a sudden everyone in the city saw missiles heading straight for them! They were being attacked! All the armies scrambled to try and shoot down the missiles.

Those women and children, and the elderly Jew Jacobs, and all the Messianic Jews all ran for cover, but there didn't seem to be anywhere to go, for the missiles were coming from every direction. They had bomb shelters, but there weren't enough of them to accommodate everyone trying to find a space to hide. Plus, it was really too late, as the missiles were right overhead.

Many thought these missiles were armed with nuclear warheads, and that they would obliterate Israel. The Jews had won every war the Arabs had waged against them, and they knew they could only lose *once* - when they saw the missiles heading straight for them, they just knew they were gonners. But the Messianic Jacobs held onto their faith in God, for He would come to save them just like He said He would. They knew God would come through for them just like He had always done. Israel would never be wiped off the map.

In that same instant, everyone heard a noise like chariots in the sky, millions of them coming over the mountaintops they seemed to leap. The Jew Jacobs and all the Messianic armies there with them, looked up to see what else was coming out of the sky besides the missiles. What they saw mesmerized them at first - the appearance was like horses, millions of horses, with riders in battle array. The Man at the lead of these horses just looked at the incoming missiles, waved his arm, and the missiles were obliterated, for Jesus could not let them harm his beloved heritage. Cheers went up all over Jerusalem. The Messianics now knew for sure their Savior would not let them down!

>~~~<

al-Mahdi had watched as his missiles were being destroyed, but he had no idea what had happened to them or who did it. He ordered his armies to move into the city to find out what was going on.

Although the unorganized armies of Hamas and Hezbollah caused much chaos in the past, al-Mahdi was extremely organized, and thus his armies were also. He signaled them that it didn't matter what happened to the missiles, they would fight this battle with guns and tanks if needed - they were prepared to fight to the death.

The Muslims crept slowly into Jerusalem, cautious about what they might find. They had watched from afar, knowing that the missiles they fired were set to explode on impact. But they did not explode - they just disappeared! So al-Mahdi's armies had moved in closer to find out what had happened.

The Israelite and Messianic armies were inside the city waiting for the attack - they had been told the Muslim armies were headed their way. They all stood ready with their weapons aimed at the enemy. Jesus and His armies had appeared on the ground now, and landed in the garden of Olivet, where Jesus dismounted first, stepping on the mount of Olivet. The second He stepped foot on the ground, it shook with the strength of a large earthquake and the hill split in two! There seemed to be no end to His army, which had dismounted from their horses and was now standing in the gap Jesus had formed from the splitting of the hill.

The enemies had come in to the city to surround the tremendous number of Jesus's armies. al-Mahdi thought this was a very big mistake by this *white* army, this maneuver that appeared to have these strange armies surrounded, but what he saw next caused the color from his face to drain quickly. The multitude of the armies before them seemed to multiply right before their eyes and was incomprehensible! There was standing room only, so to speak - there was no space between each soldier! And they glowed!

Next thing he knew, al-Mahdi's armies seemed to be confused. The first line of Muslim soldiers fell to the ground with stunned looks on their faces. Then Jesus had caused the rest to turn on their own people. Some of the Shi'a and the Sunnis turned against one another, and they were destroying one another. Then those Muslims on the outskirts of the city, ran forward to cut down the white army where they stood. But as they soon discovered, these men from the mysterious white army would not be cut down. These soldiers, all in white, lunged between their enemies' weapons and were not cut down.

The Muslims' faces turned a ghostly white, drained of all color when they saw those whom they had thought they just killed coming back at them. They couldn't outrun them, but the Muslims still thought al-Mahdi would get them through this and that they would win, so they continued in the battle, standing their ground.

There was so much dust mustered up from the ground, as the armies fought against each other. But since the armies of Jesus could not die, their number never diminished. The other Israelite and Messianic armies just stood behind them ready to fight, but found they didn't have much to do. But one by one, the Muslims were falling to their deaths. Then Jesus spoke a *word,* and waved His arm. His armies looked up, for they saw fire come down from the sky, then turned toward the multitude of the Islamic army, and their enemies lay dead, fallen to the earth.

No one had escaped. The war against Islam was won. The heavenly army then returned home in the blink of an eye! Just like that the war was over.

The Israelites had seen *Him.* They had seen the *Man* leading an army to defend Jerusalem. They had seen *Him* come out of the sky. And they knew something had just miraculously happened - they had won another unwinnable

war! And they had not known who was the leader of this
Godly army. *"Was it Michael or Gabriel, the arch angels?"*
they wondered. But they didn't ask the Messianics, because
the Israelites thought they were just as bewildered. But they
weren't. The Messianics knew it was Jesus who had just come
to save them.

The cleansing began with all the weapons, the Israelites
gathered them all up to be burned. They chose a site just
outside Jerusalem, in the desert away from any possible home
or building. They piled them up, and the pile reached up
several feet high, and hundreds of feet wide. The Israelites
and the Messianics threw their own weapons up on the pile
too, and then they were all set on fire. The fire continued and
smoldered for what seemed like months or years, but was
really only seven hours.

*T*he last harvest of the year always took place after *Yom Kippur*, the *Day of Atonement*. And the last feast of the year was *Sukkot*, or the *Feast of Tabernacles*. This feast was also known as the *Ingathering* of the final harvest.

The *Feast of Tabernacles* began on the 15th day of Tishrei, the seventh month and lasted for seven days, with the eighth day being a holy convocation - no work was done on the first day and the eighth day. But it was the *Ingathering* celebration that they were really celebrating, which happened at the end of the harvest year and was a celebration of the bringing in of the harvest - both celebrations were combined into one huge eight day celebration. While Jews considered Tishrei the first month of the harvest year, the Bible clearly states this is the *final harvest of the year*, making it the last month of the harvest year. A fitting celebration for the end of a harvest year - and a fitting celebration for what it really represents: the *final harvest* that Jesus spoke of in Revelation.

They heard it it in their spirits - that *last trumpet* - loud and clear on the first day of Sukkot. It had been a tense morning, but those seasoned Messianics reassured the new Messianics - the Jew Jacobs who had just discovered their Messiah only a few days earlier - that Messiah would fight this battle for them. So they had the confidence the Lord would win this one last battle for them - and He did in fact do just that!

Then all who called themselves Messianics - those who believed in Yeshua with all their hearts - Jew and Gentile - looked up and saw angels coming straight toward them! Instinctively, the Messianics raised their arms in the air, and each person was taken up by an angel. Those Messianics that were still alive all around the world, had been called up to meet Jesus in the air! As they ascended to heaven in a cloud, those still on the earth saw them. In a twinkling of the eye, it was - and all of the Messianics were gone!

The seventh angel had blown his shofar fifteen days earlier, but it was finally heard by those left on the earth. The angel poured out his bowl of a plague on the earth. In that very same hour, after the Messianics had been taken up to heaven, there was a great earthquake. The sun was darkened, and the moon was not casting its full light today and the earth began to rumble, slowly at first. But then it trembled violently, more so than at any other time that the earth had ever shaken. This earthquake was different - it was being felt all around the earth, and this time a tenth of all the cities on the earth fell into rubble.

Jesus had gathered all the dead from the war. He first told those who had never heard it before - He told them about why He had come to the earth - He told them what He did on the cross.

But they didn't know they were dead, and they didn't recognize Him. For Jesus wanted to give them the exact same opportunity as everyone else. For it is stated in Scripture that the gospel would be preached to those who had died without hearing the gospel. Those that believed were spared, and told to await judgment. But those who did not, Jesus appeared to them and told them their fate. He then tossed them into the lake of fire with the rest of the evil ones, with one wave of His arm.

Of course, the most evil of all was Satan, who had been in the guise of al-Mahdi, so he and his Isa were both cast into the lake of fire, too. All those who had died in the *Babylonian* massacre were there in the lake of fire already, those who were not innocent. All evil had been removed from the earth. Now the earth could be cleansed.

The few scattered people left on the earth were not from the Abrahamic tribes of Jacob, nor were they Muslims, nor Messianics. Some were those who had successfully hidden from al-Mahdi's armies, but had not yet made a decision to believe in Jesus. Some of the others who were left on the earth had called themselves *Christians* - they were those who had not truly accepted Jesus into their hearts and lives, but also had not converted to Islam. There were even others still on the earth, those from other religions - also who had not converted to Islam, nor did they believe in Jesus. And then there were those who didn't believe in anything but themselves. But they had *all* watched when the Muslims had been *reaped* from the earth by the invisible scythes.

Still wandering around, scattered throughout the earth, were these *few* survivors. They were confused and didn't know what to think. Then the earth began to shake again. For the past several years, there had been an abundance of earthquakes, in all different sizes. So people had become familiar with the ground quaking almost daily - wherever they happened to be.

But today's quakes were different. There were several quakes almost evenly spaced about the various tectonic plates on the earth; pretty much where they all met, and along the major trenches.

Since the majority of the quakes were in the ocean, tsunamis were triggered all over the globe. In turn, they triggered gas lines to rupture and explode, causing fires here and there, amongst the rubble. Then the fires spread to join other fires. The fires seemed to be growing, rather than going out.

Those who were left on the earth had heard all the same messages the whole world had heard - they had heard the good news that Jesus came to die for mankind's sin. They had chosen to harden their hearts against the one true God, and He knew the true nature of their hearts. There is no forgiveness for this choice - or even for no choice at all - they had committed the unforgivable sin. It is too late to be forgiven and they will perish to hell - for all eternity. There is no way out. It was indeed like the days of Noah. They had *missed the boat* and *God had shut the door*!

The quakes had caused the earth to open up in many places all over the world, large cracks in the earth swallowing everything and everyone in their paths.

Although the quakes began to taper off after awhile, everything was burning - grass, trees, buildings, houses, and even people. The fires were destined to continue until they had burned the whole earth.

Some of the people who had found a place to hide began to come out of their shelters to see what was happening to their earth. These people watched in horror as their homes and cities burned. All over the globe, people mourned the loss of their treasures and their earthly lives. *"How would they even begin to rebuild their homes or their lives,"* they wondered.

Even after all the destruction, and even though for as far as the eye could see, anything and everything was on fire - burning with no apparent end - it never occurred to most of the remaining people that this was the *end* of the earth - and the *end* of their lives. Soon they would be gone too, unable to escape the earthly fires. There would be no rebuilding for *them*. The fires didn't stop until all the remaining people were gone. And then they were destined to endure the eternal fires, for this is what they chose - instead of God.

⟫⟨

They had all heard the same warnings, but most didn't believe it would happen. And so it took them by *surprise*, just like in Noah's day. Instead of preparing and watching, they continued to seek after ungodly things, or just shrugged it off thinking they could continue with their selfish lives and put God on a back burner - for later. It didn't matter that they didn't believe - Jesus *did* come, and He gathered those who *were* watching for Him and took *them* to Heaven - but the *end* still came for the rest and for the earth.

The earth lay charred, smoldering and barren. As far as one could look, if there had been anyone left on the earth to look, all they would see was the black burnt wood of the ruins, and the gray ash that covered every single surface. The fire had not been hot enough to completely melt the steel in buildings, but it didn't leave much standing either - everywhere you looked, there were skeletons of twisted, warped, bent and sagging steel.

The fire destroyed all that mankind had come to depend on for communication and entertainment, too - no more cell phones, or even land line phones, no more cable TV, no more internet - all those cables, wires and fiber optics are now just a jumbled melted mess. The earth was no longer the earth it had been. Although it looks sad, hopeless and beyond repair, quite the opposite is true.

The Earth's *death* was no more final than the death of a human being. God's judgment on the earth had been held back by His own *Word*. But by His own *Word* also, He sent fire down, in many forms, to destroy the corruption, and the evil that corrupted man, woman and the earth. But redemption is God's plan, not only for mankind, but also for the earth. And redemption buys back God's original plan - his original design.

This earth was destined for destruction, but it is also destined for resurrection and restoration. The fire was not only a fire of destruction, it was a purifying fire - a fire that refines and cleanses. Much as the trees and shrubs seem to die in a *Winter* and then come back to life in the *Spring*, so will the earth again become a new and living thing - God had long ago built into creation, the healing properties of nature. And so the earth is healing itself. The earth had a *"Winter of fire"* and now it is time for the earth's *"Spring"* back to life.

So now God can begin with a clean slate. He has cleansed and purified the earth with fire, He has removed Satan and all his demons and all that was created as a direct result of sin, so now there is also no more sin on the earth. Earth's fiery *end* will open the doors to a brand new *beginning*. Now God can create His New Earth.

A new earth, that is superior and new in quality of life, will come forth. The Earth is mankind's home so they will return to it to live, but it won't be like it was when they lived on it before. It will be changed, as they will be. It will be different, but still the same - life will continue on the earth, but without corruption and sin.

><del></del><

For those who did not want God in their lives, or to run

their lives on earth, there is an eternal place prepared that is completely void of God: no light, no love, no peace, no life, no mercy, no strength and no water.

Even though those who chose to ignore God in this life, He was all around them - yet still they denied Him. If there was no God on this earth, it would look just like hell - void of any attributes of God. But God gave us a *Way* to avoid a place without Him - He gave us Jesus.

><del>~</del><

Some believe this war goes way back to the so-called hatred between Sarah and Hagar, for their sons Isaac and Ishmael, respectively. And some even think this war was between the sons themselves, Isaac and Ishmael. But there was never a battle between these two brothers. It was clear who the promise of God was for, and that was Isaac. God also promised to bless Ishmael and his people, which He did.

But the real war was between Jacob and Esau. They have been warring between each other since they were in the womb, and now the war is finally over.

This war was not between the Jews and the Muslims. This was a war between good and evil, and good triumphed over evil. It was a war between God and Satan - and God always has the last word:

> *"The earth is mine, and all its fullness,*
> *the world and those who dwell therein.*
> *I am the Alpha and the Omega,*
> *the Beginning and the End,*
> *the First and the Last.*

I am the Lord of hosts.
I am the Lord, and there is no other;
there is no God besides Me.
I am the Lord your God."

*A*fter the war, Messianic Jacob was now a mixture of Judah Jacobs, Protestant Jacobs and even a few Gentile Catholic Jacobs who had joined together as *one*. They had been taken up to New Jerusalem to celebrate the *Feast of Tabernacles*, the *Wedding Feast of the Lord*. They would celebrate in the city of Jerusalem in the new temple that was built by Jesus, according to prophecy in Zechariah, *"Yes, He shall build the temple of the Lord."* He had built the *new temple* in the *New Jerusalem*, which became His bride. In building His congregation, one person at a time, He had created His *New Jerusalem.*

The *Temple* was of a *new design* - since there was no need for sacrifices any longer, and there is no longer a need for a physical dwelling place on the earth for the Lord God. For not only does His Spirit dwell inside each believer, right beside their own spirit, making them the true temple now - the glory of God was all around them all the time!

The people had landed on the grass just down the street from the banquet hall. They then walked to the big banquet hall in Jerusalem. Everything, buildings, flowers, trees, roads, sidewalks and even some of the people's clothing, who were walking about the city, glistened in the sun - or rather God's glory, because there was no need of the sun here on Jerusalem any longer.

As they walked, the people took everything in with all their senses. It felt like they had been here for days, or weeks, or even months for all they knew, but they still couldn't help being in awe of everything they saw.

Upon entering the large beveled glass double doors of the banquet room, everyone paused to stare in amazement. There were hundreds, no, maybe thousands, of banquet tables. The room was huge - as far as the eye could see there were tables, tables, tables!

Then, one by one, those who had fought in the war began to notice that they were not wearing their war clothes and armor any longer. As each person walked through the double doors, their clothing transformed. Those who had not entered yet were still wearing their armor or the clothes they had on when they were taken up. But those inside the room, and even those just inside the doors were now clothed in white flowing robes, much like the robes students would wear at a school graduation ceremony in times of old on earth. After everyone had gone in, many of the children were making a game of running in and out of the banquet doors so they could see their clothes change back and forth.

The banquet room was open all the way around with huge white pillars spaced proportionately around the room, seemingly holding up the roof. The view from every angle was magnificent - overlooking the beautiful *River of the Water of Life* and the other buildings throughout Jerusalem. The city had truly been transformed, and they could even see the temple from there. The sight was amazing in that you could actually see the whole city from any angle, sparkling gold all the way around the huge banquet hall. There were millions of people visible, but somehow there seemed to be enough room for everyone and no one seemed to be or feel crowded as they walked slowly into the banquet room. The room appeared larger than it was because of the open air *"walls"* - or so they thought because they were still judging things by earth's standards.

The tables were larger than the typical banquet tables on earth. They had to be. They had to accommodate the huge centerpieces, and every edible delight you could possibly think of to be on each table! As you walked into the hall, the tables gave the illusion that they were rows and rows of long and unending tables. Ornately carved antique white wooden chairs lined both sides of each table. The seats and backs of the chairs were cushioned with a white brocade linen fabric. With white brocade linen napkins to match the chairs, the place settings before each chair also displayed golden utensils and cutlery with gold goblets inlaid with goldleaf flecks. The napkins had an added touch of class as they were edged with a glowing gold thread embroidery in a grapes and vine design.

The centerpieces were carved fruit and vegetable masterpieces surrounded with all kinds of fruit all around the base, and appeared to be one elongated centerpiece on each *long* table. But as each person walked up to one of the tables, they came upon *round* banquet tables with a carved fruit and ice sculpture centerpiece on each one. The transformation was all so magical!

Each centerpiece was different and unique. Some had lots of delectable red flowers carved out of watermelons, and there were also some watermelons that were beautifully carved into baskets holding other fruits. Some of those fruits were carved into flowers, and some were left in their natural state and beauty. Other melons of all kinds were carved into various animal shapes and flowers. Bell peppers of every color were placed artistically at the base of some centerpieces, some carved, some left whole.

Radishes, tomatoes, carrots and just about any vegetable or fruit you could think of had ornate carvings in them, as well as left beautifully whole. All were placed just so in the centerpieces to form the magnificent pieces of art they were. In the center of each of these fruit and vegetable wonders was an ice sculpture. Each sculpture was a different likeness of an angel, and the angels seemed to be watching over the tables, with their majestic wings hovering over as if in protection.

The tables themselves were amazing in that the center portion of each table was one huge *Lazy Susan* which was an *altar* laden entirely with delectable foods consisting of fruits, vegetables, breads, nuts, pastas, pastries and other incredible edibles. All around the centerpieces, food was presented in the most beautiful presentation ever seen. Each table's carved fruit centerpiece surrounded with loose whole fruits, in turn were held in place with vines of grapes encircling the other fruits all the way around the table. Then around the outer portion of the Lazy Susan were platters, platters and more platters of wonderful things to feast on. The platters made of pure gold cradled succulent entrees, casseroles, hor d' oeuvres, vegetable dishes, cheeses, pastries, desserts - you name it, it was there on each table!

There were cheeses of all kinds, fruit slices and berries of every color you could possibly think of too. There were platters of finger snacks of items of chicken nuggets, mini pizzas, sausage rolls, and others had cheese puffs, vegetable rolls and mini vegetable quiches. Yet another platter was filled with delightful seafood snacks, such as shrimp.

And breads galore! The breads were absolutely magnificent works of art. The breads were both leavened and unleavened: bagels, pumpernickel, matzo, rye, sourdough, bialy rolls, challah, ciabatta, kugelhopf, and so much more, including the most beautiful braided breads - braided and shaped into loaves of all shapes and sizes, along with rolls of all kinds. There were also breadsticks that were twisted, braided or seasoned to perfection. Plus there were even cornucopias made of bread, and the artistic baker had given them the appearance of being carved. It was all absolutely beautiful - and deliciously inviting!

Flowing out of the cornucopias were yummy looking pastries in the colors of a rainbow. Pettit Fours, Baklava, Fruit tarts, fruit turnovers, fudge brownies, turtle cupcakes, tea cakes of all kinds, cream puffs, Creme Brulee tarts, caramel nut buns and miscellaneous scones were just a few of the delectable desserts displayed on each table.

Even though the tables seemed to be a *fixed* size, there just seemed to be more and more food as one would turn the Lazy Susan around to choose what they wanted from the platters. As you turned the Lazy Susan, it seemed so huge, but if you watched the fruit and ice sculpture in the center and focused on one side of it, that side would pass several times as you turned the center portion of the table, but different platters of food would appear each time. It was fun just seeing what would show up with the next turn.

The tables were not numbered, nor were they assigned to anyone in particular, so everyone chose where they wanted to sit. Friends and family members gathered together and all sat at the same table, of course. After they all sat down they looked around the table to see who else was there and they were excited to see their parents and grandparents there at the same table, with aunts, uncles and cousins, too. It was just like a reunion or homecoming. At every single table, everyone's excitement was barely contained. It was all just plain fun, like being on an eternal vacation!

Everyone in the room chattered excitedly while they waited for Jesus to arrive. *Redeemed*, a Messianic rock band on the old earth, appeared near the head table. Then Jesus appeared at the head table and a hush fell over the whole room as everyone turned their attention to their favorite Person and Friend. *Redeemed* began singing their own rendition of *Psalm 100* and the combination of Jesus and the obviously anointed song, caused God's Glory to fill the room so strongly that no one could speak or move.

Make a joyful shout to the Lord, all you lands!
Serve the Lord with gladness;
Come before His presence with singing.
Know that the Lord, He is God;
It is He who has made us, not we ourselves.
We are His people and the sheep of His pasture.
Enter into His gates with thanksgiving,
And into His courts with praise.
Be thankful to Him, and bless His name.
For the Lord is good; His mercy is everlasting,
And His truth endures to all generations.

When the song was over, Jesus began speaking, "In commemoration of *Our Marriage*, we have this wonderful feast before us. Today, we celebrate the *Feast of Tabernacles* together. I have come to *tabernacle* permanently among you - just as my Father dwelt among His people in the Tabernacle in the desert.

This *Feast of Tabernacles* is a symbol of the the intimacy you have with Me, and my desire to dwell among you. Because of the blood of the *perfect Lamb*, both Jew and

Gentile are united as *one* blood-washed physical people called *Israel*. Peace was re-established via the blood of the true *Passover Lamb*. I gladly gave My life for you, and I gladly give My love to you," Jesus finished with the raising of his goblet in a toast to His bride, Israel. Everyone in the room then raised their goblets, too.

Everyone at the tables was so excited to see Jesus they couldn't stop stirring and whispering to each other. But Jesus didn't find this rude, He was honored and touched and was excited Himself to meet everyone personally.

Jesus was presenting His *bride* to His Father for the first time and this was the moment He had been waiting for for over six thousand years! He was overwhelmed with joy, which in turn spread over *His Bride*, Israel sitting before Him. The glory of God was very apparent in the room, and everyone was in reverence of their *Bridegroom* Jesus, who stood before them in person. Everyone took a moment to reflect all that had happened recently, and was happening to them right now. It was beyond words, but just the same they knew why they were here.

Jesus put up his hands, with palms down in a gesture as if to say '*calm down, I will be finished soon and will be out there amongst you all*', and He continued with his speech, "Jew and Gentile together are *One New Man*, and will always be *One people* to me - and of course, My Bride."

Jesus paused for a second and then said, "Today we celebrate the completion of all the *Feasts of God*, the fulfillment of My Father's Redemption of His people. It is also a celebration of the beginning of our eternal lives together - a celebration of the life My Father and I always wanted for you is now come. And now I present you, *Israel* my bride, to My Father in person. You are my *firstfruit harvest offering* to Him, and this *Feast of Tabernacles* is for you to celebrate our *Eternal Union* together with My Father. Eat and drink in celebration and honor of the most glorious life you could ever have imagined! The best is yet to come! My Father's love and My love are with you eternally!"

With that everyone stood, with raised hands for they were so overwhelmed with the presence of God and the joy of being with Jesus. They cheered, yelled and sang songs to Jesus, making all sorts of noise in celebration, and in all their many different languages. After a few minutes of this wild praise to God the people began to settle down and began to be aware of the food on the tables. Jesus began to make His way by the tables to meet and greet every single person in the banquet room - every single person who made up *His bride, Israel.*

After Jesus made His first round of the room, stopping to talk with and hug every single person there, He arrived back at the head table and took His seat. Then He stood up again and raised His goblet and asked for everyone's attention. There was a hush throughout the room as everyone turned to look and awaited anxiously to hear what Jesus was going to say.

"In honor of you, *My Bride, My Israel, My Inheritance*, and including those of you who were in *Egypt, my people,* and *Assyria, the work of my hands*. I toast to you a marriage blessing over your eternal lives and of course, to bless our *Tabernacle Feast*. You fought the good fight and were faithful to the end - only to begin your eternal lives with Me. I love you all beyond measure and look forward to our lives together. As Ruth once said, '*For wherever you go, I will go. Where you stay, I will stay. Your people will be my people and your God will be my God.*' Because you are here to share in this Feast, this is what I hear each and every one of your hearts saying to Me. Please enjoy your food. My loved ones, eat and be full of joy!"

Jesus then took a drink from His goblet, and everyone in the room followed suit. Then they all sat down to the wonderful feast before them. It was the celebration of the beginning of their new lives with Jesus. Now that they had met Him in person, in the flesh, it was becoming very real to them. The wonder of it all was just now sinking in and around the room you could see the joy on their faces, one by one, as they realized for the first time that this was *not* a dream. It was real! They had arrived and were here in the same room with Jesus! The feelings were beyond words, beyond comprehension. Many people had tears of joy flowing down their faces even as they ate.

When it appeared the dinner festivities were concluding and most people were finished eating, milling around the room visiting friends and relatives at other tables, some tables near the Head table began to disappear. They were replaced with a beautiful parquet wood *dance* floor, perfect for dancing the whole night. *Redeemed* began to play a lively version of Psalm 150 and the angels began to sing along.

Praise the Lord!
Praise God in His sanctuary;
Praise Him in His mighty firmament!
Praise Him for His mighty acts;
Praise Him according to His excellent greatness!
Praise Him with the sound of the trumpet;
Praise Him with the lute and harp!
Praise Him with the timbrel and dance;
Praise Him with stringed instruments and flutes!
Praise Him with loud cymbals;
Praise Him with high sounding cymbals!
Let everything that has breath praise the Lord.
Praise the Lord!

That was the only invitation everyone needed to get up and dance. Once everyone got up from the tables, the whole room was instantly turned into one huge dance floor and all you could see were heads bobbing up and down, arms clothed in white flowing sleeves flailing in the air and the room was also filled with joyous laughter, singing and waving their arms in the air in praise to God. And the most wonderful thing of all, was that Jesus was right in the center of it all!

Afterword

This story is based on the four thousand years recorded in the Bible, plus what I have gleaned from history books and articles for the last two thousand years - plus a little imagination, but also based on prophecy. This epic story covers the lives of two brothers - over a period of four thousand years (the story covers all six thousand years of the earth). They both are searching for their Father's love - at any cost. While it is based on historical fact, it is still a work of fiction - and therefore subject to my own interpretation.

While I took a few liberties with the end times events, most of this book is in Scripture - we just couldn't see it until the last five or six years. God is opening the eyes of every faithful Gentile believer and showing us things in Scripture that have always been there, but we couldn't see them until now!

I have also added some things that I learned from the Jewish point of view, so even those stories you thought you knew may sound a bit different - but I know you will enjoy those little bits I added. Since the Bible is a Jewish book, I believe it is imperative that we learn to look at it through "*Jewish eyes*" and with a "*Jewish mind.*"

From *Day One*, God has been bringing us full circle - back to *Day One*. But it has been a process. He has tried every means possible to do this, without interfering with our *Free Will* - drawing us closer to Him and closer to what *should have been* - Jew and Gentile united in Him. But God has a deadline and it is drawing near!

I believe God allowed the Church to first fall into great apostasy, and then emerge gradually back to what the first believers knew and experienced. Most things in the Bible are *patterns* for those things to happen in the future, so I believe the record of the first church in the Book of Acts is in fact a *pattern*, or *shadow* of things to come - the *first church* is now trying to emerge again!

The first church was not meant to continue as it was - simply because God knows the hearts of mankind. He knew we wouldn't be able to maintain it without the original apostles. But as we near the end of this age, God is releasing more revelation of His Word - as He said in Daniel 12:4. I also believe God will release His *full power* at the end of the age - just like the power the first church had. I also believe we will be able to translate to safety (Acts 8:39-40) and God will provide all our needs - supernaturally just like He did for the children of Israel wandering in the desert for forty years! I believe He will do this before we go up to join Him in the clouds.

Although it did happen, in a *perfect world* we were never supposed to disconnect from our Jewish Heritage. But God allowed it, for it was all a part of His plan. Some will say that we are not supposed to reconnect because it was not in the Bible, but at the time the New Covenant letters were written, there was no disconnection. The first church, including the Gentile believers, were all very Jewish in how they believed. They celebrated the festivals together, and they attended temple together. Their assemblies were actually in each other's homes, and they were not called *churches*.

But now God wants us to reconnect to our Jewish brothers and sisters. We don't *have to* do anything, but if you love Jesus I would think you would want to do anything and everything that represents Him. And I truly believe it will bring us closer to knowing Him and His Heart. Celebrating the Feasts of God, His Sabbaths and renouncing the pagan holidays that have been carried over from the Catholic Church, have brought much insight into God's Word for me. He has blessed me with knowledge beyond anything I could have found on my own!

The *Feast of Tabernacles* is also called *The Ingathering* - it is not only a remembrance of God's provision while the children of Israel were in the desert, it is also a celebration of the *final harvest*. Throughout the Bible *harvest* is always used to describe the people on this earth - those who believe in Jesus and have followed His Word. So I believe it is during this Feast that we will meet Jesus in the air. Others believe it will be during the *Feast of Trumpets*, but I think it will most definitely be during one of the Fall Feasts!

Plain and simple, God wants to dwell with us just like He did in the garden of Eden. This is the story of what I believe to be true in how He is achieving this.

We, mankind, cannot possibly believe that we *know it all*. God said He would reveal things to us at the *end of the age*. Open your minds to receive all that God wants you to know - step outside of your safe little box, and see what God has for you!

My Theories of Revelation

I have studied this book for over twenty years, but about a year ago I began to think much of what I have always believed could be wrong. Most Biblical scholars take everything in Revelation as being quite literal, but it is not literal. While the things that are to happen are definitely to happen, how they are described in Revelation are not literal.

Plus, Revelation is not in any kind of chronological order. While God is a god of order, the book of Revelation is a series of John's visions, most likely written down as he remembered them - so not necessarily in any kind of order.

For instance, Chapter 19 tells us the beast and false prophet are thrown into the lake of fire. But then Chapter 20 tells us the devil is chained and then released again after a thousand years - then he is defeated and thrown into the lake of fire - again. I can name others, but that alone should convince you that nothing in this fascinating book is in any kind of order.

I have recently come to find that "Mystery Babylon" is in fact the "beast empire," based on Revelation 17:10-12. Just as in Daniel, John is speaking of the seven beast empires, and he refers to Babylon as just that - the beast empire. The seventh empire was the Ottoman Empire, and that is the empire that will be revived (Revelation 13:3 & 17:11).

God is the God of the living, not the dead (Matthew 22:32). Therefore, those people in Revelation 20:4-6 are alive *in heaven*. I believe there is not going to be a future "millennium" on earth. In fact, I have found evidence that the "thousand years" could actually be the thousand years right after Jesus came the first time. My theory for this is *that millennium* ended for the Messianic Jews about the year 1099, when the Christians began to persecute and kill the Jews - even Messianic Jews. I could be wrong, but what I do know for sure, is that there is not going to be a period of time of one thousand years after which Jesus releases evil on us again. This evil has already be unleashed on us - it is here now.

And this hatred has not let up, even today. Although it is off by about twenty years, I think it pretty much states there was one thousand years of relative peace, after the destruction of the temple. Both our calendar and the Jews Calendar is off - by how much, I cannot say. But I know that they are both wrong.

"Babylon falling" happens all at the same time as everything else - plagues are poured out on her (Revelation 18:4 & 8). Plagues are poured out on the beast empire - trumpets and bowls. And since we are talking about the trumpets and bowls, they are one and the same - the angel blows the trumpet and then the bowl is poured out - they all say the same things. As for the seals, although they say something different, I think when the seal is broken by "the Lamb," the angel blows the trumpet and the bowl is poured out. So I think they pretty much happen at the same time.

And the war (or wars)? There is only one war - the one in Revelation. The war between the North king (Seleucid dynasty) and the South king (Ptolemy) was the *pattern* for this war. Although many battles have taken place on this hill, this particular war does not happen in Har Megiddo (Armageddon) - Israel's enemies only *gather* there. The battle happens in Jerusalem - on or near the mount of Olives.

It is very possible that Revelation has another meaning, or more than one meaning. We cannot assume we know everything already about this book, plus those of you who are afraid of it should not be - there is nothing to be afraid of and I have found my life to be blessed simply for studying it.

Read Ezekiel 37 - many believe it is speaking of Israel becoming a nation again. Now read Revelation 11:11-12 - they are worded very similarly. Coincidence? I don't believe there is such a thing as *coincidence*. They could be speaking of the same event.

God tells Daniel to seal up his prophecy (Daniel 12:4), but that *"new knowledge will be released at the end."* In Revelation, He tells John *not* to seal up his prophecy - *"for the time is at hand,"* Revelation 22:10. I truly believe we are now at "the end of the age." All signs point to now, or the very near future - in other words, in our lifetime!

And when you study, keep in mind that this all began in the Middle East, and it will end in the Middle East. Stop thinking of America, or Europe, or any nation that is not in the Middle East. You can try to reason that the eagle mentioned in Ezekiel is speaking of America, but its not. Think Middle East!

AND remember - the Bible is a Jewish book - we must *not* use our *"Greekness,"* BUT try to read it with "Jewish eyes and a Jewish mind." We also must look at Revelation through the Passover & the Tabernacle - "the *Lamb*" is mentioned at least 25 times in Revelation - that *is* our hint!

Don't stay stuck in last decade's teachings - search and study through the Scriptures. And when you're done, search and study again! There are many things in Revelation that have only just begun to be released. The only way you're not going to miss them is if you begin to look at this wonderful book with new eyes! Be open for what God wants to show you!

Although the nations in Ezekiel 38 and 39 are located in and around Turkey, and the Mahdi will most likely be recognized first from there, Persia is the nation that we should also keep our eyes on today. The Revolutionary Guards of Iran, under the leadership of the Ayatollah and Ahmadinijad, are behind all the terrorist organizations around the world - including the United States. I, for one, will be watching this very dangerous nation. They will not nuke Israel, for Islamic prophecy states the Mahdi will reign from Jerusalem, but they could nuke the *Great Satan* (America) and other enemies!

Ancient Jewish Wedding

I believe that God is calling Gentile Believers in Jesus back to their Jewish roots, their rightful heritage. Proverbs 25:2 says: *It is the glory of God to conceal a matter, but the glory of kings is to search out a matter.* So lets dig deep into God's Word for the true meaning of the Ancient Jewish Wedding.

Selection of the Bride: In ancient Israel, brides were usually chosen by the father of the bridegroom. The Father would send His most trusted servant to search for a bride for his son. Genesis 24:2-4 We have not seen Jesus, but God's servant, the Holy Spirit, has revealed Him to us. 1Peter 1:8

The Bride Price: Brides in ancient times were purchased. The price was paid to the father of the bride, both to compensate him for the loss of a worker, and to show him how much the bridegroom loved and valued the bride. Jesus paid a very high price for His bride. His blood that was shed on the cross was the payment for His bride. 1Corinthians 7:23

The Betrothal: The betrothal is like an engagement today, but with a greater sense of commitment. The couple actually enters into a covenant. This covenant is serious, final and sealed in blood - and it is legally binding. Once the couple entered into this Betrothal, they were married in all aspects except for the consummation of the marriage. This betrothal is the contract (*Ketubah* in Hebrew). The *Ketubah* contains all of the bridegroom's promises to his bride. The bride cherishes her *Ketubah*. Our *Ketubah* is God's Word! Our *Ketubah* shows us all we are entitled to as a part of the Bride of Messiah.

The Bride's Consent: Although a bride was selected for the bridegroom, she still had a choice. In Genesis 24:57-58, Rebekah was asked concerning Isaac: "*Will you go with this man?*" And she said, "*I will go.*" She gave her consent - her "*I do.*" God is a gentleman and He never forces anyone to say "*I do*" to His Son. Have you said your "*I do's*" to Yeshua (Jesus) yet?

The Cup of the Covenant: After the Ketubah was accepted, a cup of wine was shared to seal the marriage covenant. A second cup of wine would be shared many months later during the marriage ceremony.
   The *Third Cup* that Jesus took during His last Passover meal, was not only the *Cup of Redemption* - it was also the *First Cup of the new marriage covenant* with His Bride.
   In Matthew 26:29, Jesus is speaking of a *Cup* that He will drink with His bride on the day of the Feast of Tabernacles, which is the marriage ceremony and celebration.

Gifts for the Bride: The Betrothal included the giving of gifts by the bridegroom to His bride. Many times the bridegroom gave a coin or something of value to his betrothed bride. God's Holy Spirit is our spiritual gift from Him. Through Jesus, we, the Bride, receive many gifts: forgiveness, eternal life, gifts of the Spirit, and many more. What bride would say to her bridegroom who comes bearing gifts, "No, I cannot accept them"? Yet many of us do that to our Bridegroom - we do not accept His free gift.

Mikvah: A bride in ancient, and modern Israel today, experiences a *"mikvah"* prior to her wedding. The word *mikvah* means a pool of living water which the bride uses for ritual purification. This immersion in water is part of a bride's physical and spiritual preparation for the wedding ceremony. The mikvah represents a separation from the old life to a new life. The bride of Messiah also goes to the living waters of the mikvah. When believers in Jesus are immersed in water, it is a separation from an old life to a new life. "Old things pass away...all things become new." Revelation 21:4-5

Departure of the Groom: Once the marriage covenant was sealed, the bridegroom left his bride to go to his father's house to prepare a wedding chamber. He would be gone for up to twelve months. Our bridegroom has gone to prepare a wedding chamber for His bride. While we wait for the return of our Bridegroom, we need to stay faithful, watchful and spiritually alert. This is the hour to pray and fast! *"I go to prepare a place for you, and if I go and prepare a place for you, I will come again and receive you to myself; that where I am, there you may be also."* John 14:3 *"Can the friends of the Bridegroom mourn as long as the Bridegroom is with them? But the days will come when the Bridegroom will be taken away from them, and then they will fast."* Matthew 9:15

The Consecrated Bride: The Jewish bride was set apart, consecrated, separated unto her bridegroom - the one who purchased her. So, while waiting for his return, she was to stay faithful. It was probably easy to stay faithful at first, but when his return was delayed, the temptation would be great. After awhile, the bride may even start to question his return. "Scoffers will come in the last days, walking according to their own lusts, and saying, 'Where is the promise of His coming?'" 2Peter 3:3-4 We are His consecrated bride, awaiting His return. We cannot fall into temptation. We must be ready at all times for the return of our Bridegroom!

Return of the Bridegroom: Jewish bridegrooms usually came for their brides late at night, near the midnight hour. The sound of the shofar would break the silence of the night and there would be great shouting and dancing in the streets. Since the father is the one who tells the son when he can go to his bride, only the father knows when this will be. *"But of that day and hour no one knows, not even the angels in heaven, nor the Son, but only the Father."* Mark 13:32 *"But the day of the Lord will come as a thief in the night,..."* 2Peter 3:10 *"Watch therefore, for you do not know what hour your Lord is coming."* Matthew 24:42 *"And while they went to buy, the bridegroom came, and those who were ready went in with him to the wedding; and the door was shut."* These are all referring to the events of a Jewish wedding - Jesus called believers in Him, His bride. Many times He used the Jewish wedding to explain to us what is about to happen.

The Huppah: The second half of the ancient Jewish wedding ceremony, or huppah, is also called the "hometaking." The huppah of ancient times was a special room built in the bridegroom's father's home. The huppah symbolized the new home to which the bridegroom would take his bride. The bride and bridegroom were escorted to the bridal chamber where they would be alone for seven days. The spiritual parallel to the huppah for the bride of Messiah begins as we are lifted up off the earth to be taken to our heavenly wedding chamber where we will spend *seven days* with our Bridegroom. Many think this seven days is actually seven years. *"Come my people, enter our chambers and shut the door behind you, hide yourself as it were, for a little moment until the indignation is past. For behold the Lord comes out of His place to punish the inhabitants of the earth for their iniquity."* Isaiah 26:20-21 While the wrath of God is poured out on the earth, the bride of Messiah will be hidden away with her Bridegroom.

The Marriage Supper: Following the seven days in the bridal chamber, the bride and bridegroom joined their guests for a joyous marriage feast. The Feast of Tabernacles is that marriage feast. It is a seven day feast. I believe we will spend that seven days (or years) with our Bridegroom during this feast. We will have a marriage feast with Jesus! *"Let us be glad and rejoice and give Him glory, for the marriage of the Lamb has come, and His wife has made herself ready. Blessed are those who are called to the marriage supper of the Lamb!"* Revelation 19:7 & 9.

A Theory of Counterfeits

Similarities:

Islam	Catholicism
Prayer Beads	Prayer Beads
Spread by force	Spread by force
Muhammad	Hitler
Hates Jews	Hates Jews / Holocaust
	Spanish Inquisition, etc.
Infidels - unbelievers	Infidels - unbelievers
Supreme Leader	Pope

Opposites:

Muslims	Messianic Jews & Christians
Allah	God / Jesus / Holy Spirit
Quran	Bible
Sharia Law	Law of Moses
Ishmael is son of Promise	Isaac is son of Promise
Violence	Peace
Friday is holy	Saturday is holy

Eschatology:

7-9 year Peace Treaty	7 year Peace Treaty
Islam is future of world	God reclaims the world
Bismillah head/arm bands	Mark of Beast
All nations surround Israel	All nations attack Israel
Isa will claim to be Jesus & will convert many	Falling Away
al-Mahdi is political, military & religious leader	Antichrist is political, military & religious leader
Isa will enforce Islam	False prophet enforces false religion
Shari'a Law	New World Order
Islam is world religion	Universal world religion
Islam denies the Father	Antichrist denies the Father
Islam denies the Son	Antichrist denies the Son
al-Mahdi & Isa behead	Antichrist beheads
Israel is target	Antichrist targets Israel
al-Mahdi on white horse	Antichrist on white horse
Islam denies cross	Antichrist denies cross
Islam practices deceit	Jesus warned of deceit
Islam will be final empire	Antichrist has final empire
Dajjal - antichrist	Jesus - real Messiah

Theories based on Daniel's Prophecy

This is only a theory, I am not attempting to set a date for the end of this age. We must take in consideration the fact that both the Gregorian and the Hebrew calendars are inaccurate. There are several years, if not hundreds, missing. I chose the year 2023 for my story because of this theory.

638 Jerusalem was taken by the Muslims - 50 years later the Dome of the Rock, a shrine, was built over where the temple once stood - making it impossible to build the temple again on that spot. And the al-Aqsa Mosque was known as a *temple* by the Knights Templar.

   688 - year the shrine, Dome of the Rock, was built on temple mt
  1260 - years - Revelation 11:2, 3 & 11; Daniel 12:7
   1948 - Israel became a nation again

   688 - the temple cannot be built while Dome still stands
  1290 - years - Daniel 12:11
   1978 - year peace treaty was signed between Israel & Egypt

   688 - Quran quotes on inside of Dome deny Father & Son - a
         symbol of Allah & Islam in the place of the temple
  1335 - Daniel 12:12
   2023 -

Catholic church theory (the numbers don't fit as well, but keep in mind our calendars are off and both happened in the 7th century):

   606 - Bishop Boniface III was first to call himself Pope,
         which means "Father" & usurps God's authority
 1260 - Daniel 12:7, Revelation 11:2,3 & 11
 1866

   606 - Seventh century, same as Islam taking Jerusalem.
         Present organizational form of Catholic church
 1290 - Daniel 12:11
 1896

   606 - interesting number, don't you think?
 1335 - Daniel 12:12
 1941 - in 7 years, Israel is made a nation again

Jesus was born in a Jubilee year. I have no idea if 2023 is a Jubilee year, but it is said that Jesus will also return in a Jubilee year.

Second Babylon Theory

What is interesting is that the Catholics gave us the idea that Rome is *Babylon* - in their attempt to convince all that they are the succession of Peter. They state that Peter was in Rome when he wrote he was in *Babylon* (1Peter 5:13). But Peter was actually in Babylon, Egypt, where he also mentions Mark, who was the bishop of the church in Alexandria, Egypt. When you study all the false doctrines and all that the Catholic church did to God's people, it paints a pretty convincing picture of the Catholic church being *"Mystery Babylon."* It is also ironic that Peter, whom the Catholics think the church is built on, wrote only two books - one filled with warnings of false teachers.

Babylon *is* Rome or Vatican City, where the pope and other leaders live, for it is the leaders who have led their followers astray with many apostasies. The numbers don't fit as well, but our calendar and the Jewish calendar are not accurate. The facts *do* fit however - keep in mind that Islam copied much of the Catholic religion, but twisted it. There is a very good possibility that these two entities will join together (Rev. 17 states that Babylon is linked to the beast empire).

Babylon usurps God's authority, placing himself in God's place: The Pope did this in 606. Islam sort of did this in 688, but will actually do it as the al-Mahdi at end of age.

Abomination of Desolation is set up in temple: The Church of Sepulchre was built in 326, and restored in 630 after being captured by Muslims. Islam built Dome of Rock on temple mount in 688.

Babylon is a whore: God always refers to His people this way when they went after idols. Catholic Church was once the First Church, but began to chase idols at the end of the first century - and the apostasies snowballed from there. Islam has always gone after idols, but were never *God's people*, so they do not fit this one - or do they?

Babylon is Royalty and rich: The leadership of the Catholic church has considered itself royalty since fourth century, and they are the richest institution on earth. Islam's leaders didn't become royalty until 1926, and they have only been rich since the discovery of oil in 1938.

When Babylon is burning she can be seen from sea: Both Vatican City (Rome) and Mecca can be seen from sea.

Babylon killed God's people: Both have killed God's people, the Jews, but only the Catholic Church did it Jesus's name.

Babylon committed fornication with kings: The Catholic church and kings have a long history together - kings using the church to kill others, especially God's people. Mecca also has a long history with kings and leaders of nations.

What is Sharia Law?

Just as the law of the Jews governs their every day lives, Sharia Law governs the lives of Muslims. It is the law of the Caliphate of Islam.

Sharia Law is the mysterious law of the antichrist that will eventually govern the whole world. The Mahdi is not only head and Imam over all Islam, he is the essence of Sharia Law.

We have all wondered how the false prophet would get the whole world to worship the beast - the Mahdi and Sharia Law explains it all. It is a religion, government and politics all rolled into one very evil entity.

Sharia Law is the fusion of religion and politics, which is the essence of Islam. It is the idea that there cannot exist a law that is not the expression of Allah's will.

It is a hijacked version, and quite opposite, of God's Law. It is derived from the Quran and the Hadith. Sharia Law is the ultimate "one world order" and is already on its way to being adopted even in American courts.

It relates to all of Allah's commands concerning the activities of man. And it is dangerous, for Islam allows killing in certain cases so one who kills an unbeliever in Allah, would be acquitted - or never charged at all.

Sharia Law does not benefit any society for it contains too many harsh rules and punishments. Canada and Australia are already in danger of Sharia taking over their courts.

I urge you to study the things found in this book, and see for yourselves. Many of our states already have Sharia Law in our US Courts - soon it will be the only law. I suggest you read "*A Time To Betray*" - it happened first in Iran, but it will spread to the entire world at the end of this age.

This is not to scare you, but to inform you. We must be informed and aware of what is going on in this world so we can be ready for our Messiah when He comes to get us.

We cannot pray this away, as some think, for it is God's plan. In the past there was time to pray for God to change things, but we are at the end of the age - there is no time to change things any longer.

This Sharia Law is the "one world order" that will take the world by storm in a very short time. Be warned, it *will* happen. Even if the violence stopped, and the conversions to Islam stopped, non-Muslim nations simply are not sustaining their populations - in about 30-50 years Islam will completely take over the world. Islam is the future of the world!

Be a "watchman on the wall" and be ready!

The Feasts of God

The Feasts of God, are actually "Appointments with God."

Feasts of Passover and Unleavened Bread

The Feast of Unleavened Bread is a seven-day holiday, beginning the day after Passover. Together, Passover and the Feast of Unleavened Bread are called the *"Eight Days of Passover"* according to Jewish tradition. They are celebrated together since unleavened bread is also eaten on Passover. In the New Testament they were referred to as simply "Unleavened Bread" which Jesus knew to include Passover.

Unleavened bread is the perfect picture of Jesus the Messiah. The bread is without leaven (sin), as Jesus is without sin. The bread is striped and pierced, as His body was beaten and pierced for our sins (Isaiah 53:5). In addition, the Feast of Unleavened Bread symbolizes Jesus' burial. His body was placed in the grave but did not see corruption as He rose on the third day (Psalm 16:10 & Matthew 28:5-6) and carried our sins away (Hebrews. 9:26-28).

A time of remembrance of the time the Lord brought the children of Israel out of Egypt, Passover and Unleavened Bread together picture the sacrificial death of Jesus and the burial of His body, which God the Father raised on the third day before it decayed; which we will see in the Feast of Firstfruits.

What most know as the *Lord's Supper* was actually Jesus's last Passover meal. It was a feast that He and His disciples celebrated every year, and on this day the *Cup* Jesus picked up was the *Third Cup*, which was known as the *Cup of Redemption* by the Jews. This *Cup* was placed on the Passover table, but no one ever drank from it - until Jesus came and picked it up.

When Jesus said *"Do this in remembrance of Me...."* He was telling His disciples to remember Him whenever they came together for the Passover meal, for He was the fulfilling of Passover - Just as stated by John the Immerser in John 1:29 *"Behold, the Lamb of God!"* Jesus and all His disciples continued to celebrate all of God's feasts. (Matt. 26:17, Mark 14:12, Luke 22:15, John 10:22, Acts 2:1, 18:21, 20:6, 1Corinthians. 5:7-8, etc.)

Feast of Firstfruits

Firstfruits marks the beginning of the grain harvests in Israel, and it is on the 16th day of Nisan - the Third Day - the same day Jesus was raised from the dead.

A sheaf of barley is not only a thanksgiving offering to the Lord, it represents the entire barley harvest and serves as a pledge of faith that the rest of the harvest will be brought in.

Jesus rose from the dead on the third day of the Passover season

(Nisan 16), on the day of Firstfruits, completing the prophetic picture the Spring Feasts painted of His work of redemption: death (Passover), burial (Unleavened Bread) and resurrection (Firstfruits).

Paul states in 1 Cor. 15:20-23: *"But now Christ is risen from the dead, and has become the firstfruits of those who have fallen asleep. For since by man came death, by Man also came the resurrection of the dead. For as in Adam all die, even so in Christ all shall be made alive. But each one in its own order: Christ the firstfruits, afterward those who are Christ's at His coming."*

The Scriptures state that the resurrection of Jesus is the guarantee and the beginning (firstfruits) of the final *harvest*, or resurrection, of all mankind. He fulfilled the prophetic meaning of this holy day by rising from the dead to become the firstfruits of the resurrection, and He did it on the very day of Firstfruits.

Feast of Shavu'ot (Pentecost)

This is the Feast Jesus's disciples were celebrating in the Upper Room, as described in Acts Chapter Two. Although it is known by the Jews as the last Spring Feast and marks the beginning of the summer harvest, it also marks the day the Word was given to the Jews on Mount Sinai.

The fulfillment of Shavu'ot was the promised Holy Spirit which descended, indwelt believers - a day when the Word was given to Jesus's believers the final time. The Word now dwelt inside each and every one of them, as Jesus promised (John 14:16).

The two loaves that are part of the offering on the Shavu'ot Feast day, contain yeast and symbolize that the Body of Christ would be made up of Jews and Gentiles. This demonstrates the fulfillment of God's covenant with Abraham to bless all the nations through him (Gen. 12:3); and that two would come together as one nation.

Just as faithful Judah brought the firstfruits of their wheat harvest to the Temple on Shavu'ot, so the 3,000 Jewish believers on the Day of Pentecost were the firstfruits of the Church.

One of Jesus' parables about the kingdom of heaven refers to wheat and tares – a message that the true assembly of believers, like wheat, would exist along with false professors of the faith, like tares among the wheat, until Messiah returns and separates them (Matthew 13:24-30; 34-43).

I believe the wheat will most likely be those who embrace their Jewish roots, but continue to celebrate in the New Covenant that Jesus fulfilled for us. The tares will be those who falsely claim to be Christians, and unbelievers.

A shofar is blown on this day, and is known by the Jews to be the *"first shofar."* The *"last shofar"* is blown during the Fall Feasts. (1Corinthians 15:52).

Feast of Shofars (Trumpets)

The Feast of Shofars (also called Rosh Hashannah by the Jews) is the only Jewish holiday occurring on the first day of the month. Just as the seventh day and the seventh year are holy according to Mosaic law (Ex. 20:8-10; Lev. 25:4), so is the seventh month, Tishrei, the Sabbath of months. Jews in ancient Israel announced the new moon with short blasts of a trumpet, but the new moon of Tishrei was announced with long blasts, setting it apart.

The shofar sounds long blasts, while the silver trumpets sound short blasts over the sacrifices. Besides the sacrificial ceremony, the trumpet had many uses for Israel: To gather an assembly before the Lord (the rapture of the church). (Num. 10:2-4 & 1Corinthians. 15:52). To sound a battle alarm (God will defeat Satan's rebellious followers at Christ's return) (Num. 10:9 & Rev. 20:9). To announce the coronation of a new king (the coming of Jesus the Messiah) (2Kings 9:13 & Rev. 11:15)

Because Jesus fulfilled the Spring Feasts at His first coming, it is believed that the three fall festivals – Feast of Trumpets, Day of Atonement, and Feast of Tabernacles – will be fulfilled at the Messiah's second coming. Jewish tradition holds that the resurrection of the dead will occur on this day.

Day of Atonement (Yom Kippur)

Known also as Yom Kippur, this day is Israel's most solemn holy day. God originally designated Yom Kippur as a day in which "you must practice self-denial" (Lev. 23:27, 32), and it was an especially significant day for Israel's priesthood.

On this day only, the high priest enters the Holy of Holies and stands in the presence of God's glory. Many animal sacrifices were offered on this day. Besides the daily burnt offerings with their required grain and drink offerings, additional offerings were made, including a bull, a ram and seven lambs for the people, and a ram for the priesthood (Num. 29:7-11).

The goat sacrificed had to be spotless, and the worshiper would transfer his sins and the sins of his family onto this goat. The goat for Jesus, whose blood is shed, symbolizes the substitutionary death of the Messiah. The goat symbolizes the finished work of Jesus in taking away our sins, never to be remembered again. Just as the High Priest takes the blood of the unblemished goat for God into the Holy of Holies to make atonement for the people, Jesus entered the heavenly Holy of Holies with His own blood as the once and final payment for our sins.

Before Jesus, the Day of Atonement was a long and drawn out ceremony. But, with the coming of Jesus, this day is no longer needed, just as the Temple is no longer needed.

According to the traditions of Israel, the fulfillment of the Day of

Atonement will be a dark day. Israel's prophets warn of a coming day of judgment for the nation. Amos 5:18-20, Zeph. 1:14-16, and Joel 2:31 all speak of the day in which the Lord will turn off the heavenly lights, pour out His wrath on the wicked, and bring Israel to repentance and into the New Covenant. On the Day Atonement, the skies will grow dark, and Yeshua will reveal Himself to the Jews - they will rejoice and know that their Messiah has finally come for them!

Feast of Tabernacles (Sukkot)

The Feast of Tabernacles, or Sukkot, or "The Feast," is the seventh and final feast God gave Israel. It is the most festive of all the feasts and is mentioned more often in scripture than any of the others. The word "*Sukkot*" in Hebrew is transliterated as "*Tabernacles*."

Throughout this seven-day feast, God's people are required to live in temporary shelters to remind them of God's provision during the forty years of the children of Israel's desert wandering. God provided all their food, their clothes never wore out, and neither did their sandals (Deut. 29:5). God wanted the Israelites to become totally dependent on Him.

This festival is also called the *Feast of Ingathering* (Ex. 23:16; 34:22) because it is observed after all the fall crops are harvested. This happy feast commemorates God's past provision in the desert, and His present goodness in providing the fall harvest.

It is during this ceremony that Jesus stands up and shouts. (John 7:37-38) The Jewish leaders are infuriated; and a debate ensues among the people, many of whom do not realize, or will not believe, He is the Son of David, born in Bethlehem, the Messiah (John 7:40-44).

In the Year of Jubilee, land reverts to its original owner, slaves are set free, all debts are canceled, and the land rests. What a wonderful picture of the results of Messiah's sacrificial death: Jesus canceled our sin debt, redeemed us out of the slave market of sin and set us free, promised us a place in heaven, and gave us rest.

Something to ponder: Some believe Jesus was born during the Feast of Tabernacles. If that's true, it more fully illustrates the truth that Jesus is the *Tabernacle of God*. John 1:14 says, "*The Word became flesh and took up residence (tabernacled or dwelt) with us.*" Jesus will again tabernacle with us when He returns in power and great glory. God's people will enjoy intimate, face-to-face fellowship with their Savior, celebrating this feast with Him in heaven!

God's Sabbaths

One very neglected commandment is the Fourth Commandment: "*Remember the Sabbath day, to keep it holy. Six days you shall labor and do all your work, but the seventh day is the Sabbath of the Lord your God. In it you shall do no work: you, nor your son, nor your daughter, nor your manservant, nor your maidservant, nor your cattle, nor your stranger who is within your gates. For in six days the Lord made the heavens and the earth, the sea, and all that is in them, and rested the seventh day. Therefore the Lord blessed the Sabbath day and hallowed it."* Exodus 20:8-11

The Gentiles think it is not commanded of them. But if Jesus said it, then it is true. Throughout the New Testament, all the disciples kept the Feasts. They were in Jerusalem for Shavu'ot (Pentecost - Acts 2:1), and for all the other Feasts. The only thing that we aren't supposed to be, is circumcised, which was a sign of the Old Covenant. We are under the New Covenant now. We are also not bound to the 613 rules and laws the Jews have ascribed to the Law. Keeping the Sabbath is the fourth commandment.

We must not forget that Jesus is Lord of the Sabbath (Mark 2:27-28). And He is our Sabbath (Matthew 11:28-30). God made the Sabbath for man - not the other way around! He wants us to have a day of rest. To rest our bodies and souls from a week of tiring work. You don't have to be ritualistic, but if you take a day of rest (Sabbath not only means "rest," it also means "seventh," as in the seventh day - Saturday), you will truly be blessed.

A day of rest does not mean going shopping, or going to church or going on vacation - it actually means R-E-S-T. Its taken me a couple years to figure out what that really means, but I have come to believe that rest means *rest*. I tried all kinds of things, but found that I truly felt rested and received the most from God when I simply sat back and relaxed, expecting to receive from God. That's it. And don't forget that the unfulfilled Feasts will be fulfilled in the Seventh (Sabbath) month of Tishrei! Yeshua (Jesus) is truly coming to give us rest!

Feast of Dedication (Hanukah)   or   Festival of Lights

The *Feast of Dedication* is only recorded in the Bible briefly, in John 10:22 where it is mentioned only by name. It happened some time after Malachi was finished, but before Jesus was born, so it was a Festival that Jesus observed. It is included in the Apochrypa Jewish histories.

Antiochus IV Epiphanes attacked the city of Jerusalem and defiled the temple. The king ordered the Jews to reject their God, their religion, their customs and their beliefs, and to worship the Greek gods. Antiochus killed many of the Jews as a terrifying warning to all who would not deny their God and worship *him,* Antiochus IV Epiphanes.

Antiochus placed a statue of the Greek god Zeus in the Temple, and sacrificed a pig on the altar in the Holy of Holies. When Jewish priests refused to eat the meat of the pig, Antiochus had them killed. Eventually all Jewish observances were outlawed.

Under the leadership of Mattathias Maccabeus, a Jewish priest, along with his brothers, a band of Jews revolted against the cruelty of Antiochus. They refused to bow their knee to his pagan god. Mattithias's son, Judas Maccabeus, continued the revolt when he died.

Finally in 165 BC the temple was freed, but before the temple could be used again for sacrifices and worship, it had to be cleansed of its defilement, and then rededicated.

A part of the cleansing process was to relight the temple menorah. According to the Law, it was to burn continually before God, and could only be lit from consecrated oil. But most of the oil had been defiled by the Syrians. The Jewish priests found only one small jug of oil, only enough to light the menorah for one day. It would take eight days to prepare a new supply of consecrated oil, but they lighted the menorah anyway.

The oil that should only have lasted for one day, kept the menorah burning for eight full days! This day was declared to be a miracle, and an eight day celebration was formerly announced that this feast was to commemorate this oil miracle each year on twenty-fifth day of Kislev.

Tabernacle of Intimacy

Courtyard

The **Fence** around the Tabernacle represents mankind's separation from God.

There is only one **Entrance** into the Tabernacle - one entrance through the fence. Jesus is that One Entrance.

The **Brazen Altar** was where the worshiper transferred his sin to an unblemished Lamb, and then a priest sacrificed it to God for the worshiper's sins. Yeshua (Jesus) was our unblemished Lamb Who was sacrificed to God to atone for all mankind's sins.

The **Brass Laver** was made from mirrors to represent God looking at us and showing us our sinful selves through the Law. It was where the priests cleansed before going into the Holy Place. It is where mankind comes before the Lord to be cleansed of their sins.

Holy Place

The **Golden Menorah** inside the Tabernacle was made of One pure piece of gold, with seven flames, which represents the One Spirit of God manifested seven ways.

The **Altar of Incense** is to be lit continually. It represents the prayers of the saints that reach to God continually.

The **Table of Showbread**, (Bread of Presence or the Bread of Face). It represents God always with us. Jesus's name "Immanuel" means "God with us."

Holy of Holies

The **Veil** separates the Ark of the Covenant from the Holy Place and the priests. Only the High Priest goes into the Holy of Holies - once a year. Yeshua (Jesus) is our High Priest who presented His own blood in the true Tabernacle in Heaven. When He died on earth, this Veil supernaturally ripped in two, removing that separation from God for all mankind, and making it possible for all mankind to go before God in the Holy of Holies - through Jesus, the only entrance.

The **Ark of the Covenant** is where God dwelt among the Children of Israel while they were in the desert for forty years - He tabernacled (dwelt) with them. The presence of God was among them the whole forty years, and He stripped Israel of all earthly ties to bring them closer to Him.

In the Ark of the Covenant are **three** things, one is **Aaron's Rod**, which represents God's authority - the authority of God in your life.

Also in the Ark of the Covenant is a **Jar of Manna**, which represents God's supernatural provision. It represents mankind's faith in God to provide all their needs. We are to put our lives into Jesus's faithful hands, and He will provide everything that we need.

The final thing in the Ark of the Covenant are the **Two Tablets of the Ten Commandments**. These Laws represent the nature of God. If we keep these commandments, God will bless our lives.

Who is Jesus?

Are we just dressing "Jesus Christ," the Gentile God, in Jewish clothing? Yeshua's Name (Jesus) was given by an angelic messenger from Adonai Elohim (Lord God) and reveals the special relationship and ministry He has with His Jewish People.

"...an angel of the Lord appeared to Joseph in a dream and said, 'Joseph, son of David, do not be afraid to take Mary home with you as your wife; for what has been conceived in her is from the Ruach haKodesh (Holy Spirit). She will give birth to a son, and you are to name him Yeshua (Jesus), (which means 'God saves') because he will save his people from their sins." Matt. 1:20-21

If you search your heart, you will find that Yeshua was very much a part of Israel and the Jewish People ...that He taught from the Torah, the Books of Moses ...that His words, His world and the New Testament are very much a legacy of Israel and the Jewish People.

But who is He really? He is the fulfillment of God's plan to save His people - all His people. When Adam and Eve invited sin into this world, they caused all mankind to be born sinners, with a dead spirit - separated from God. But God wanted His people back - He wants to reconnect with us. So He set into motion a plan, and that plan began with Abraham.

God chose Abraham, a Jew, over all other people on the earth. Through Abraham, God would give His promise which would ultimately bring Jesus into this world. Jesus is God in the flesh. God needed someone with perfect blood to be shed for the sacrifice for mankind's sin. Although He set up the Tabernacle with the sacrificial system for the Jews, it was only temporary.

So God came to earth as a Man, so He Himself could shed His blood and be sacrificed for our sins. When He died He took all mankind's sin onto Himself, the veil of the temple tore in two, making it now possible for us, sinful mankind, to go before God - but we must go through Jesus. Jesus is the only way to God. Jesus was raised from the dead, which made it possible for mankind to be resurrected from the dead at the end of this age - to live eternally with Him.

The hope of a Messiah, a Redeemer, is at the heart of the Jewish People. It is throughout their liturgy, literature, and binds them together throughout history. It is also the greatest gift to all mankind - for the Gentiles were promised salvation *through* the Jews.

We are unable to perceive the things of God by the natural realm, but God gives us revelation through His Spirit - if we accept His gift. God desires for us to understand that His Spirit is real, and lives inside us if we have accepted His gift. We need to stop searching for Him outside ourselves, because the only thing out there is darkness. Eternal life is a gift from God. Jesus has offered us the gift of eternal life - but we must receive it. Are you ready to receive God's gift of eternal life through Yeshua (Jesus)?

Is there a God?
Chance or Divine Design?

I would like to say a few things to those of you who, after reading this book, still do not believe in God.

First of all it is pretty arrogant of us human beings to think that we simply appeared here on this earth - nothing created us, there is no higher being than us. In other words, we worship ourselves. So every human being does believe in a god, of sorts.

Are you an evolutionist? Well, Darwin's theory was never proven beyond the theory stage - it was never proven that mankind evolved.

How do you explain nature? The very fact that in winter, nature seems to completely die, and then mysteriously comes back to life in the Spring - that in itself tells us there is some divine designer.

How do you explain DNA? Each person and animal has a unique DNA all their own. How can you possibly explain that DNA evolved from a monkey or a sponge - and became a human being? My DNA is mine - it did not evolve from anything. God designed it especially for me. And He designed your DNA just for you.

How do you explain the design of the many beautiful animals in this world? Like the zebra or the giraffe?

How do you explain science? God is the one who invented science. So science will always prove He exists.

How do you explain the design of the human bone? Compared to reinforced concrete, the human bone is more flexible and has more strength to resist crushing compressive loads.

How can you explain the heavens? All the planets orbit around the sun in precise order, and timing. Nothing holds them in place, yet they stay where they are. The earth spins around 24 hours a day, yet stays on its axis forever.

How do you explain corn? The kernels of corn on an ear of Indian corn, or maize, are set in rows, generally straight, but sometimes spirally. These rows are always arranged in an even number. Never odd!

How about the bee? A bee has the number 3 throughout its design and life. In 3 days the egg of the queen is hatched. It is fed for 9 days (3x3). Its reaches maturity in 15 days (5x3). His 2 eyes are made up of 3000 small eyes, each having 6 sides. Under his body are 6 wax scales. It has 6 legs, each composed of 3 sections. Its foot has 3 triangular sections. Its antenna have 9 sections. Its stinger has 9 barbs on each side. Is this design? or is it chance - evolved from the cell that also made the monkey or a sponge?

Man's pulse beats on the seven-day principle - six our of seven days it beats faster in the morning than in the evening, but on the seventh day it beats slower. Man is supposed to rest on the seventh day because he is designed so that every seven days he needs rest.

Need purpose for your life? Jesus is the only One who can give mankind purpose for life - for He was why mankind was created!

Is Hell Real?

If you believe what is written here, then you do by the Spirit of God. If you do not believe these words, you probably never will - until it is too late. But that is your own choice, because God gave us free will.

God made Hell for Satan and his demons (Matthew 25:41). God never intended man to go there, so He is not the one who sends people there - we do that all by ourselves.

Once Lucifer (Satan), and the third of the angels that went with him, were thrown to the earth for rebelling, God knew that mankind, whom he had not created yet, would fall for the devil's deception. He had to also create a system that would eventually save mankind, and give him freedom from sin.

So He set up a sacrificial system (see the Tabernacle page) that would temporarily take away man's sin. And then, when the time was right, God Himself would come down to earth to become the ultimate sacrifice for mankind's sins. That is what Yeshua (Jesus) did.

And God made it so simple for us, so anyone can be saved - but only if they go through the One Door that He made for us - Yeshua (Jesus). There is only One way to heaven, because there is only One way to God.

But God gave us free will - and we have the right to exercise that free will and reject what God has given us - namely, Jesus. But, you can believe in a false Jesus and still go to hell. Jesus warned us that there would be many of these (Matthew 24:24), and that we should not believe in them.

If you want nothing to do with God, there is a place prepared for you that has nothing to do with God - Hell. Hell is void of light, because God is light. Hell is void of love, because God is love. And so on. Hell is a place void of anything that is God. Hell is void of all God's attributes.

An analogy you might understand: Walk up to a huge and expensive house and knock on the door. When the owner answers the door, you say, "Hi, I'm moving in with you." What do you think the owner would say? "No, you're not! I don't know you."

So, if you don't know God, what gives you the right to move into His house? Getting into God's house, heaven, has nothing to do with being good. You must _know_ Him - i.e. you must have a relationship with Him. It is based on relationship, not whether or not you are good. And if you don't want anything to do with God, why would you want to spend eternity with Him in heaven?

We are a sinful people. We are born into sin. We are not sinners because we sin. We sin because we are sinners. And because God gave us *free will*, we must *choose* Him in order to get into heaven. We must establish a relationship with Him. If you deny God - Yeshua (Jesus) - on earth, you do not have the right to move into His house in heaven.

But you cannot "earn" that right either - you must simply choose to believe in Yeshua (Jesus). You must believe that He died for your sins on the cross, and then was raised from the dead by God, and went to heaven to present His own blood in the real temple in heaven.

God gave us the directions to His house, and there is only One Way there - through Jesus. But we are always trying to get there another way, thinking we can do good deeds to get there. We choose to ignore the simple directions God gave us.

Sin cannot exist in God's presence, or in heaven. Hebrews 12:29 states that God is a "consuming fire." That means that if man, who is sinful by nature, was to go before God without the blood of Jesus protecting Him with His righteousness, that man would not be able to exist in God's presence. God's presence would consume him.

John 1:12 states that we must *receive* Him, and *that* gives us the right to become "children of God." It is very simple - all we have to do is believe in Yeshua (Jesus). We must believe that He died for us and that He was raised from the dead, and is alive in heaven - waiting for us.

All mankind *can* be saved from hell - if they just choose to believe in Yeshua (Jesus). So, yes, Hell is very, very real. But we don't ever have to go there - it is so simple, just choose Yeshua (Jesus)!

Prayer for Salvation

Let me say first, that there is no right - or wrong - way to pray to God for your salvation. No matter what you pray, pray from your heart and Jesus will hear you. All He wants is your willingness. Please read this whole page, and then come back to the prayer when you are ready. The following prayer is only a guideline:

"Yeshua (Jesus), please show me my heart. Show me my life through the mirror of the Law. Save me Lord God from your wrath and hell.

I admit I am a sinner and that I need You in my life. I need a Savior. I need you, Jesus.

Please Yeshua, come live in my heart and make me a new creature. Teach me Your Word and Your ways. Show me how to put You first in everything that I say or do.

Thank you Father for including me in Your family!

In Yeshua's (Jesus's) name. Amen."

The Bible says that we must believe in Yeshua (Jesus), and believe that He died on the cross for our sins, and then rose again, and lives inside each believer. That is all you have to believe! It is that simple!

By doing this, you are allowing God to bring life to your spirit. You were born with a body, soul and a spirit, but your spirit is dead until God comes to live inside you - right beside your own spirit, giving it life. Yeshua (Jesus) is our life - without Him we have no life. But with Him we can have eternal life - literally!

But it does not end with your spirit being brought back to life. You need to find yourself a Messianic Church that celebrates the Feasts of God and has renounced all pagan holidays and practices. You must also read your Bible so the Word can renew your mind. And do your best to keep God's commandments, which are already written on our hearts, and when your spirit came to life God made you aware of these commandments.

They have always been there, you just didn't know it. But they alone cannot save you from God's wrath and hell. We need God's forgiveness so that He will cleanse us from all unrighteousness so we can be in the presence of God!

Resources

Although this novel was written for the genre of Fiction, it is based on historical facts, as best as I could compile them in order to put them in novel form. Here are a few of the books, videos, websites and teachers I used to gather information in order to write this novel:

"Holy Bible" - Published by Thomas Nelson Publishers, 1983,
      New King James Version
"Complete Jewish Bible" - Translated by David H Stern;
      Jewish New Testament Publications, 1998
"The Iron Lance" novel by Stephen R. Lawhead - The Celtic Crusades
"Son of Hamas" autobiography of Mosab Hassan Yousef-
      by Mosab Hassan Yousef & Ron Brackin
"The Islamic AntiChrist" by Joel Richardson - The Islamic Mahdi as
      the AntiChrist
"9/11 to 666" by Ralph W. Stice - Current events, Biblical prophecy &
      the vision of Islam
"The Tabernacle" by Rose Publishing - Jesus in the Tabernacle of God
"The Book of Jubilees" translated by R.H. Charles - An account of
      Genesis by a Sadducee Jew
"The Coming Economic Armageddon" by David Jeremiah - A look at
      the US's possible financial ruin
"The Twelfth Imam" novel by Joel C. Rosenberg - Present day novel
      based on current events in Iran
"Constantine" by Paul Stephenson - the life and history of the Roman
      Emperor Constantine I
"Worlds at War" by Anthony Pagden - 2500 year struggle between East
      and Western Europe & Asia
"Dungeon, Fire and Sword" by John J. Robinson - The Knights
      Templar in the Crusades
"The Last Crusaders" by Barnaby Rogerson - Last hundred-year battle
      center of the world
"The Age of Feudalism" by Timothy Levi Biel - history of beginning
      and end of Feudal Power
"The Devil's Disciples" by Anthony Read - Hitler's people
"War of the Jews" by Josephus - Account of the destruction of temple
"Antiquities of the Jews" by Josephus - an account of Jewish history
"The End Times and Mahdi" by Harun Yahya (pen name for Adnan
      Oktar) -Turkish author & possibly the Mahdi...just a *hunch*.
"Eusebius's Ecclesiastical History" by Eusebius Pamphilus, translated
      by C.F. Cruse - Account of the first three centuries, including
      Constantine's reign
"God's War on Terror: Islam, Prophecy and the Bible" by Walid
      Shoebat & Joel Richardson - Islam through eyes of ex-terrorist
"Hitler" by Ian Kershaw - a look at Hitler's bond with the German
      people, and the result of the Nuremberg laws

"Awakening to Messiah" by Messianic Rabbi K.A. Schneider - A
teaching on Jewish Roots of Gentile believers & testimony
"The Messianic Church Arising" by Robert D. Heidler - restoring the
Church's Covenant Roots
"Jewish Voice Today" - A magazine Publication of Jewish Voice
Ministries International
"Why Not Women" by Loren Cunningham & David Hamilton - an
explanation of the Corinthians, the Timothys & Colossians
& Ephesians where they concern women - a bondage perpetrated
on women when Jesus took that bondage away.
"A Time To Betray" by Reza Kahlili - a true account of a CIA agent
inside Iran's Revolutionary Guards

"Jewish Voice" - Jonathan Bernis, President - a Messianic Jewish
website - teachings & brings gospel to Jews
"Discovering the Jewish Jesus" - Rabbi Kurt Schneider, Messianic
teacher - a Messianic Jewish website: teaches Jewish Heritage
"It's Supernatural" - Sid Roth, founder - a Messianic
Jewish website: brings gospel to Jews

Teachings of:
Jonathan Bernis; Jewish Voice - website: jewishvoice.org
Kurt Schneider; Avat Adonai - website: avatadonai.org &
discoveringthejewishjesus.com
Sid Roth; Its Supernatural - website: sidroth.org
Joel Richardson; Joel's Trumpet - website: joelstrumpet.com
Foundations Ministries - website: fourndationsmin.org

"Unlocking the Prophetic Mysteries of Israel" - DVD presented by
Jonathan Bernis, guest speakers Bill Koenig & Randall Price
"Understanding the Times" - DVD presented by Joel Richardson - a
study of Islam, Islamic & Biblical eschatology 2010
"The Return is Near" - DVD presented by Joel Richardson - current
events, Islam & Biblical eschatology 2011

If you wish someone to come speak at your church about the Messianic
Movement, your lost Jewish heritage or Biblical eschatology - please
contact:

Jewish Heritage: Rabbi Jonathan Bernis, Rabbi Jack Zimmerman or
Ronna Cohen at: jewishvoice.org;
OR Rabbi Kurt A. Schneider at: discoveringthejewishjesus.com

Biblical Eschatology: Joel Richardson at joelstrumpet.com

These five people are who I have been learning from. They are very
informative and Biblically accurate. They would be happy to come to
your church to speak to you!

www.ingramcontent.com/pod-product-compliance
Lightning Source LLC
Chambersburg PA
CBHW050537260626
47157CB00002B/335